GROOMED

GROOMED

SHINING A LIGHT ON
THE UNHEARD NARRATIVE OF
CHILDHOOD SEXUAL ASSAULT

SAMANTHA LEONARD

Trigger Warning:

This book describes the sexual grooming process and acts of sexual assault. Content may be triggering for some individuals.

NEW DEGREE PRESS

GROOMED

Shining a Light on the Unheard Narrative of Childhood Sexual Assault

ISBN 978-1-64137-242-8 *Paperback*

978-1-64137-243-5 *Ebook*

To my mother, father and sister

Thank you for believing me.

A Special Thank You to Peter Skolnik for providing legal expertise.

Another Special Thank You to Ozana Castellano for editing the manuscript and being my "spell check."

CONTENTS

"But no matter how much evil I see, I think it's important for everyone to understand that there is much more light than darkness."[1]

— ROBERT UTTARO, *TO THE SURVIVORS: ONE MAN'S JOURNEY AS A RAPE CRISIS COUNSELOR WITH TRUE STORIES OF SEXUAL VIOLENCE*

1 Uttaro, Robert. *To the Survivors: One Man's Journey as a Rape Crisis Counselor with True Stories of Sexual Violence.* CreateSpace Independent Publishing Platform, 2013.

INTRODUCTION

You know that pleasure you get when someone makes you feel special?

The involuntary excitement that usually happens the instant you decide you like someone, I mean *really* like them. You want them to like you back. They are popular. You feel warm inside because they do you a favor... or maybe you feel important because they light up when they see you or give you a compliment. You trust them because they listen to you and take an interest in you.

They give you attention, affection and appreciation.

You get the fluttery sensation in your stomach and you can't stop thinking about them. You are understandably all-consumed by the praise and attention.

Most of us have experienced these lustful feelings.

The sensation sweeps you off your feet and leaves you feeling helpless. But, I am not talking about true and genuine lust between two people. It's the other kind.

The feeling is so overwhelmingly good that you know you would be to blame if anything were to go wrong. You feel as if you must owe this person the world.

You may, as many survivors do, experience that pleasure that gives you an almost, but not quite, sinful thrill. So, you keep it to yourself and relish in the innocent bliss of your own private world.

Now imagine you are a child—perhaps ten or eleven years old.

And imagine these feelings and this pleasure are not coming from a peer crush. Instead it's an adult, likely someone you've known, your parents know, and you've come to see as important in your life. They are a trusted adult.

You've been selected.

You've been manipulated.

You've been groomed.

And now you're at risk for one of the most devastating crimes committed to children.

Sadly these crimes will affect more than one in ten children in America.[2]

Childhood sexual assault is reaching epidemic proportions, and it is happening behind closed doors. Many victims of childhood sexual assault do not disclose or report what was done to them, and their stories are never heard; they never get a chance to feel validated in their pain or learn the respect they deserve. Based off the assault that is reported, it is estimated that one in ten children will be assaulted before they turn eighteen. However, research also tells us the 73 percent of child victims do not tell anyone about the abuse for at least one year, and 45 percent of victims will not tell anyone for at least five years while some will never tell at all.[3]

There is no clear-cut formulation to pinpoint the next child that will be targeted; there is no cookie-cutter profile of who

---

2 "Sexual Abuse Facts & Resources" Cachouston.org. https://www.cachouston.org/sexual-abuse/child-sexual-abuse-facts/. (May 2019).

3 Ibid

the next perpetrator will be, and there certainly is no simple, all-in-one, quick fix on childhood grooming. The key to solving this flaw in our communities is to start recognizing it—like the flu, the common cold or the head lice going around school—and to start taking intentional steps to prevent it.

I am writing this book in hopes that you will lean into discomfort to expose childhood grooming and guide today's parents, teachers, coaches, guardians and children themselves on how to spot problems and red flags in our community.

The tales of grooming are each individual and gripping in their own way. Over the past year, I have spoken to and researched the stories of eight individuals, including myself, who were the victims of childhood sexual assault.

And in each case, the stories were unique.

But sadly, I was able to find some very common and consistent patterns. On average, from my interviews, research and personal experience, I have learned that these victims:

- knew their perpetrators for twenty months on average before the first sexual encounter
- were on average twenty-five years younger than their perpetrator_

And so, while every story is unique, many share some very common traits.

This book is woven together through a single, fictionalized story crafted from the stories of these survivors and me. Most were fearful to share their stories, had suffered through the court systems, had lost friends and family support through their decisions to come forward or to not come forward, and are afraid even today.

The central story of this book—including all names, characters, and incidents portrayed within—are falsified. No identification with actual persons (living or deceased), places, buildings, and products is intended or should be inferred. Utilizing the location of Jersey Shore was done for effect and should not imply any significance to that city. The dates were selected at random, but the timetables and timelines, the stages, and the shared activities are based on the common patterns I observed across the interviews.

The story of "Blair" is a composite of my experience and those of other victims I interviewed. But to the extent that the experiences were mine, they are all factually accurate—things I told the therapist and the police, and testified about at my abuser's trial. He was found "not guilty." But the truth is the truth.

Stories have power—and so the story in this book is designed to tell it as one collected story to unmask the truth.

The truth that underlies each story is that the abuse is never the survivor's fault.

Grooming leaves traumatic scars. It is a malicious form of manipulation used especially in child molestation. It is designed to prepare victims for abuse and then shame them into secrecy. They feel positive emotions toward the offender because the offender gives them gifts and time. The offender understands the victim...perhaps more than the victim understands themselves.

No matter the perceived magnitude, the body is forever changed after trauma and abuse. Every sexual assault survivor deserves to be heard, understood and loved in the most genuine way. We all hold the power to listen to each other and start conversations to change the culture around sexual violence.

Grooming is betrayal.

The experience is clearly traumatic for the victims themselves. I've also learned that the pain and suffering extend to the family members, teachers, coaches, guardians and others who feel they let the victims down by not recognizing the signs.

Why did they not recognize those signs? Oftentimes, this is because grooming isn't one observable action. It's a collection of actions over an extended period of time that leads to the ultimate betrayal. Darkness to Light is a nonprofit that offers child sexual prevention trainings that can help educate schools and communities to continue this conversation.[4]

This book is written to show the collection of actions to help others see grooming before it leads to assault.

This book is written to help others avoid this pain.

Victims of grooming are vulnerable in some way: maybe they don't have great self-esteem, their parents work seven days a week to make ends meet, or their mom is battling cancer. They have a void that needs to be filled. That's when the offender swoops in to save the day. [5]

Then, when they are dominated by the impression that this person is safe and loving, the abuse slowly and gradually seeps in.

"He friended me on Facebook and sent me harmless messages. They were innocent…so I turned the webcam on when he

4 "Resources" d2l.org. https://www.d2l.org/resources/ (May 2019).

5 "Sexual Abuse Facts & Resources" Cachouston.org. https://www.cachouston.org/sexual-abuse/child-sexual-abuse-facts/. (May 2019).

asked...I mean I said no at first but he was so nice to me...I was only eleven..."[6]

"I saw that my daughter was friends with him on Facebook, but I had met him. He was her coach...he seemed so nice, almost too nice..."[7]

"After a couple weeks of talking on the webcam, he showed me his penis. I didn't tell anyone until I found out he had done it to someone else...he would be charged with grooming thirty-eight girls online"[8]

The above excerpts are from a story that was published in 2017 on The Independent's website, an online adaptation of a UK newspaper. The article on Internet safety talks about a mother's struggle with allowing her eleven-year-old daughter to have a Facebook account. The mother was a social worker and considered herself "clued up on child protection." She made sure her daughter's account was private and even had her daughter's password. She warned her daughter about pedophiles. She never would have guessed that the

---

6 H, Hannah. "Internet Safety: A Mother's Story of How a Pedophile Groomed Her 11-year-old Daughter Online." *Independent*. 6 February 2017. https://www.independent.co.uk/life-style/health-and-families/internet-safety-day-hannah-h-mother-paedophile-online-grooming-11-year-old-daughter-facebook-webcam-a7560801.html (May 2019).

7 Ibid

8 Ibid

cheery man in his twenties at the local grocery store who lived around the corner would groom her daughter online. [9]

Grooming is not a term that can easily be defined or explained. It doesn't have one narrative or three steps you can take to avoid it. It is camouflaged as charm and niceness. Groomers don't fit the "pedophile" stereotype; they don't drive around in white vans handing out candy to children. Instead, they are usually well-liked, well-to-do people who prey on vulnerable children, their families and the community by gaining people's trust.

For this book, I interviewed:

- School teachers, college students, writers, filmmakers, translators, consultants

- People who have attended University of Delaware, Open University, Freie Universität, Georgetown University

- People who suffer from eating disorders, anxiety, depression and self-harm

- People who testified against their perpetrator and were found guilty, others were not found not guilty, others

9 Ibid

never reported, some were told they could not prosecute, and some died before they could report and I spoke to their families

These people have different experiences as survivors and working with survivors. These men and women survived and continue helping survivors. They do not wish to be named or identified, but they do wish to connect with survivors to prevent future assaults and to empower communities to do the same.

Sexual violence comes in many shapes and sizes. Some people experience the violence in their homes with their partners, others feel the agony and shame in the workplace, and others are walking on college campuses wondering where it all went so horribly wrong. Sexual grooming is another way in which people, especially children, experience sexual violence. Grooming does not get dropped off at your doorstep by a drone in a fixed package. Every survivor of the grooming process has their own unique story. However, some characteristic trademarks of the grooming process are important to know so we can recognize them, educate our children on them, offer empathy and validation to those who have experienced grooming, and intervene before another child is assaulted. Forensic psychiatrist Dr. Michael Welner outlines the six stages that can lead up to sexual molestation as the following:

1. Selecting the victim
2. Gaining the victim's trust
3. Filling the victim's needs
4. Isolating the victim
5. Sexualizing the relationship
6. Maintaining control[10]

This book will walk you through the "collective" story based on interviews with victims and experts to lay out how someone would most typically experience these stages.

This is not my story. This is our story:

- I am not writing this book to be brave.
- I am not writing this book to indulge in self-pity.
- I am not writing this book to shame perpetrators.

---

10 "Behaviors of Sexual Predators: Grooming" www.icmec.org. https://www.icmec.org/wp-content/uploads/2016/05/Behaviors-of-Sexual-Predators-Grooming.pdf . (May 2019).

I am writing this book to bring light into a dark space.

To let people know that 93 percent of child sexual abuse victims know their abuser.[11]

Time and time again, people use hindsight to see the signs and remember the gut feeling they had that something was fishy. The truth is, victims are not the only people being groomed; perpetrators are also grooming our communities. They are neighbors, teachers, coaches, mentors. They are well-liked members of the community who use their charisma to stay under the radar. I challenge you to listen, to question, to educate, to be vulnerable and to change the narrative around sexual violence.

Let's talk about this epidemic.

Let's learn to recognize the signs of abuse.

Let's listen to survivors and remind them they are not to blame.

Let's learn from their stories and protect our children and friends.

Let's keep love loving.

---

11 "Children and Teen Statistics" www.rainn.org. https://www.rainn.org/statistics/children-and-teens (May 2019).

(Of course, all of the tips given in this book are no substitute for using your own intuition and moral guidance to question relationships and distance yourself or a child from an adult. Remember, the only person to blame for an assault is the perpetrator. However, we hold the power to slow down, look for the signs and act on them. We can make our communities a safer place.

If you are suspicious of child sexual abuse, contact child protective services or call the Child Help Line at 1-800-4-A-CHILD. This resource serves the US and Canada, twenty-four hours a day and seven days a week with professional crisis counselors who provide assistance in over 170 languages for information, referrals and crisis intervention.[12])

---

12 "The Childhelp National Child Abuse Hotline" www.childhelp.org. https://www.childhelp.org/hotline/. (May 2019).

PART 1

SELECTING THE VICTIM

OCTOBER 2013.

TWENTY MONTHS BEFORE FIRST SEXUAL ENCOUNTER.

Marissa was my best friend on the entire earth.

She was rushing around her room, trying on outfit after outfit, deciding which combination of Hollister's clothes to wear. Marissa was a short, skinny ten-year-old girl with long strawberry blonde hair and freckles scattered across her nose and the tops of her checks. We were about to leave for Fall Festival at our elementary school where every classmate, parent, teacher and coach would be. Together we sank into Marissa's comfy mattress covered in polka dot blankets, picking out outfits and gabbing about the fifth grade in Ms. Tilly's class.

"Blair, do you like the cut-off jeans or the navy pants better?" Marissa asked, looking at herself in the mirror and holding each pair of jeans against her. Her wavy long reddish locks hung down around her petite shoulders.

"Definitely the navy pants for the party, but you know how your mom feels about V-neck shirts. Maybe you should wear a different t-shirt?" I suggested, looking up from my phone. I had just finally gotten a phone after Marissa convinced both my mom and my dad that it was a absolute necessity. My parents had been divorced since I was little, and getting them both to agree was harder than trying to eat all the vegetables on my plate. I looked at my pin-straight brunette hair in the mirror. It was tied back in a ponytail, and I had on a pair of jeans and a cropped Forever 21 tee with a palm tree on it.

Good enough, I thought.

"Navy pants and V-neck it is! Let's go see who is there. I hope there is still pizza when we get there!" Marissa headed for her bedroom door.

We scurried down the stairs and were greeted by Marissa's mom.

"Are you two all ready for the bash? We are already late!" Mrs. Martin said, looking around and trying to gather her belongings.

"Yup! Ready!" Marissa clutched her iPhone and headed for the door.

Mrs. Martin looked up, saw Marissa's shirt, and rolled her eyes. "You know I would prefer if you covered up a bit more, Marissa."

"Oops! No one goes to these parties anyway." Marissa cringed and looked to me for comfort. I smiled indifferently, not wanting to upset Mrs. Martin or Marissa, and shrugged.

Together we hopped on our pastel-colored beach cruisers, dropping our phones in the big baskets attached to the fronts of the bikes. This unseasonably warm fall afternoon in the oceanfront town of Glenvale was perfect for pedaling over to the elementary school a few blocks from Marissa's home. Glenvale was one of the few shore towns that had real community year-round, good schools and, of course, high taxes. The homes in Glenvale were older and close together, but they had the charm of dollhouses lined with white fences.

Together we came pedaling into the school yard, and Marissa made a beeline for the snacks under the white tents. I followed, as usual, picked up a paper plate and reached my hand into the chip bowl to scoop out a handful of salt and vinegar chips. But, in that moment, I was distracted by an unfamiliar face. A beautiful unfamiliar face. A young woman with a mass of long brunette hair entered the tent, wearing a white tennis outfit and aviator-style Ray-Bans. She held a pretty, two-year-old girl on her hip. Behind her waltzed in a tall, handsome man with a stroller. His light hair, green eyes and suntanned skin made him hard to miss.

"Lizzy!" Marissa yelped. She jumped out of the snack line and raced toward the beautiful woman and her perfect-looking family. "I am so happy to see you!" She looked to the woman holding the girl. "Can I play with Lizzy?" Marissa asked.

"Of course, sweetheart," the woman replied and gently bent down to release the girl.

I was curious. *Who were these people?* I had been Marissa's best friend for years and had never met them. Marissa wasn't just my best friend; she was my only friend. *How could I have missed this alluring family?* I wandered over, awkwardly positioning myself next to Marissa.

"Hi," I waved quietly to the little girl.

"Blair, this is Lizzy and her sister Elena," Marissa said pointing to the stroller the man was holding. They are my tutor's daughters. Aren't they sooooo cute?"

"Yeah, they are adorable," I gushed, grinning from ear to ear.

"You are too kind, girls. Will you be okay with Lizzy for a moment?" the woman asked as she walked out onto the courtyard where the parents were hanging out.

"Oh no, it's Marissa! I know you two must be up to no good!" the man who had walked in with the beautiful women exclaimed. He had on a pair of khaki pants, a light blue, short-sleeve polo and sneakers. His messy blond hair was perfectly tossed into place. Elena cooed in the stroller in front of him.

"Oh shut up, Mr. Campbell," Marissa said, glaring.

"You're such a silly goose, Marissa! You know you can call me Jack. Mr. Campbell is my dad! Looks like you've got a partner in crime now," the handsome man with the stroller said and looked over at me standing stiffly behind Marissa. I could feel his energy; he radiated a positive energy that I felt just standing next to him.

"Oh, this is Blair. She is my best friend. We've got to go now. We are taking Lizzy into the bouncy house!" Marissa picked Lizzy up and paraded the two-year-old through the crowd of people to the other side of the courtyard. I followed.

When we arrived at the bouncy house, it was crowded with younger kids flying up and down, having the time of their lives.

"Ya know, Lizzy, I am going to start seeing a lot more of you now that your dad tutors me in math." Marissa looked down at the darling child who resembled her mother. Then Marissa explained that she had been recommended to see an outside tutor by her teacher, and Jack was highly sought after. I still found it strange that I had never met this interesting and lovely family in a town where everyone knew everyone.

"Jack is a professor. He teaches at a *college,*" Marissa told me with her eyes wide, trying to shake off the fact that she needed a tutor.

Tutor? Did Marissa really need a tutor? Numbers got mixed up in my head all the time. This year I actually started getting pulled out of math class to get extra help with a special teacher. I did not like talking about it...

I want a tutor. I need a tutor... I thought.

"Tutor?" I blurted out what I was thinking. "Can I come to tutoring with you?"

"We'll have to check with Mr. Campbell and see. I know he told my mom he is booked, but he loves me, so maybe he'll make an exception for you!"

A small pang of envy tickled within me. *This family loved Marissa?* I didn't know why...but I wanted them to love me too. I also couldn't lose Marissa to these people.

We walked back to the tent and handed Lizzy off to Jack. I sat down at a table in the courtyard and looked down at my phone, hoping someone had texted me. No one had. Marissa came and sat with me at the empty table.

"Oh no, double trouble is back," Jack teased. "I should have known I would find you two off on your own! Why don't you come join the party?"

I let out a nervous laugh.

"We are bored! There are more parents than kids here," Marissa insisted, trying to defend herself. Truth was, we often isolated ourselves from the other kids, but it was rare to find us apart from each other.

"Silly gooses! I don't know...I think you two could pass as adults! You're getting pretty big!" And then Jack was swept away by his two daughters, Lizzy and Elena. The whole courtyard was now crowded with parents, teachers and coaches chatting and kids running around. Jack had been invited since he apparently tutored many kids in this small town. We sat on the edge of the courtyard, looking out onto the party and then down at our phones. The comment Jack had made about us looking older and being trouble makers kept creeping into my thoughts. People had told me they thought I was mature for my age.

No one has ever told me I looked older… I thought.

"Oh my gosh! Isn't Mrs. Campbell so athletic and pretty?" Marissa's comment interrupted my thought. "I heard she was a tennis champion before she had Lizzy and Elena, and her husband Jack is so nice—whenever he tutors me in math, he would even joke that I am prettier than Mrs. Campbell."

We both giggled, but a tinge of jealousy crept into my throat. It felt odd to call him Jack, but he would correct both of us if we slipped up and called him Mr. Campbell.

"My mom told me Mrs. Campbell used to play on the Olympic tennis team," she continued. "Mrs. Campbell said she can help me practice my tennis if I wanted, ya know, since I am so sporty already…wouldn't that be awesome?"

"Whoa, yeah, that sounds incredible."

"Yeah, their family is the coolest. I am so glad Jack is my math tutor," Marissa gushed.

* * *

"I wanted to be the next great mentor to young people...I wanted to change lives,"[13] said a pedophile convicted of molesting children in an interview by WFAA, a news station in Dallas, Texas.

In the WFAA's interviews, two men convicted of sexually assaulting children shared that the process of grooming starts the same:

THE OFFENDER MUST BREAK DOWN THE CHILD'S MORAL FIBER.[14]

Pedophiles look for children who are vulnerable, easy to access or sexually appealing to them. Many times, they prey on the child's needs and get involved with the child's family to determine how likely they are to get caught.[15]

They build trust with the child's parents.

---

13 Huffman, Charlotte. "Two Child Sex Offenders Explain How They Picked Their Targets." www.wfaa.com. https://www.wfaa.com/article/features/originals/two-child-sex-offenders-explain-how-they-picked-their-targets/287-434667495. (May 2019).

14 Ibid

15 Georgia M. Winters & Elizabeth L. Jeglic. "Stages of Sexual Grooming: Recognizing Potentially Predatory Behaviors of Child Molesters," Deviant Behavior, 38:6, 724-733, https://www.tandfonline.com/doi/full/10.1080/01639625.2016.1197656

They are often in positions to be a positive role model for children.

Tips to parents for selecting a trustworthy caregiver:

- **Choose group situations and have multiple adults supervise children.**
- **Ask to observe interactions.**
- **Let caregiver(s) know you may pop in unexpectedly and actually show up without notice to see how things are going.**
- **Stay curious, regardless of the age of the caregiver (teens too can be perpetrators of abuse).**[16]

16 "Tips for Hiring Caregivers" www.d2l.org. https://www.d2l.org/wp-content/uploads/2017/03/Tips-For-Hiring-Caregivers-2017.pdf. (May 2019).

NOVEMBER 2013.

NINETEEN MONTHS BEFORE FIRST SEXUAL ENCOUNTER.

"Blair, I have to talk to you," my dad uttered nervously. *This was weird, Dad never broke serious news to me...* "I need to tell you that your Uncle Joseph passed away yesterday. Mom is taking care of the funeral arrangements today." He looked visibly uncomfortable, waiting for me to react. I could see him exhale after getting the statement out as quickly as possible. He quickly changed the subject, "Don't worry, he passed away peacefully. Mom and Grandma were there... Today, we are going to visit my mother."

"WHAT, no, no, no, no, no...!" I cried as tears and started streaming down my face. "Where is Mom? I need to be with her!" I sobbed.

I should have known it was going to happen last night. Guilt sank deep into my stomach. I should not have been with Marissa last night. Every Friday afternoon I spent at my Uncle Joseph's house. It was tradition. My mom always made her brother a big casserole and brought it over to him. We ate it together, and Uncle Joe made us laugh until we cried. Marissa would come along sometimes too. But, not last night... I wondered if my mom cooked for him like normal. She loved preparing meals. She was a master chef. Uncle Joe and I both worshipped her cheesy lasagna. In return, he always made me a special goodie bag with chips, salted pretzels, and peanuts, and if I was lucky, I would find a dollar bill at the bottom of the bag. But my fifty-five-year-old uncle had not been in good health the past couple of weeks. He had a sudden heart attack and was not able to recover. Apparently, he passed away in the comfort of his own bed, surrounded by my family.

How could I have been having a sleepover when my uncle was dying? My mind raced.

I was devastated.

There was no better word for it than sadness. It swept through my body. I was sad for my uncle, but I was even more sad for my grandmother and my mom. I craved their affection, and I wanted to comfort them back. I wanted to wrap my arms around them and be sad with them.

"Blair, it is going to be okay. Your mom needs to take care of all the funeral arrangements with her own mom," he said evenly. "We are going to have a great day up at your grandma's. You and Marissa can go play with Bear, your favorite dog! Go get your jacket," he said and faked a toothy smile.

I don't remember my parents ever living together, but sometimes I fantasized about what it would be like to have two parents under one roof—to have two people say goodnight to me and be there for breakfast in the morning. It kind of scared me because I was so close with my mom. My mom and I were a team. We were best friends. Sometimes it just felt unnatural with Dad.

My eyes flickered. I stomped my feet. My body did not know what to do with itself. "But I just want Mom," I tried again, puckering my face, and turned to go back into the house to grab a jacket.

This was typical, Dad swooping in when Mom needed a break.

Even though it was just twenty minutes from Glenvale and I was supposed to go to my dad's house every other weekend, if I had plans with Marissa, I could usually get out of going. No wonder I didn't even have a toothbrush here. My dad wasn't a bad guy, but I just preferred sleeping in my own bed. "Please, Blair, I will get you Pop-Tarts at the store this week," my mom had begged me to spend this weekend at his house.

"Only if Marissa can come," I bargained.

"Fine," she had said and arranged for us to go over after school yesterday.

The ride to Grandma's house was mostly quiet. Frustration and sadness filled the car. My tears eventually subsided. I was left with red puffy eyes and a seat full of soggy tissues. I looked into my dad's rearview mirror and was embarrassed by how squinty my eyes were from weeping. Country tunes played on the radio, and I rested my head against the seatbelt strap until we arrived, hoping the redness in my face would go away.

I don't think my dad knew how to deal with tears. Marissa didn't either. I decided I had to try to forget the news that my Uncle Joe was gone, at least temporarily. I was going to have to make the most of the day. I did not want to ruin Marissa's day as she was so nice for coming. So… we played with Bear, my grandma's Labrador. Grandma said we were now big kids and could play outside by ourselves. I was unamused by the proclamation of being a "big kid," but Marissa got me to play catch for a while, and we raced Bear running laps up and down the yard.

"Thank you for cheering me up, Blair," Marissa said later on in the day. "I was terrified this day was going to be miserable, but that's why you are such a great friend," Marissa smiled. I was shocked when she then came right out and said, "You don't let things get you down for too long."

I tried to force a grin. It worked; I was able to mask the sadness I was feeling. I sat for a moment on the soft green grass, fighting back unexpected tears. I thought about how funny Uncle Joe was. He always made me laugh until my stomach hurt. "Stop being funny! It hurts!" I would giggle when he was really on a roll...usually poking fun at my mom. He just had a calming presence and always made me feel at home. Home was something I longed for. I wished my mom was here. *Poor mom,* I thought.

* * *

THE OFFENDER FEEDS ON THE FAMILY'S VULNERABILITIES.

Single family households have been identified in research at John Jay College as especially prone to be targeted by pedophiles for selecting victims to groom.[17]

However, the list of vulnerabilities is not short and sweet. Offenders look for drug addiction, mental illness, domestic violence or neglect.[18]

They prey on life and its rollercoaster of experiences. They are watching, waiting for your home to take a fall and before you get back up, they pounce.

Remember, no survivor is at fault for being sexually abused and to that point, no parent or caretaker is to blame either.

We are listening to stories to learn and empower ourselves to ask questions and intervene.

---

17 Georgia M. Winters & Elizabeth L. Jeglic. "Stages of Sexual Grooming: Recognizing Potentially Predatory Behaviors of Child Molesters," Deviant Behavior, 38:6, 724-733, https://www.tandfonline.com/doi/full/10.1080/01639625.2016.1197656

18 Ibid

GRIEF IS A VULNERABILITY.

Children perceive losses, and they grieve and internalize the loss of something external. That means they may not show it on the outside, but they may feel it on the inside. It is important that as children grieve, they get support, whether it be grief counseling or conversations within the family.

SILENCE IS NOT THE ANSWER.

Psychiatrist Gail Saltz says, "As a parent, you can't protect a child from the pain of loss, but you can help him feel safe. And by allowing and encouraging him to express his feelings, you can help him build healthy coping skills that will serve him well in the future."[19]

Continue to talk about the person who died, ask about the loss and discuss the feelings the child is having. Chances are they will grieve and regrieve throughout childhood as they progress through developmental stages. These conversations open doors to remind children that all feelings are okay and discussion is welcome. [20]

---

19 Ehmke, Rachel. "Helping Children Deal with Grief." www.childmind.org. https://childmind.org/article/helping-children-deal-grief/. (May 2019).

20 Jackson, Kate. "How Children Grieve—Persistent Myths May Stand in the Way of Appropriate Care and Support for Children" *Social Work Today. https://www.socialworktoday.com/archive/030415p20.shtml.* (May 2019).

MARCH 2014.

FIFTEEN MONTHS BEFORE FIRST SEXUAL ENCOUNTER.

Soon enough, fall came to an end. Marissa and I went into winter hibernation mode for the coldest months of the year, and my uncle's death was something my mom and I talked about from time to time. But after the funeral, life continued. I was not in the same homeroom as Marissa this year—our guidance counselor knew enough to separate us chatter-bugs; not that it mattered because Marissa and I still sat together at lunch and met between practically every class. Marissa's mother was constantly on her about making other friends, but that only pushed us closer together. We were inseparable. We loved fantasizing about growing up, getting married at the same time and raising kids in Glenvale when we were grown-ups. So, when Marissa signed up for the middle school tennis team in the spring, I begged my mom if I could join too.

"Mom, I really want to join the tennis team!" I declared, almost out of breath, running into the kitchen one day after school. "Marissa is joining and I never thought I'd try it…I know I hate sports, but don't you think it'd be fun? I could even get one of those cute tennis skirts! What do you think?" I blurted out quickly.

"Slow down there, kiddo," my mom smiled gently and pulled me in for a hug. "Of course you can join. I am surprised, though, since you've never shown an interest in tennis before."

"Yeah, well I think Mrs. Martin wanted Marissa to sign up for something now that we are fifth graders."

"Sounds good to me… you know I support anything you do!" My mom looked at me and smiled proudly.

Glenvale Middle School had a spring tennis team that anyone could join for fun. This meant you didn't have to be "good" at tennis. It also meant that every day after school, Marissa and I changed into our gym clothes and met outside to run endlessly around school grounds, learn how to hold the racket, do practice drills and, of course, chat. For us, it was mostly a social hour to hang out and get evil eyes from our coach for not paying attention. Today was our first match. Marissa stood next to me and leaned over to whisper in my ear, "You think Coach Reagan will notice if I don't take out my earrings?"

I could see Marissa's mom standing in the bleachers, looking way too excited. "Nah, probably not. They are super small studs," I whispered back and looked down at the used "Glenvale Middle School" polo we were handed today. Hideous. I cringed looking at the old beat-up shirt and old tennis shoes Marissa loaned me. My stomach got queasy. I hated the idea of an audience watching me, and I never wanted to be the competitor. I made sure my mom knew she was not invited; I was terrified of having anyone watch me. I begged and pleaded with her not to come to my matches because it was too much pressure. I just wanted to play for fun with my friend!

"You can pick me up afterward...it's only a practice match anyway. The real ones don't start until I make the real team," I told my mom who agreed reluctantly. I knew it was easier for my mom not to have to take off work. She often worked in the evenings for her job as a nurse. Luckily, I was usually able to hang out at Marissa's house on those days.

Marissa leaned against the caged court. "I can't wait to get this over with. I am sooo hungry!" she exclaimed.

"Me too!" I scrunched my nose and groaned, shuffling back behind all the players who were eager to get on the court. The practice matches had started, and I was so thankful Marissa and I were doubles partners in the last match. Hopefully that meant the parents would leave by then. My heart was already pounding. I mostly feared having real competition. I wasn't afraid of losing; I just hated the pressure that a match added to the game. I just wanted to have fun.

"Marissa and Blair!" Coach Reagan called out. "You're up in the last doubles match."

We ran out onto the court. My stomach dropped. Marissa approached Coach Reagan, who was initiating a coin toss to determine who would serve first. Marissa then bounced over to me. I was standing with my legs crossed on the other side of the court. Then she heard someone shout our names, "Marissa and Blair!"

It was Mrs. Campbell. She was standing next to Marissa's mother and Jack, clapping and cheering us on too. Lizzy and Elena were sitting on a blanket.

I guess I can't beg Marissa's family not to come, I thought.

I immediately felt my stomach turn knowing that not only one person, but three people were watching me.

Adrenaline surged throughout my body, and I picked up my racket and zoned in on the match. I could not help but continue to wonder what the Campbells were doing here. I had seen them around several times at Marissa's house since Jack was tutoring Marissa, and their families had begun to become friends. Mrs. Campbell had also offered to help Marissa with her newfound interest in tennis. It seemed like they started to appear frequently in Marissa's family's circle. I couldn't help but feel like Jack noticed me, took an interest in me. The last time I was over at Marissa's, he asked me if I had a boyfriend. When I said no, he said, "You will soon."

He must think I am pretty. No boy other than my family members has ever called me pretty before. But he didn't actually say I was pretty…I must be overthinking it… I thought repeatedly.

I was now yelling "love-30" and serving the ball. We were losing. The other girls had way more focus and skill than Marissa and me, who were chasing after the ball like dogs chasing a squirrel. When the match finally ended, I exited the court and saw Lizzy and Elena still on the picnic blanket.

"Give me a high-five, pal!" Jack exclaimed, holding his palm up while standing with Lizzy and Elena. "You have got a pair of legs on you!" he remarked.

What did that mean? I wondered. *I wasn't any good at this tennis thing.* I looked around for Marissa, who was walking toward her mom and Mrs. Campbell standing off to the side.

"Here is a bottle of water, Blair," Jack reached into the diaper bag on the blanket and pulled out a cold, unopened water bottle.

"Oh…thanks." I took the bottle from him and chugged the water down.

Marissa appeared next to me. "What's for dinner at your house?" she asked.

"Probably meatballs," I answered. My mom was also the queen of homemade meatballs and spaghetti. Anything Italian was her specialty.

"I want PIZZA!" Marissa exclaimed.

"PIZZA!" I echoed, my eyes wide.

"Danielle, let's go pick up some pizza with everyone to celebrate their first match!" Jack called over to his wife and the other mothers standing a few yards away.

"Pizza it is!" the women agreed.

I smiled. I thought this guy Jack seemed so cool. He was always just acting like a kid and showing up to make everything more fun. I decided I liked that he was in the neighborhood.

I reached for my cell phone to call my mom and tell her I'd be over at Marissa's for dinner. "So, how was the match, honey?" she asked.

"Fine," I responded quickly. "I got to go, though… we will talk later. Bye, Mom. Love you!"

"Okay, honey, I love you!" she answered.

Marissa and I raced to her mom's minivan and headed off to celebrate finishing our first match.

* * *

It was only a few short days before I would see Jack again. I was sitting propped up against Marissa's headboard on a Saturday morning after sleeping over the night before. Mrs. Martin yelled from downstairs, "Girls! We got bagels!"

That bolted us out of bed. We raced downstairs and plopped down at the white breakfast nook with its floral cushions. In front of us was a brown bag of warm bagels and a choice of cream cheese or butter. I grabbed a pre-cut poppy-seed bagel and smeared a decent amount of butter on each side. "What are we going to do today, Maris?" I asked with a mouthful of bagel.

"I want to go swimming! It's so hot out!" Marissa said loudly enough so her mother could hear. Easter was two weeks ago and the spring sun was hot—and so was the heated community pool. I was also still getting used to this whole tennis thing. My legs were always sore between the daily practices and the gymnastics classes Marissa and I took a couple of evenings a week. A pool sounded really nice.

"You know I am taking Lily over to the community pool with the Campbells to go swimming… you both are invited too if you want to go swim with your sister and me," Marissa's mom told us. "But you'll be hanging out with the babies and mommies."

Marissa had a baby sister, Lily, who was a year old just like Elena.

"Yes, we'll go! Blair and I can play with Lizzy. When are we leaving?" Marissa asked eagerly.

I felt an involuntary excitement run through my core when Marissa made this declaration. I was excited to hang out with the Campbells and get to go swimming. That whole family seemed so popular, and everyone in town liked them so much. Jack and Mrs. Campbell also made me feel so welcome; I couldn't help but want to spend time with them.

"We are going to have a blast!" Marissa looked to me and started to move away from the kitchen table. "Let's go get ready!"

"I don't want to see you come down in any of those skimpy two-piece bathing suits, Marissa! And make sure you bring a change of clothes!" her mom yelled as we scampered back up the stairs.

* * *

As you see here, Blair completely bases her self-worth on what other people think of her.

Blair is normal!

She is a young person trying to make sense of the world and who she wants to be in it. In my interviews I found that:

OFFENDERS TAKE ADVANTAGE OF THIS VERY NORMAL PERIOD FOR CHILDREN WHERE THE CHILDREN QUESTION T HEMSELVES AND THE WORLD AROUND THEM.

Help children develop their self-worth; let them know that who they are is incredible. Use encouragement and praise to reinforce their uniqueness.

It is important all people—girls and boys alike—know they are worthy of love and respect.

Here are some helpful phrases for kids provided by Darkness to Light:[21]

- "Your whole body is a private part if you want it to be. You get to decide who touches you."
- "No one should ask you to keep a secret. If they do, you should tell me."
- "No one should ever touch you where your bathing suit covers."

---

21 "Tips for Hiring Caregivers" www.d2l.org. https://www.d2l.org/wp-content/uploads/2017/03/Tips-For-Hiring-Caregivers-2017.pdf. (May 2019).

- **"It's not okay for someone to ask you to touch their private parts, with any part of your body."**
- **"You can tell me anything and I will believe you."**

* * *

Marissa was right. We did have so much fun. As soon as we arrived at the pool, we were greeted by Jack and a gaggle of kids. One of them was Reese, a boy in the fifth grade we had never talked to. He lived next door to the Campbells and apparently spent a lot of time at their house hanging out. Jack practiced tennis with Reese since there was a court in Reese's backyard.

"Hey, Reese," Marissa said and kept walking right past him. I smiled and waved over at Reese while following Marissa outside. Jack was playing with Reese and his friends at the basketball hoop near the entrance of the pool club. "Oh no, trouble has arrived," he sang as Marissa and I wandered over to the pool.

Marissa rolled her eyes at him, and we hopped into the warm pool. We claimed the corner of the pool closest to Marissa's mom, who was sitting with Mrs. Campbell.

"Can you do a flip underwater?" Marissa asked and then dove underwater to show me her flip.

"Duh!" I blurted when she came up for air and I mimicked her flip.

"I bet you can't hold a handstand," she challenged.

We were in our own world pretending to be water gymnasts, with Marissa's mom a just a quick glance over our shoulders. However, when I looked over my shoulder, I noticed Jack had his eyes on me. I felt safe knowing he was watching out for us in the pool. However, our solo pool session was put to an end when five sweaty, dirty boys jumped in.

"Hut, hut," one of them declared and threw a football across the length of the pool.

We winced at the water splashing everywhere and made our way toward the stairs.

"Let's get out, Maris; we can suntan for a little bit while the boys take over!" As I stepped out of the pool in my black Old Navy bikini, I accidentally locked eyes with Jack, who was looking at me. He did not look away immediately. His eyes lingered for another second until he looked away. My stomach turned a bit. I did not know how to react. So, I did not. I wrapped a towel around my waist and sat on a poolside chair.

"So, how was the water, girls?" Mrs. Martin turned to us, breaking her intense conversation with Mrs. Campbell.

"It was SO fun!" Marissa gushed. "Blair and I practiced our gymnastics in the water, so now we are going to be ammm-mazzzzzing in class next week!"

"Oh, I am so sorry I missed all that fun. I guess I will have to watch out in class next week!" Mrs. Martin smiled at us both.

"I just ordered some pizza for you troublemakers!" Jack shouted across the yard, walking toward us. I could still feel his eyes on me. "Blair, I know you like pepperoni on your pizza, so I made sure I got a pie with that."

That was so nice of him. Why was he so nice to me? I wondered. *He didn't get Marissa's favorite toppings; she always ordered sausage...*

Then Reese walked toward us. "Hey, Jack," he called out. "Heads up!" and he threw the football at him.

"Great throw, dude," Jack exclaimed. "Come on over and talk to these pretty girls. You know Blair and Marissa...right?"

"Hi," Reese awkwardly muttered and walked over.

Jack's wife approached the table. She managed to look beautiful wearing an old camouflage hat, a black tank top and denim shorts over her bathing suit. Her thick brunette hair flowed down her back, and her face looked flawless even without makeup. She held her sweet daughter, Lizzy. "Hey, honey, the food you ordered is here…looks like we are feeding the whole pool club today!" She laughed as she set Lizzy down on the ground and started to wipe the table.

Marissa and I sat with Reese and Jack and ate our pizza. "So, Reese, do you have any girlfriends these days?" Jack teased, and Marissa and I laughed.

"No," Reese blushed and looked at Jack.

"Aww, that's okay, bud. I know you'll be turning girls down left and right in a few years," Jack said, patting him on the back. Jack got up from the table to help his wife with Lizzy.

We sat with Reese for a while before Mrs. Martin announced that it was time to get the little ones home. I liked Reese. I realized that he was in my class this year and that he only lived around the corner from me.

"I'll see you on Monday," I said to Reese before Marissa and I were off to our next adventure.

* * *

The next Saturday afternoon, my mom took the shift watching Marissa and me. It was rare that we spent a weekend apart from each other. Marissa would come along to my grandma's house and even was invited on weekend trips with my mom and me. Of course, I was always invited to Marissa's family's parties and activities too. We were like sisters.

"Blair, do you wanna go for a bike ride over to Reese's house? We can see if he is home and if he wants to go over to hang at Jack's house?" Marissa suggested as we sat out on my back deck, listening to the latest Arianna Grande song. My home was similar to the others on the street. It was a little smaller than the rest, but only my mom and me lived there, even though Marissa was a frequent visitor.

The front of the home was yellow with white shutters. In the summertime, the window boxes would be flooded with flowers cascading over the edges. At this time of year, there were small buds emerging in the planters.

"Sure," I answered. The warm sun shined on us. It seemed like we were now spending every weekend with the Campbells in some capacity. It also was still common to see Jack at my tennis matches with Marissa's family. They had become buddy-buddy with the Martins overnight.

"I could call Jack and see if he is home," Marissa suggested. "I have his number from tutoring."

It felt a little weird to call our adult friend to hang out…

"Nah, we can just ride over," I responded. "Are you going to ride your new bike?"

"Yes, let's go!" Marissa hopped up and started toward the garage.

"Moooooom, Marissa and I are going to go on a bike ride!" I opened the sliding door off the deck into the kitchen, stuck my head in and shouted.

"Where are the two of you going?" she said. "You know I don't like you two going off where there are no sidewalks."

"We are going to our friend Reese's house," I said. "He lives just around the corner. I will bring my phone."

"Well okay, just be home for dinner…and answer your phone if I call you!" she said sternly but then smiled. "Love you girls!!"

My mom was a worrier. I knew she meant it when she asked me to pick up my phone if she called. My mom reluctantly got me a phone in the fourth grade when my dad finally got on board because I spent so much time out of the house; she wanted to be able to call me.

"I love you too, Mom!" I yelled back. "Bye!" I slammed the sliding door shut. Marissa and I shuffled down into the garage to grab our bikes.

I hopped on my bike easily, and Marissa tiptoed onto her new bike. It was a little big for her, but her parents told her she'd grow into it and that it'd be perfect next season.

"This bike makes me feel like a mom," Marissa laughed.

"Well, you'd be one tiny mama!" I giggled at the sight of my ten-year-old friend on her bright yellow, shiny new bicycle.

We were off; Marissa was leading the way.

"Ouch!" Marissa fell to ground, and the bike tumbled on top of her. We were turning the corner onto Reese and Jack's street.

I jumped off my bike and stood next to my friend.

"O-M-G, are you okay, Marissa? You are bleeding!"

"Ahhhh, I am okay. But I need a Band-Aid badly," Marissa said. I could tell she was okay, but the sight of blood made my insides squirm.

I looked down at Marissa's knee with a large scrape on it. It was bleeding pretty badly. I felt nauseated...

I looked around and could see Jack's house from where Marissa had splattered.

"Let's go see if the Campbells are home," I suggested. "Maybe they can give you a Band-Aid and clean you up. Can you make it down the street?"

"Yeah, I'll make it. Can you walk up to the house though?"

"Yeah, of course," I said, looking over toward the Campbells' house and saw Mrs. Campbell walking out of their Spanish-style home toward her sliver Mercedes. She had on a sundress and her usual Ray-Bans. Their home blended well with the other homes on the street. They had bought it brand new and kept up with landscaping as per neighborhood ordinances. My favorite part of the home was the tennis court in the backyard; it was the only home in town that had a full-size court on the property.

"Oh look, there is Mrs. Campbell! I will go get her!" I exclaimed. Marissa immediately hopped up and walked her bike over to the driveway.

"Oh my goodness, girls!" Mrs. Campbell looked surprised. "What are you doing here?"

"Hi, Mrs. Campbell," I said nervously, looking up at the beautiful woman in front of me. "Marissa and I were riding bikes in the neighborhood, and Marissa just fell. Would you happen to have a Band-Aid?"

"Of course, girls! Come in please. I will clean you up, Marissa," she soothed.

Together we walked up the driveway into their home, past their grand staircase, and through the foyer. We stood in the bright kitchen where Mrs. Campbell told us to wait while she got a Band-Aid. I felt as if I was standing in a New England bed and breakfast. Light poured into the kitchen with its white cabinets and gray-scale granite countertops. Fresh flowers delicately adorned the island.

"Hey there!" Jack came out from the office and greeted us. "What have you two troublemakers gotten into this time?" he laughed.

"We were just riding bikes in the neighborhood, and Maris fell and scarped her knee. See." I pointed at the blood on Marissa's knee.

"I was just on my way out, but thank god I ran into these girls!" Mrs. Campbell came into the room carrying a Band-Aid and wipes. "Here you go, Marissa. This should clean it up."

"Thank you so so so so so much!" Marissa laughed apologetically. "I am such a mess sometimes!"

"Not to worry, Marissa, and here, take my phone number in case you are in the neighborhood and ever need anything!" She started to recite her phone number. "And Blair, take it too. You know you can always call me."

"Yeah, take my phone number too…" Jack intervened. "In case she isn't around. I am always here."

I punched in Mrs. Campbell's phone number and made a contact for her and then did the same with Jack's number. Marissa already had Jack's number from her tutoring sessions.

"You know you guys can call for any reason," Jack said again after Mrs. Campbell excused herself to go run her errands. "Even if you are in trouble, I will come and get you."

"Yeah, yeah," Marissa giggled. "But you know us…we never get into any trouble."

Jack started to walk toward the front yard. "Do you guys need a ride home? I can throw your bikes in the back of the Jeep," he offered, motioning over to his SUV.

"Marissa, are you going to be okay getting home?" I asked.

"I am fineeeeee! I can ride home," Marissa persisted.

"Okay, why don't we just go home since your knee is hurt and all."

"Yeah, let's go back to your place," Marissa agreed.

The whole ride home I thought about how weird of an experience that had been.

It felt so natural that Jack would interact with us like friends and give us his phone number.

I wondered if I would ever need to call it.

Probably not, I decided.

We returned to my house, and my mom was shocked by Marissa's knee injury.

"Why didn't you call me?" she exclaimed.

"We stopped at Marissa's tutor's house... Jack," I said.

"Jack? You call him by his first name?" I saw concern in her eyes.

"Yes, he says his dad is Mr. Campbell. He is really nice. His wife is really nice too. She gave Maris wipes and a Band-Aid."

"Well next time, if one of you falls and gets hurt, just please call me. Even if you go to a friend's house for help, I want to know what is going on."

"Yeah, okay, Mom," I said and headed to the deck to listen to pop hits on the radio for the rest of the afternoon.

* * *

Sitting in the back seat of my mom's SUV, I listened to my grandma cackle about her social misstep at lunch. I hadn't heard my grandma laugh so hard since Uncle Joseph died.

"Geez, oh man, I think I'm going to wet myself." She slapped her knee in genuine delight.

My heart was happy with my mom and grandma at the flea market that day. The three of us ladies were a good team. We used to go on day trips and enjoy each other's company more often. "Girls Trips" my grandma called them. It seemed like I had been spending more time with Marissa lately, so we hadn't had as much time just the three of us. Today, I was allowed to pick out a new purse, and we all snacked on warm pretzels and apple juice.

"I can't believe we thought that man was our waiter!" My grandma laughed about asking a young man to refill her water at the diner with her girls, only to find out he was just another customer.

"That's so funny, Grandma," I giggled in the backseat. Marissa didn't tag along today. My mom said we were just having a "family day."

Suddenly, my mom's phone started to ring. "I wonder who this is," she said. "I don't recognize the number...hello," she picked up. "Hi, Danielle! Yes, I have heard about you guys. I know Blair has spent quite a lot of time over at your home. I'm glad we are getting to speak."

My mom was talking to Mrs. Campbell. This was odd. What did she want from my mom?

"Oh, this afternoon? We are just getting back from the flea market with my mother and Blair. I will have to ask if she is up to it. Hold on," she said. "Blair honey, Danielle Campbell is on the phone. She is wondering if you would like to come over their home tonight to practice tennis with Marissa on their court. Apparently, Marissa and her mom are over there now."

She wants me to come over? I thought she wanted to help just Marissa with tennis…

"Sure, yeah, I'll go over. Tell her thanks!"

I had wanted a to get better at tennis now that Marissa was taking it seriously and also because Mrs. Campbell was always there watching. I was feeling a little behind, and Mrs. Campbell was a star.

This way, I could practice without all the pressure. Plus, the Campbells were so…I don't know…cool…

* * *

Within the hour, my mom dropped me off at the Campbells' home. My grandma was still in the car, but we had stopped at home for me to change into more comfortable clothes. Mrs. Campbell came outside.

"Hi, Mrs. Beam," she flashed her perfect white smile. "Nice to finally meet you! We love Blair. She and Marissa are so great with the kids, and they are both promising tennis stars. She is welcome here any time."

"Oh thank you, Danielle. You can call me Cathy by the way... Blair is a good kid. You just let me know when you'd like me to come and get her and what I owe you for the lesson," she looked at me and smiled.

"Oh, don't worry about that. It is my pleasure. I miss my tennis days, and Marissa and her mother are here. You know, you are welcome to stay."

"Oh, I am actually going to drop my mom off right now. Maybe another time," My mom answered.

"Another time then!" Danielle smiled.

"Alright, well I will see ya later, Blair. Have fun!" My mom smiled and blew me a kiss.

I gave my mom and grandma a hug goodbye and hopped out of the car. "See ya!" I said and walked up the paved driveway and into the Campbells' home. There I found Marissa.

"Blair and Marissa darlings, I just wanted to tell you how great I think it is that you are taking up tennis; it really helped me build my confidence when I was your age." She looked over at the tennis court behind her. "The court is yours all afternoon, ladies. Mrs. Martin will be right here cheering you on.

"Thank you!" Marissa and I said in unison. Marissa seemed comfortable here; it seemed to me she was here a lot. I wondered when she had time to come over to the Campbells.

Suddenly Jack came through the back patio door, carrying boxes and boxes of food. "Hey guys! I got food!" he shouted, and Marissa and I ran off the court into the house. Lizzy and Elena were with him and seated at the table ready to eat dinner.

"Hi," I smiled. "Wow, you got pizza!"

"Oh, I decided to get you some chicken tenders too. I thought you'd like that."

I did like chicken tenders, way better than pizza…I wonder how he knew that? I thought.

"Oh, thank you!" I felt flattered but was not all that hungry. I had eaten a snack at home before coming over. But I figured I had better eat some of this chicken since he got it just for me. Mrs. Campbell and Mrs. Martin soon entered from the back patio, and we all sat down to eat at the large round kitchen table. I started to wonder why I was there since we had only practiced for a couple of minutes. But I was having fun, I had chicken fingers, Marissa to hang out with, two adorable kids, and I felt comfortable there. The only weird part was that I had not been invited by Marissa.

I guess they like me.

Jack's high energy made the house feel like an arcade. He was constantly moving around and wanting to play with us. The entire time we were eating dinner, Marissa was talking to Lizzy about going to daycare and all the friends she was making. Marissa's mom and Mrs. Campbell were busy feeding Elena and picking at their salads.

"Blair, have you seen the whole house?" Jack asked while making continual eye contact with me. He then asked, "Did you know we have a movie theater downstairs?"

"No, I didn't know," I answered.

"Maris, you have seen the house… right?"

"Yeah, I am here every Wednesday for tutoring; I've seen the place a million times!" Marissa said a bit flippantly.

"Well then, let me give you the grand tour, Blair!" Jack said and gazed into my eyes again. When he looked at me, it was like he was trying to say something he wasn't saying out loud. I wanted to know what it was.

"Okay, come on, Lizzy; come with us on the tour!" I exclaimed in my high-pitched "kid" voice.

"Oh Lizzy sees the house every day," Jack waved his hand. "We'll be right back."

I followed him out back on the paved patio deck, past the swing set, out to where the tennis court was located. "We are planning to get a trampoline built into the ground right here," he said, pointing in front of the tennis court. I realized then that they had a large backyard; it was probably the largest in the neighborhood because of how far back it extended.

"What do you think, Blair? Should we put a trampoline in here?" he said, walking a few steps ahead and marking the ground with a rock. "Or here maybe?" He moved a few steps back and marked another spot on the ground.

Something about this conversation gave me a rush. I felt special. This adult, this really cool adult, was asking my opinion on his house. *Why did he want my opinion?* I stood for a moment and took a breath in. "I don't know really. I think maybe put it back farther, so you don't get hit with tennis balls."

"See, that is what I think too!" Jack exclaimed. "But Danielle wants the trampoline to be closer so we have more yard space…I think that's bogus! The yard is huge!"

"Yeah, I mean, I think it will look good either way. Your yard is so nice," I said, looking around at the colorful landscape that covered the back of their home.

"That's not all though; let me show you the rest of the house," Jack said. "You've got to see the movie theater!" he said, moving inside through a side door.

"You really have a movie theater?" I asked, following behind him.

"Yeah, I did not really want this house when we first bought it, but Danielle really wanted it, so I made it happen. Someone else actually had an offer on the house, and I called and made them an offer they couldn't refuse. I figured I could make it fun when I got here."

"Oh really? That was so nice that you did that for her! I am sure she was so happy." Wow, Jack really seemed like an awesome husband.

"Yeah, she was...for a while. She wants me to stop adding toys now," he said, seeming a bit frustrated. "Do you have a favorite movie?" he asked, changing the subject.

"Yes, I love *Frozen*!"

"Oh, I have watched that one so many times with Lizzy in here." He laughed, opening the door to a giant room with a high ceiling and rows of comfy recliners. "My very favorite movie is *Titanic*. It's an old one by now, but have you ever seen it?"

"No, I haven't," I said shrugging.

"It is so good. Maybe you'll like it when you're older."

"I bet I would like it now. I like watching shows with my mom, and people say I am so mature, ya know, because my parents are divorced."

"Oh well, maybe you would."

Jack continued to walk me around his entire house: his and Danielle's bedroom, Lizzy and Elena's room, and all the bathrooms. He kept saying, "So what do you think?" and asking me what flowers I thought he should plant in his backyard and the kind of art would look good on various walls. All the while, I couldn't help but feel my stomach flutter.

This man cared what I thought...was this wrong? Because it felt good...

We walked back to the living room to find Marissa playing with Lizzy and Elena.

"Hey there, kiddos!" Jack yelled.

"Daddy!" Lizzy yelled out. The little girl leapt into his arms.

With that, Mrs. Campbell and Mrs. Martin walked into the room with Elena. "We had a stinky baby!" they laughed "How is everything going here?" Mrs. Campbell looked at Marissa and Lizzy.

"Good!" Lizzy yelled and smiled.

"I can see that, sweetie!" she looked at her daughter kindly. "How are you two, Blair and Marissa? Everything okay?"

"Everything is great as usual," Marissa said.

"Yeah, I got the grand tour of your home. It's so pretty. I just love it!" I looked up at her and smiled.

"Alright. Well, Jack, what do you say we start to clean up for the night?"

"Yes, girls, we are going to head out," Mrs. Martin nodded toward the door, looking at Marissa.

Mrs. Campbell squatted down next to Lizzy. "It was such a pleasure having you guys. Come again!" she said, picking Lizzy up.

"Oh! Before you guys go, I have some tutoring materials for you, Marissa—and you too, Blair," Jack said and walked toward Marissa and me with blue reusable grocery bags. I stood behind Marissa, who was staring at her phone. He handed Marissa one bag and me another. "Blair, I have some extra, so I figured I'd give you one too. You can use these workbooks and check the answers in the back if you want to practice your times tables at home. See how fast you can do your mental math! You know if you ever need some extra help, I can schedule you in!"

"Thanks!" Marissa looked up from her phone and grabbed the bag, heading for the car.

I looked into the bag and pretended not to realize there was a *Titanic* DVD at the bottom. "Thank you," I looked up at Jack and whispered.

"Come on, sweetie. I can drive you home now," Mrs. Martin called.

"Bye, Blair," Jack said causally, walking into the house.

I hopped into the back seat of Mrs. Martin's minivan.

"Everyone buckled?"

"Yesss," Marissa and I moaned. We started the two-minute drive back to my house.

"Thanks for coming over, Blair. We love having you around," Mrs. Martin said.

"Thanks!" I hopped out of her car and walked up my driveway and into my house.

"Hi, Mom! I'm home!" I shouted and ran into my room.

"How did it go, honey?" she called out. I could tell she was cleaning up from her dinner.

"Good!" I shouted. "I can't wait to go back. I want Mr. Campbell to tutor me like he does with Marissa. He said he could!"

My mom stopped what she was doing and started for my room; she knocked gently before opening the door.

"Come in!" I appreciated when my mom gave me my privacy.

She sat down next to me on my bed and looked at me with those calming eyes. "Is that something you would like, Blair? A tutor?"

I breathed in through my nose, *I really needed help in math.* "Yeah, Mom, I hate being one of the kids getting pulled out of class for extra help. "

My mom let out a sigh. It almost looked like tears were forming in her eyes. "I know, honey. I hope you know how smart you really are; it's okay to ask for help sometimes. I will call Mr. Campbell and see what I can set up," she said while still looking as me with those loving eyes. She hugged me, stood up and asked, "What are you up to tonight? I am still cleaning up from my dinner."

"I think I'll pop a movie in my TV and call it a night," I said looking over at the TV monitor in the corner of my room and the tall shelf of DVDs.

"That sounds like a relaxing night," my mom said as she kissed me on the head and left my room, closing the door behind her. I reached into the bag Jack had given me and pulled out the *Titanic* DVD. I didn't know why, but I did not want anyone to know Jack had given it to me. I opened it up and popped in the movie before drifting into a deep sleep while rooting for Jack and Rose to make it out alive.

* * *

OFFENDERS NORMALIZE THE RELATIONSHIP.

In this situation, Jack Campbell used the story from *Titanic* to plant the seed in Blair's head that forbidden love is daring and admirable and introduces secrecy.

Sex counselor Marlowe Garrison explains by saying, "Secrecy is developed early on for non-sexual aspects of the relationships."[22] This normalizes the idea of secrets and makes the child feel special. Therefore, the child is more inclined to keep secrets.

Colleague Michael Dawn, also a sex counselor, says, "[With] romance, you're not going to have a feeling that

22 Webster, Emma. "What Is Sexual Grooming?" www.allure.com. https://www.allure.com/story/what-is-sexual-grooming-abuse. (May 2019).

you've been taken advantage of, or you're doing something to pay back someone. [Romance is] a mutual feeling; and in a grooming circumstance, it's not really a mutual feeling... The whole idea of the grooming is it's a slow process and that's why, psychologically, [it] can be so damaging—especially if the [victim] is young because they don't always know what they're falling into."[23]

In the movie, Jack and Rose are forbidden from dating because Jack is from a lower economic class than Rose. Here, Jack Campbell drew a connection between Blair and himself because they are forbidden from loving each other because of their age difference. This association with *Titanic* not only normalized the relationship but also glamourized it. In addition, the fact that he had just given her the DVD in secrecy meant he wanted to normalize any future secret interactions without Blair knowing she was actually being groomed.[24]

23 Ibid
24 Ibid

APRIL 2014.

FOURTEEN MONTHS BEFORE FIRST SEXUAL ENCOUNTER.

I held on to the side of the seat as tightly as my fingers could grip as the bus rattled and shook riding over bump after bump. I hopped on Marissa's bus after school today. We didn't have practice today, so I asked my mom if I could go over Marissa's house instead.

"Of course, Blair," she laughed when I called. "Where else would you be?" she joked.

We always liked to sit on the wheel seat of the bus where there were the most bumps. This was the first year we had ever taken the bus together. The ride was such a thrill.

"Ahh!" we'd shriek throughout the bus ride, gripping each other and the seats around us. By the time we got to Marissa's house, we were giggling enough to annoy everyone around us. We didn't care; we had each other. We walked off the bus together, wearing our backpacks and zip-up sweatshirts. It was a wet spring day, the warm sunny air cooled by a fresh rain. Walking up the driveway, I noticed Jack's Jeep parked outside. Neither of us mentioned it. Marissa swung open the door into her home and dropped her bag on the ground. "I'm home!" she screamed.

Through the kitchen window, we could see Marissa's dad and Jack sitting on her deck. Marissa's dad was a doctor and had odd hours, so sometimes he was home during the day. Marissa and I walked through the kitchen and stepped out onto the back deck. "I am home!" she stammered again.

"Oh hey, Maris! What are you doing home so early?" her dad asked. "Jack just stopped by to help me tune up my brakes on the Audi. He is a man of all trades. Isn't he?" her dad exclaimed.

"Yeah…" Marissa rolled her eyes, not caring about her dad's car. "And I am home because practice got canceled today…"

"You know I have to head over to the hospital soon," Marissa's dad said. "Do you want to stay here with your grandfather and your sister or go over Blair's house?"

"Oh no…" Marissa murmured, looking over to me. "Can we go to your house?"

"Yeah, of course," I smiled. "I'll just ask my mom to come get us!"

I started dialing my mom.

"Oh hey, girls. Why don't I drive you over to my place? I finished working on the test you took for me, Marissa; I can give it back to you," Jack suggested. "And then I can drop you at Blair's. No big deal."

"Okay. That works," I said and hung up the call before my mom answered.

Marissa's dad, Paul, and Jack cleaned their workspace in the garage. Marissa's dad had on a pair of work gloves and safety googles. Jack was just in his regular polo and khakis.

"What have you troublemakers been up to?" Jack asked, looking me straight in the eyes and smiling. He cocked his head slightly while looking at me and then turned to Marissa's dad before anyone could notice the extended gaze. "I better get going, Paul. Let me know if you have any trouble with those brakes. They should be good to go."

"Thanks, bud. Are you sure I don't owe you anything for the help? It would have cost me a fortune to take it into the shop," Marissa's dad looked at Jack and asked.

Jack rolled his eyes. "Paul, don't even worry about it. I would never take money from you for a favor. It's not a problem."

Jack started to walk toward the door. "Alright, girls, hop into my car. I'll drive ya over to my place, grab the test for you to take home, Marissa, and then I'll drop you at Blair's."

"Sounds good," Paul said. "Thanks again for all your help."

The three of us, Jack, Marissa and I, left through the front door.

"Shotgun!" Marissa yelled and ran over to Jack's car, hopping in the front seat.

I opened the back door and slid in. Jack got in the car and turned the key to start. Katy Perry's "Roar" started blasting through the stereo. Marissa started dancing in her seat, and I started to sing along. Jack laughed as we pulled out of the driveway. He stepped on the gas harder, put the windows down and sped around town in his Jeep. When we pulled into his driveway, he turned the music down and laughed. "You girls are so much fun!"

"One more song!" Marissa shouted and continued wiggling around to the music.

"Sure!" Jack turned the music back up as he pulled out of his driveway to take us for another spin around the block. It felt like such a rush riding around in the car with him and Marissa. For some reason, it felt rebellious even though I was with a trusted adult… we couldn't have been doing anything wrong. As we pulled in the driveway a second time, I felt my phone start to buzz in my back pocket. It was my mom. "Hey!" I picked up quickly. I probably should tell her I was going to be home soon with Marissa.

"Hi, honey, I was just out at the grocery store, and I wanted to see if you needed to be picked up. I saw you tried to call a few minutes ago."

"Hey, Mom! I'm actually about to be dropped off. I am at the Campbells picking up a test for Marissa, and then Jack is going to drop us off," I told her while Marissa and Jack waited for me to get off the phone to go inside.

"Oh, that's okay, Blair. He doesn't need to come out. I'll come pick the two of you up since I'm already out."

"Okay, Mom, I'll see you soon!"

"Alright, love you honey. See you soon!" she said, and I could hear her smile on the other end.

"My mom is going to come get us from here! Jack, you don't have to take us home," I said. I didn't think my mom had ever met Jack before. She had met his wife dropping me off, but she hadn't encountered Jack yet. I wondered what she would think of him. I wanted her to like him.

We walked into Jack's home and no one was home. "Everyone is out and about today," Jack said, spinning around in his kitchen, loving having the place to himself. I felt empowered in this big house with just Jack and Marissa; I felt like we were in charge, like Marissa and I could do whatever we wanted here. "Help yourself to whatever is in the fridge, guys," Jack said, walking into his office.

"I want a cookie AND fruit snacks," Marissa said, looking at the freshly baked cookies on the stove top as she started to search for snacks in the pantry. She grabbed a cookie and some gummy bears and walked over to the couch, plopping down and kicking her feet back. I grabbed a warm chocolate chip cookie as well and followed. When Jack reappeared with the test for Marissa to take home, he had a cookie in his hand too.

"Don't be fooled by these cookies," Jack said. "Danielle only uses the prepackaged dough. She doesn't like to cook herself."

Marissa and I laughed. Danielle seemed like the perfect wife. Even if she didn't like to cook, she didn't need to. They had such a perfect home and family. Jack seemed the ideal dreamy husband; he provided for the family and was so good with the kids. He seemed like a kid himself most of the time.

Then my mom pulled up out front. She didn't pull into the driveway but just waited on the street, and we filed outside when we saw her car. Jack followed us outside to greet my mom.

"Hey, Mrs. Beam! Great to finally meet you!" A huge smile spread across Jack's tan face as he jogged across the yard in his khakis and polo. "I'm Jack, Danielle's husband."

"Hi Jack, I'm Cathy," she said. "You've got such a beautiful home here," she remarked. "Also, I've been meaning to call you about tutoring Blair. She's been getting pulled out for extra help in math and really wants some extra practice. She doesn't like getting singled out in class."

"Oh my gosh, of course, I would love to help Blair. She is so smart, Cathy. Everyone just learns differently, you know?" Jack said. "Do you want to come in and see my house and where I tutor? I'm happy to show you around and set something up."

"Oh no, I really better get going. I've got a load of groceries in the car, but let's talk soon. Here is my number," she said and pulled a piece paper and pen out of her bag and started to scribble her number before handing it to Jack.

Score...I thought...I am finally going to get tutoring like Marissa! Marissa and I hopped in the back seats while they continued talking.

"Alright, alright," Jack said. "But, seriously, anytime you wanna come over, you're more than welcome. We've always got kids running around here. This house is like the neighborhood house and Blair is always welcome too... Marissa, do you have the test I gave you?" he looked to the back seat to ask.

"Yeah, I got it," Marissa said, holding the paper.

"Oh yeah, Cathy, if Marissa and Blair ever want to come over and hit the tennis ball around in the yard, they are more than welcome to do that too. Danielle doesn't get out there as much as she wishes with the one-year-old, but she hates seeing the court empty," he said.

"Oh, well, thank you, Jack, that is so kind," my mom said and smiled. I could tell she just wanted to get home now.

"One last thing, Cathy," Jack said. "Quick opinion, do you like the rose bushes we've got out front here, or do you think they are too unruly? We're thinking about taking them out and just putting in some perennials," he added.

"Oh, Jack, I think your home looks beautiful as is. You've done a great job with it. I think the bushes look great," my mom reassured him.

"Oh, you're too sweet, Cathy. Really, I just hire people to do it," Jack said. "I barely do any of the gardening myself."

"Well you and your wife have good taste!" my mom said and put her hands on the wheel.

"Alright, well you have a good afternoon! See you guys later!" Jack waved into the back seats.

On the car ride home, Marissa and I gabbed about school and Jared, the boy who was texting her.

"He asked when my birthday is," Marissa gushed. "What the heck should I say?" She put her phone down and looked to me for guidance.

"You should tell him to guess," I told her, trying to think of a "cool" answer.

"Oh, good idea! That will keep the conversation going," she chimed and began typing.

My mom loved listening to our stories in the back seat. Within minutes, we were back at my house, helping my mom unpack groceries. I loved my house. As much as I loved hanging out at Marissa's house, I was happy when we hung out here. It was my comfort zone; I was always happy and comfortable here.

* * *

"Parents shouldn't be embarrassed to talk about things like this. It's harder to abuse or trick a child who knows what you're up to,"[25] one offender says.

---

25 Huffman, Charlotte. "Two Child Sex Offenders Explain How They Picked Their Targets." www.wfaa.com. https://www.wfaa.com/article/features/originals/two-child-sex-offenders-explain-how-they-picked-their-targets/287-434667495. (May 2019).

OFFENDERS DO NOT JUST GROOM CHILDREN. THEY GROOM COMMUNITIES.[26]

Take it upon yourself to learn the signs, the red flags and stay involved. Have a healthy curiosity about people and trust your gut instincts. Groomers use their charm and niceness to appear innocent, like Jack who does favors for others, tutors kids and takes an interest in people. They are hard to detect. Research conducted by John Jays Criminal College shows people are generally poor at picking up on grooming while it is happening, so we must educate ourselves and remind the children in our lives that there are safe people to talk to.

Listen to children.

Believe them.

Children will often report abuse to someone other than a parent. If you work with children, recognize your role as a listener and protector. Also consider the message you send when you ignore someone's call for help. Be a role model for caring and compassion to promote open communication.[27]

---

26 Georgia M. Winters & Elizabeth L. Jeglic. "Stages of Sexual Grooming: Recognizing Potentially Predatory Behaviors of Child Molesters," Deviant Behavior, 38:6, 724-733, https://www.tandfonline.com/doi/full/10.1080/01639625.2016.1197656

27 "Step 3:Talk about it." www.d2l.org. https://www.d2l.org/education/5-steps/step-3/ (May 2019).

PART 2

GAINING TRUST

OCTOBER 2014.

EIGHT MONTHS BEFORE FIRST SEXUAL ENCOUNTER.

"But, please, Mom. I really want an iPad," I dramatically pleaded with her.

My mother—for whom I developed the affectionate name "Nurse Cathy"—sat next to me in the driver's seat of our dark red SUV. I started calling her Nurse Cathy because I spent so much time listening to her tell me stories about grouchy patients who never knew her name. I had a good relationship with my mom. I loved her because she was my mom, but I also genuinely liked spending time with her. She worked her tail off at the hospital in Glenvale to make sure I always wore the latest fashions and never longed for anything. My dad worked in construction, I think, but we did not talk about his work much.

"Honey, you have a phone and you have an iPod Touch that I got you from Christmas last year; you don't need an iPad. What can you do on an iPad that you can't on a phone or iPod?"

"Ahhhh," I groaned. I knew my mom was right. "I know, I know, I just think they are sooooo cool!" I smiled thinking about myself with an iPad.

"One day, honey, but for now you have a perfectly good phone and iPod. You know, not everyone your age even has a phone," she said. "You are only eleven years old, my dear."

"I know I am..." I let out a sigh. I knew she was right. I also knew I had begged my mom for the phone and the iPod I had. I looked down at my iPhone in its sparkly purple case. *She was right.*

"Alright, you're here, my dear. Give me a kiss!" She stuck her neck over the center console of the car, and I gave her a goodbye kiss. "Study hard. Let me know if you need anything. I love you, Blair."

"Bye, Mom. I love you!" I clicked the handle on the car door and pushed it open. Hopping out, I was now standing in Jack's driveway. It was getting a lot colder now. Halloween was around the corner, and I could feel bitter air around me. I had been over to Jack's house a couple of months now for tutoring. All summer long, I went over Jack's once a week to "stay sharp" he said. I had a lot of fun there. I would just hang out with Lizzy, Elena, Jack and usually some other neighborhood kids. Danielle was usually out. "Group tutoring" he called it. We'd do some worksheets, and Jack would check them over with us. Then after an hour, my mom would pick me up, and I would give Jack some money from her. They only weird part was talking about it with Marissa. I did not think she liked that I was going over for tutoring and at different times than her. We didn't talk about it much because, apparently, Jack recommended that we be in separate groups. And our moms thought it was a good idea too.

I walked up to the door and rang the bell. Danielle immediately opened the door. "Hi, Blair!" she said and smiled. "Come in, come in. It is chilly out there," she said as she stepped out of the way and welcomed me into her warm home. Today she had on a tight pair of skinny jeans and tall fall boots. They were brown and had embroidery laced up the sides. She wore an oversized sweater on her athletic body, and her silky brunette hair was perfectly in place as usual.

She had just a touch of mascara on and maybe some blush on her cheeks. She was flawless.

"I love your boots, Mrs. Campbell. Where did you get them?" I asked after I was done analyzing her whole outfit.

"Oh, you know, I ordered them online. I was just happy they fit my wider calves. I have such a hard time finding boots that fit with these calf muscles!" she said. "Well, honey, you know the drill. Jack is in his office, and I'm actually running out. I'll see you later!" She picked up Elena and put her in a baby car seat.

"Okay, thank you!" I looked up at Mrs. Campbell and smiled.

She walked out the door, and I turned to the living room past the kitchen. I could see Lizzy sitting at the TV with a headset and a brand-new iPad.

"Hi, Lizzy!"

"Yyyaaaayyyy, I get to play with Blair!" Her little baby teeth smiled widely, and she clapped her hands together. She was dressed up in a fairy costume.

"Blair!" Jack appeared from his office.

"Daddy!" Lizzy giggled and shot up.

"Hello, my fairy princess," he said and spun her around. Her legs flew up in the air, and she laughed hysterically. He put her down and looked at me. He did that thing again where he looked into my eyes intensely; I was starting to get used to it.

"Hey, Blair. It's just us today," he said, moving closer to me and smiling. He always had so much energy; he always seemed so happy.

"Hi," I said. I looked down at Lizzy and reached for her tiny hand. She grabbed on, and I put my high-pitched "child" voice on. "Is that your Halloween costume?"

"Yes, I am a fairy princess," she explained and started twirling an imaginary wand around.

"I wanna play with you and Daddy down in the basement." She bounced up and down.

Jack looked at me apologetically and took a deep breath. "Do you mind if we give her five minutes to play before we get started? I'll just throw on a movie for her after that."

"Oh, I don't mind. Sounds like fun!" I looked at Lizzy and smiled.

"Okay, let's go get your fairy Barbies!" I followed Lizzy down the stairs and into the depths of their basement. It was the ultimate kid zone. The walls were covered with a floral mural with fairies dancing in the sky. The space seemed to have every toy a kid could imagine between life-size Barbie cars and buckets of books. I looked over at Jack, who was following behind me, and took a moment to stare at the miniature amusement park I was standing in.

"Hey, Lizzy, let's put your Barbies in their hot pink car!" Jack picked up a toy car and brought it over. "Vroom vrooooom," he said as he drove the car back and forth.

"Go, Barbie!" Lizzy cheered him on.

"Vroooooooo!" Jack continued flying the car up into the sky and over Lizzy's head and then over mine. He looked at me again. "What's up, Blair?" he asked.

"Nothing," I smiled my default smile. "I am excited for Halloween."

"Oh yeah, I am going to have a Halloween party. You should come!"

"When is it?" I asked, finally focusing on him instead of the fanciful surroundings.

"Tomorrow, on Halloween night."

"Oh I don't think I can." I frowned. "I usually go over to my uncle's house to hand out candy, but this year since he died, I'm going to my grandma's house," I explained. Out of nowhere, I felt a sadness creep in that I would not spend Halloween with my fun-loving uncle. I stared at the wall for a moment, thinking about him, and then caught myself zoning out. "I am going to be a princess this year. I have a tiara and Cinderella dress." I turned my frown into a smile quickly.

"Oh that's a bummer. So I am going to miss out on that costume?" he shrugged. He actually looked disappointed. "I was really hoping you'd come."

"Yeah, but that's okay. There is always next year," I said. Now my heart was muddled. I felt guilty for now wishing I could go to Jack's Halloween party.

"Oh yeah. Well, if you're busy tomorrow, then come on over tonight. I have a haunted maze set up for the neighborhood! It is super scary!"

"No way! You have a maze at your house? Where is it?" I looked at him, surprised. That sounded *so* fun! I was immediately distracted from my confusing emotions.

"Yeah, silly goose. It's no big deal. Marissa and Reese will be here. You should stay!"

"But we have school tomorrow!" My stomach sank thinking about staying up late on a school night. My mom probably wouldn't mind, but I knew I would be tired the next day, and I would worry the whole night about not waking up for school on time.

"No, relax. It's getting dark early. We'll go after dinnertime!"

"Okay, okay, as long as my mom says it's okay," I said.

"Yes, we are going to have so much fun!" I pulled out my phone to call my mom and ask if I could stay a bit later tonight.

"I wish I had an iPad," I said as I dialed. My mom picked up, and I told her Marissa was coming over later. I asked if I could stay to play in the maze with Marissa and Reese.

"What kind of maze?" she asked.

"You know, like a haunted maze, the scary ones for Halloween. I don't know, Jack has it planned out," I told her. "Mrs. Martin can probably bring me home."

"Well I guess that's okay," she said. "Are you sure it's all okay with the neighbors?"

"Yeah, yeah, of course, Mom!" I reassured her.

"Well, okay, I will see you later then."

I hung up the phone.

"You want an iPad?" Jack asked. "Because you know Lizzy just got a new one, so we have her old one. I could give it to you."

"Really?" My mind filled with hopefulness, wishing for this iPad.

"Yeah, that old thing is of no use to us anymore. It would be one less thing lying around the house if you want to take it off our hands."

Lizzy was playing with her Barbies off by herself in the corner now.

"You know, you'd have to ask your mom, and I would have to reset the iPad for ya, but it would be no problem. I could even download some good math apps for you."

"Really?" My eyes widened. *I wanted an iPad so badly. I really hoped my mom didn't mind. I know she worked really hard to get me my phone, but this was no big deal, right? And I had the phone for a couple of months now. I really wanted the iPad.*

"Yeah, no sweat off my back," Jack shrugged like it was no big deal. "I'll tell ya what! You talk to your mom about it, and I will reset the iPad for you and have it the next time you come over."

"O-M-G!" I was so excited. "Thank you, Jack!"

"No problem, kiddo," he said, smiling. "You're so good with the kids that I love having you here. Now let's get back to the real reason you are here, tutoring!"

"Thanks!" I felt a little nervous when he said that. I could not tell if it was excitement or nervousness. I think I was just excited for my new iPad!

* * *

"I TOOK HER INNOCENCE,"[28] SAID THE SCHOOL TEACHER WHO WAS HIGHLY REGARDED IN HIS NORTHERN TEXAS TOWN BEFORE HE WAS CAUGHT ASSAULTING HIS STUDENTS.

The problem with grooming is that at first, it looks just like an involved coach, a mentor, a good teacher or role model.

---

28 Huffman, Charlotte. "Two Child Sex Offenders Explain How They Picked Their Targets." www.wfaa.com. https://www.wfaa.com/article/features/originals/two-child-sex-offenders-explain-how-they-picked-their-targets/287-434667495. (May 2019).

Groomers are often well-liked people. They are smart, cunning and clever. Almost like spies, they collect information about the child; they learn how the child's family operates and determine how to fill the needs of the child. In this story, Blair, even though she comes from a loving home, is a target. She is curious, and she is looking at others to help her find her way in the world.

Children are often told to always trust adults in certain "higher-level" roles (teachers, mentors, coaches, tutors, religious leaders, babysitters, etc.), and because they get to see the groomer mixing in with other caretakers comfortably, a natural trust starts to develop between the child and the groomer.

The groomer is an expert at cultivating relationships with not only the victim, but also the victim's family and the community intended to aid their sexual pursuits. They flood the child with gifts, time and secrets to solidify the private nature of the relationship. Then, groomers use this special trusting bond to gradually begin to control and manipulate the child. Research from a study conducted at John Jays College of Criminal Justice concluded that accidental touches and "innocent" brushes are usually the first forms of physical contact and are intended to desensitize the child to the contact. They also may use psychological

avenues to desensitize the child, like talking about sex and showing them porn.[29]

Dr. Shan Jumper, a forensic psychologist from Illinois, stated, "People like to believe they could spot someone who is a source of danger to their child. In fact, most child molesters are known to the families, look pretty average and are often quite charming versus being the 'creepy looking guy who lives down the street.'"[30]

The solution we need to embrace is unlearning.

It starts with you.

I challenge you to practice unlearning some of the stereotypes you have around child sexual abuse—whether it is believing that school is a safe zone; or that a little league coach could never be a predator; or because he/she is a dad/mom, they could never abuse a child; or that abusers give off creepy vibes.

---

29 Georgia M. Winters & Elizabeth L. Jeglic. "Stages of Sexual Grooming: Recognizing Potentially Predatory Behaviors of Child Molesters," Deviant Behavior, 38:6, 724-733, https://www.tandfonline.com/doi/full/10.1080/01639625.2016.1197656

30 Ibid

DITCH THOSE LIMITING BELIEFS!

These frameworks are blinding us from seeing the signs that are right in front of us. Realize that this mental model of what child sexual abuse looks like it not serving us. Catch yourself relying on these stereotypes and redefine child sexual abuse in the context of what we know today. According to RAINN, we know that every eleven minutes, child protective services finds evidence for a claim of child sexual abuse. We know that one in nine girls and one in fifty-three boys under the age of eighteen will experience sexual abuse or assault at the hands of an adult. We know that 93 percent of perpetrators know the victim, 59 percent are acquaintances and 34 percent are family members. We know that child sexual abuse survivors are four times more likely to abuse drugs or experience PTSD, and they are three times more likely to experience a major depressive disorder. Now we can use this knowledge to inform our thoughts and actions. Catch yourself dismissing worry or concern and remind yourself of the statistics.

Stay curious.

Take action.

Caretakers, if you notice an adult taking special interest in a child, let them know you see them. For example, a simple, "I see you really have taken a liking to Blair. Maybe it would

be good for her to develop relationships with other tutors," lets the people in that child's life know that there are watchful eyes around, or "I do not let Blair over at adults' homes unless another adult is present. Will Danielle be home too?" could be an appropriate way to set boundaries.

* * *

"I am hungry," Lizzy groaned.

It had been hours since I arrived at Jack's house, and he'd offered me Lizzy's iPad. We had finished up my tutoring session and had been playing with Lizzy in her fairy costume, coloring pictures and acting out stories all afternoon, but it seemed like no time had passed. Jack had hung with us mostly the whole time while I was waiting for Marissa and Reese to come over.

"Alright, let's get you a snack, Lizzy. What do you want?" I asked.

"Cheesy fries!" Jack exclaimed.

"Fries!" Lizzy smiled clapping her fairy wands together. "The gooey ones!"

Jack walked over to the kitchen, pulled out a bag of frozen steak-cut French fries from the freezer, and snatched a bag of shredded cheese out of the fridge.

"This is about the only meal I can make," Jack said, looking over at me. "Just wait, Blair, you'll love my cheesy fries."

I watched him prepare his special French fries on a baking sheet, talking Lizzy and me through, step by step, on how he makes his signature fries. Within minutes, Danielle would come walking through the door with the Martins.

"Oh, you and your fries again," Danielle said, carrying take-out into the house. "I got some food for you and the kids, honey," she said and came over to give Jack a kiss.

"Oh thanks, Dani," he said. "You're the best!" Jack smiled.

Wow, I was in such admiration of this couple. They seemed to have it all: a perfect marriage, house, kids, cars, everything.

"Hey, Blair!" Marissa walked through the door. I felt kind of funny being here already since I usually came over with Marissa and her family. I had been coming over for tutoring quite often, but Marissa's family had never come over while I was in tutoring. I wondered what they were thinking.

"Hi, Marissa!" She appeared at my side, walked over the to the table and sat down.

"I am so excited for the haunted maze!" Marissa said.

"Me too! It's going to be so much fun!"

Suddenly the house seemed to be full of kids. Marissa's younger sister was there, her dad was there, I saw Reese had come over with his younger brother, and they were all in the living room huddled around the football game on TV. Reese was the boy in my and Marissa's class who lived next door to Jack. He had pale skin and shaggy dark brown hair that probably should have been cut weeks ago.

"What is all this?" I asked, looking at Marissa and all the people in the living room.

"These are my famous cheese fries!" Jack said waltzing over with a huge tray of fries.

"My specialty just for you guys!" he said.

Marissa and I reached over for a fry. They were delicious… the crispy potatoes were covered in gooey cheese and crisp cold tomatoes. I was in heaven.

"Let's go, guys!" Jack called out. "We've got some scaring to do!"

I saw Reese and his friends huddled around the TV start to migrate toward Jack. *Oh my god, we were really going through a haunted maze. I actually was terrified of haunted houses, so I hoped this wasn't too scary.*

I felt a rush of adrenaline. I looked at Marissa. "This is crazy!" I said, trying to disguise my fear with excitement. Flashes of "fright fest" at the local amusement park were running through my head. *I had sworn I would never do another haunted house.*

"It's fun!" Marissa giggled. She went over to the assembly of neighborhood boys.

"Let's go!" Jack called out again and started to parade out of his house into the backyard.

"Oh my god!" I could hear Danielle remarking. "We are having a Halloween party here tomorrow! We cannot have this eye sore of a maze set up...there won't be enough room for the people."

"Don't worry, honey. I'll call the landscapers tomorrow. They will have it all put away and ready in time," Jack rubbed her back before walking out back.

Marissa and I were having a ball. It might have been cold outside, but this was a blast. It seemed like there were endless amounts of places to turn and things popping out at us. Jack had the whole tennis court set up with doorways and cornstalks defining the maze. Marissa and I held each other's hands and squeezed them tightly to stay safe. Reese threw a toy spider at me and ran away.

"Hey!" I said to Reese, watching him run in the other direction. I picked up an ear of corn off a stalk and tossed it in his direction playfully.

"Hey!" he echoed. "You're pretty good at throwing," he said, sounding surprised.

"You are not so bad yourself," I said, feeling flattered. Looking at Reese, I saw he had a red lifeguard sweatshirt on. I wondered if he was going to lifeguard training this year.

"Yeah, Jack practices my throwing with me," Reese said. "We both really like baseball, so sometimes he'll come out and practice with me."

"Yeah, you seem really close with him," I said.

"Yeah, he is the best. Jack is just like a big brother to me," Reese said, pegging a corn stalk at Jack. Jack caught the ear of corn and started jogging away.

"Come on, guys! Check out the new trampoline!" Jack shouted and ran across the maze to the new trampoline.

He put the trampoline in exactly where I told him to…even though that wasn't what Danielle wanted…

The gaggle of kids—Marissa, Lizzy, Reese, his brother, their three friends and I—followed Jack and took turns on the trampoline for the next hour. Jack would show off different tricks that we were allowed to try and other ones like back flips that only he could do.

After a while, I started to get really cold. I tucked my hands up into my sleeves and crossed my arms. I was done. I stood close to Marissa, and we both watched the boys do their damage. Jack walked over to us.

"What's wrong, girls?" Jack came bouncing over, smiling from ear to ear.

"I am just a little cold," I said, crossing my arms.

"Here, you take my sweatshirt." He took off his zip-up and handed it to me. "I am sweating anyway. You girls were doing awesome, but let's call it a night."

"Okay," I said, feeling relieved.

"Finallllly!" Marissa exclaimed.

By the time we came in through the patio doors and into the house, the rest of the parents were sitting around the table gabbing as usual. Marissa and I stuck together like glue. It was time to go home now, and Marissa's parents were dropping me off.

"Good bye, guys! Thanks for coming!" Jack waved everyone off. *I had so much fun today,* I thought.

"Bye, Blair, thanks for staying tonight!" Jack said. "And I am not ripping you off! I will get that iPad to you!" he said.

Wow, could today have gotten any better? *I got to hang out in this awesome house, play with an adorable little girl, eat greasy fries, run around with my best friend in a haunted maze and get iPad for doing it all? This was the life.*

* * *

Red Flag!

- **Adults who prefer to be in the company of children rather than other adults.**

Here, Jack clearly loved having kids around all the time and used the "big brother" label as a way to mask his manipulative techniques. Have a curiosity about the people who go out of their way to connect with the children in our lives. Do not be afraid to acknowledge how your child might be vulnerable. Be aware of your blind spots and guard against them.

If you suspect a child is being groomed, immediately limit the child's interactions with that person as much as possible. Talk to the child and use age-appropriate language to discuss the child's relationship with the individual. Let the individual in question know you are watching by questioning them on how their time is spent with the child. If you discover that a child has been abused, check in with the child and report the abuse as soon as possible.[31]

31 "Grooming: Protect Your Child from Sexual Predators." www.boystown.org. https://www.boystown.org/parenting/article/Pages/victim-grooming-protect-your-child-from-sexual-predators.aspx. (May 2019).

NOVEMBER 2014.

SEVEN MONTHS BEFORE FIRST SEXUAL ENCOUNTER.

I was sitting on my bed. The low-rise skin-tight jeans I had on were itching against my skin when my phone buzzed. I saw Jack's name pop up. I felt a little nervous that he was texting me. My stomach dropped and this felt wrong…but why? I wasn't sure…

Jack: Hi Blair! It's Jack. Do you still want the iPad? I can fix it up for you.

Phewww...totally innocent, I sighed.

Blair: Yeah! My mom won't mind! Thanks so much!

Was he going to text me again?

Jack: Do you want to come over for tutoring tonight? I can call your mom if you want. I am busy later on this week when you usually come.

Tutoring tonight? Of course! If I can get the iPad...

I stood up from my bed and raced through the hallway lined with baby photos and into the kitchen. "Mom! Can I go over to the Campbells' for tutoring tonight instead of on Friday?" I told her that Jack just texted me and asked. I wondered how she would react. My mom was standing over the kitchen sink, loading up the dishwasher. The kitchen smelled like pork chops and mashed potatoes. Classic meal by Nurse Cathy.

"He texted you?" my mom asked. Jack's wife Danielle usually called my mom to set up tutoring.

"Yeah, he had my number from when Marissa fell off her bike in front of his house... he was asking me about the iPad he is going to reset for me. Lizzy got a new one, and he is giving me her old one."

"He is giving it to you?" my mom turned off the music she had playing on her phone and turned around. She looked at me.

"Yeah, I was telling him how badly I NEED an iPad!" I put my hands together in prayer position dramatizing the "need" I had.

My mom rolled her eyes, "Well, that is very of nice of him, and make sure you thank him," she said. She raised her eyebrows and continued looking at me.

"Do you want to go to tutoring tonight?" she asked.

"Yeah I'll go, and I will thank him! Can you drop me off?" I asked.

"Yes, of course. Let me know when you need to go," my mom said and turned back toward the sink full of dishes.

* * *

When I pulled up in front of Jack's house, his Jeep was gone. That was normal. He sometimes rolled up right on time for our tutoring, and I was a few minutes early. His house was so close to mine, we always overestimated how long it took to drive there. I kissed my mom goodbye and hopped out of the car. I felt the brisk air on my skin and sped up to the front door. There were no more remnants of the haunted Halloween maze we played in last week. Halloween had come and gone.

I knocked on the door. Mrs. Campbell instantly appeared, looking stunning. She had her hair blown-out, her makeup perfected and wore a fancy black dress. I couldn't believe she just had baby Elena a year ago. She stayed at home with the kids now, but I thought she could easily still be a tennis pro in my eyes.

"Hey, hon! Come on in!" she waved me inside. "It's getting cold out there, huh? I better throw on a jacket!" she said while grabbing a soft black leather jacket from the closet and throwing it on casually.

"You look so great, Mrs. Campbell. Your outfit is so pretty," I cooed.

"Oh you're so sweet, honey. You know, you're so beautiful, honey."

Wow...She thinks I am pretty and she is a champion. I felt so flattered.

"I am going out with my family tonight and dropping these two off with a sitter," she said pointing at Lizzy and Elena. "Jack should be here any minute though... he told me you'd be coming," she said as she welcomed me into the house.

I envied how perfect her life seemed. I felt lucky that they wanted me to be a part of it. I wanted to be a part of it.

"Okay! Thank you. I hope you have fun tonight! You deserve it," I said in admiration.

Lizzy came running over and wrapped her tiny arms around my legs, hugging me. "Hi, Blair," she said, looking up at me with a big grin. I loved how much Lizzy looked up to me; she really liked having me around. I felt so grown up having someone look up to me the way she did.

"Hey there, Lizzy," I squatted down in my too-tight jeans and gave her a proper hug. "How is preschool treating you?"

"Good! I am learning the ABCs, but I already know them!" The now three-year-old smiled.

"Oh my gosh, WOW! Can I hear them?" I looked at her big eyes and sang along as she recited the ABCs. We clapped together and moved to the kitchen table where Mrs. Campbell was waiting to leave. There was a brand-new coloring book and crayons. Lizzy squealed with excitement over the pony coloring book and started humming to herself as we sat and colored together. I wondered when Jack would get home.

Right on time, Jack pulled up, and I saw his headlights pour into the window. Lizzy knew her daddy was home and raced to the door.

"Daddy, Daddy, look!" She held up the series of pictures she had just colored, some of them accidentally falling to the ground.

Jack's face lit up at the sight of his daughter's drawings. He got down on the floor and praised her, giving her a high-five and a hug.

"Blair, you are so good with Lizzy," Jack said and looked up at me. "Really, she loves you, and I love having you around."

My heart fluttered. I didn't like that his praise made me feel so good, but it did. *How could I possibly make this perfect family even better?*

"Really, I didn't do much. It's not a big deal, and I like hanging out here too," I said, looking down at Lizzy so I could break the intense eye contact Jack was making with me.

"Seriously, you are special, Blair. You're so mature for your age. I would never believe you are only eleven," he praised.

"Yeah, people tell me that a lot. I think it is because my parents are divorced." It felt good to talk about that.

"Yeah, I would love to get to know your mom better. She seems sweet," Jack smiled and looked into my eyes.

Wow, he cared about my mom, I thought.

With that, Danielle was out the door with Lizzy and Elena, off to her night out with her family.

"Well, I have the iPad I promised ya," Jack said and walked over into his office. He came out with the iPad. He sat down on the bench in his front foyer and motioned for me to sit next to him. He scooted closer to me. My jeans were touching his. It felt a little too close for me, but he leaned over with the iPad and started to show me how it worked.

"Now see here," Jack said and popped a small chip out of the pad. "This is a sim card. This card has my number and all my info on it," he explained, still sitting with our hips touching. "I am just going to pop it out, and then you can use it with Wi-Fi."

"Wow, thank you so much!" I was so excited to play with it. "I have the practice questions for you!" I said, finding an excuse to stand up and retrieve my Vera Bradley tote with my tutoring folder inside.

"Thanks, Blair," he said, looking at me intently as I gave him the paper. The corners of my lips curled into a soft smile. I felt so happy, but also nervous. *I am so happy to be here*, I thought, *but I also don't feel like I deserve this iPad.* I also wasn't sure why Jack was sitting so close to me. *Is he flirting with me? No, never... he would never flirt with me... WHAT AM I EVEN WORRYING ABOUT?* I reminded myself that Jack was married, with two kids, and thirty-six years old.

"Did you see Danielle before she left tonight?" Jack asked, walking toward me and playing with my new iPad.

"Yeah, who was she going out with? She looked really nice... she always looks really nice..."

"Yeah, yeah, everyone always oohs and ahhs at Danielle...I think she was going on a date tonight," Jack said casually.

WHAT? my eyes widened.

"She has a boyfriend?" I eagerly questioned.

"I don't know," Jack shrugged. "I wouldn't be surprised...most married couples aren't faithful anyway these days."

I was shocked...how could that be true?

"Really, who do you know that is married and cheating in town...anyone I know?" *This was good gossip.*

"Ah yeah, you know the Taylors? He has been cheating on his wife for years...and the Mallys? They have an open relationship and hook up with other couples in town...they asked Dani and me to hook up with them once...but we are not into that kind of stuff."

My mind was blown...how could that be true? These were all seemingly perfect families; how could this be so normal? What did he mean by hooking up anyway?

"Ahhh, there is so much you'll learn as you start to see the flaws in adults... grownups have problems too," he said.

I was still so in shock.

"So the Mallys actually wanted to hook up with you and Danielle? That's crazy!" I exclaimed.

"Yeah, they have quite the sex life," Jack laughed.

Sex, he said the word *sex*. We were completely alone. It felt wrong hearing him say it, but he trusted that I was adult enough to hear it. I didn't know much about sex. I had never even kissed anyone before besides a tiny peck on the lips, so I definitely did not know from experience. I learned about making babies in health class really quickly once and had seen my fair share of sex scenes in movies. The most awkward was watching the sex scenes in *Grey's Anatomy* with my mom. *Gross,* I thought.

"So does that mean that you don't love Danielle?" I asked. I thought it might be intrusive, but I was interested, and he was open.

"No, I mean, of course I do. Well I did; we were in love, and she is the mother of my children, but now we are married and it's different. We are like living partners. It sounds bad, but you'll understand one day…it's how marriage works."

I thought about my own parents. Their marriage hadn't worked out…did they cheat on each other? I never really knew why they got divorced. I didn't remember them together ever. My dad worked a lot, and it wasn't my priority to see him at night. I didn't get to see them interact much; my mom was always the one around.

"Wow, I am sorry, that sounds so terrible… so, does that mean you have had girlfriends?"

"It's really not so bad…and um, I wouldn't say I have had girlfriends…I have never developed feelings for anyone…but I do have my own fun," he said smiling. He was being vague now. I figured I had better stop asking questions. I didn't really know what to say next. *Was it safe to assume that no one told the truth?* My earth had totally been shattered by this idea that marriage wasn't real or it wasn't what I dreamt it was.

"We're way off track here, kiddo," Jack laughed. "Let me show you some games you can practice adding and subtracting decimals with on there."

* * *

LOOK FOR VERBAL GROOMING.

This can be jokes of a sexual nature, flattery, sexual innuendo, provocative discussion about personal life, inquisitive conversation about the child's personal life. Remember that taking interest in one's life can be loving, but it also can be a powerful way to manipulate someone.

"It is grooming because you're gaining their trust on a sexual nature, and that opens the door to commit a sexual offense,"[32] an offender and former school teacher admits.

---

32 Huffman, Charlotte. "Two Child Sex Offenders Explain How They Picked Their Targets." www.wfaa.com. https://www.wfaa.com/article/features/originals/two-child-sex-offenders-explain-how-they-picked-their-targets/287-434667495. (May 2019).

LOVE IS ABOUT AFFECTION, PLEASURE AND RESPECT.

GROOMING IS ABOUT POWER AND CONTROL.

Let the children in your life know that people they love can hurt them. Be ready to listen even when days are hectic; let them know you care. Take opportunities to teach children the difference between a joyful surprise and a shameful secret. Let them know that secrets make it hard to protect them from harm and often exclude others.[33]

Teach children how to say "no." Teach children that their "no" should be respected whether it is play, hugging, kissing, even eating. For example, if a child does not want to hug a relative goodbye, respect that decision and know that respect is important for the safety of the child.[34]

* * *

I hopped up and down, struggling to get my unitard on for gymnastics class. A tank unitard was necessary today because I had class with Miss Jasmine, and she didn't like it when we were not in uniform. Sometimes Marissa and

---

33 "Stop it Now: Everyday Tips to Keep Kids Safe." www.stopitnow.org. https://stopitnow.org/ohc-content/tip-sheet-4. (May 2019).

34 Ibid

I would just wear a t-shirt and shorts, but our teacher did not like that. I finally got the unitard up and took a second to catch my breath. *Okay. Now where are my shorts?* I went digging into my messy drawers looking for my black hipster shorts. *Ah, here they are...* I pulled on my shorts and then threw my hand-me-down sweatpants from my cousin on over my uniform to shield my legs from the cold air. *Almost ready to go,* I thought. My phone buzzed in my pocket.

Jack's name popped up on my screen. I looked around to see if anyone could see he his name had popped up even though I was standing in my room alone. I was uncomfortable but intrigued. I opened the text.

Jack: How is the iPad working for you?

Relief...he is just asking about the iPad. I start to type back.

Blair: Great, I am loving it!

I responded, but I was unsure where this conversation was going...was it supposed to be going anywhere? I did not want to sound awkward...or rude...

"Blair, honey...it's time to go to dance class!" my mom yelled down. I could hear the smile in her voice.

"Okay mom!" I shouted up to her. *I wonder if he is going to respond again...*

Jack's name appeared on my screen again. I was eager to open it.

Jack: Good, let me know if you need any help with it! See ya soon, kiddo!

I stood for a moment deciding if I should respond. *I'll ask Marissa*, I thought. *She'll know what to say.*

I closed out of the messages, picked up my pink drawstring bag with a gymnast on it and ran outside to the car. It was getting colder outside and darker earlier. *I hate the winter*, I thought.

My mom followed behind me. I always felt like I was waiting for her. It took my mom forever to get out the door.

"Alrighty!" my mom cheered as she entered the car. I was looking down at my phone. "Let's get you off to class... there are no parent meetings tonight. Right, honey?"

"Nope, just a regular practice tonight," I answered.

"Okay, sounds good," she answered. We were on our way to go pick up Marissa. Since Maris and I were in all the same classes, our moms alternated who would take us home from dance and who would pick us up. It was our turn to pick up.

"Hey, Maris!" I waved to her as she opened the SUV door and climbed in.

"Oh-my-god!" she bellowed.

"What's up?" I asked.

"My sister is soooo annoying! She will never shut up!" Marissa complained.

I laughed, thinking of her cute little sister who ruled her house.

"Oh no, what has Lily gotten into this time?" I inquired.

"She is just a little terror!" she remarked.

"Oh, I know your mom and dad have their hands full at your house," my mom chimed in.

We were pulling up at the gym now. Marissa and I hopped out and hurried inside. I gave my mom a kiss before I left.

"Marissa, I have to tell you something..." I looked at her when we got in the gym. She was taking off her sneakers and digging through her bag to find her hair tie.

"What, Blair?"

"Jack texted me today...he was just asking about my new iPad...but has he ever texted you before?" I asked.

"Oh yeah, he texts me sometimes...it usually has to do with my dad or my family coming over...something silly."

"So you don't think it's weird?"

"Honestly...it would be weird if it were any other parent... but not Jack...he is just like a big brother."

She was right...he acted more like a big brother than a tutor...

"True...you're right," I said as I shuffled through my bag looking for my water bottle. I put my phone away, and we headed into class together. Well at least I had nothing to worry about... *I mean, what was I worrying about anyway?*

DECEMBER 2014.

SIX MONTHS BEFORE FIRST SEXUAL ENCOUNTER.

It was officially Christmas season. Festive lights started to go up on houses. Teachers started baking more and constantly bringing in their homemade cookies to school. My mom was hounding me about what was on my Christmas list. I wanted a dog, of course. She was certain I did not need one… I had enough going on between tennis and gymnastics and tutoring. I did not have time to take care of a dog. Oh well… maybe next year…

Fall tennis practices at school season had finally come to a close. Thank goodness because it was SO cold outside. We even had some snow fall last week. It seemed like winter came overnight. I sank into the couch at 6 p.m. that Thursday night, and it was already dark outside. My mom was in the bathroom, taking a shower, and I turned on ABC Family channel to watch the Twenty-five Days of Christmas.

A text came in; it was Jack. It was pretty normal for Jack to text me, especially about coming over for tutoring...even though his wife still called my mom to schedule. He wanted me to come over tomorrow night... tomorrow was Friday. I responded that I could come, knowing I wouldn't have anything else going on unless it involved Marissa. But I would have fun over Jack's house anyway.

* * *

Tomorrow came quickly, and I went over Jack's house for tutoring. Mrs. Campbell had cleared it with my mom too. This time he was there when I got there. He was bursting with energy as usual. When I walked in the door, he was on Xbox Live with Reese yelling at someone on the headset and getting into the game. When he saw me, he looked up.

"Blair!" he exclaimed. He shot up from his game, hit pause and walked over. Danielle wasn't home.

"Hey there!" I smiled. I instantly felt happier. The winter always set me into a fog and made me drag through my days a little bit, but Jack's energy woke my body up.

He came over with Reese tailing behind him and gave me a quick side hug. His arm was warm. "Let me make some hot chocolate for us all, and we can get to work on your assignments this week," Jack said and released me from the brief embrace.

"Okay, that sounds good!" I LOVED anything chocolate, and the little marshmallows he added in the mug were the perfect touch.

Jack started to ask me about my Christmas list, and I told him about the dog I wanted that was not going to happen.

"Oh well, I wish I could give you an old dog of ours, but I don't think it works like that," Jack laughed pouring Reese and me hot chocolate. "We were actually thinking of getting a dog though."

"Are you serious?" I said. *That would be soo awesome if they got a dog. Then I could walk over all the time and play with it.* "What kind of dog?" I asked.

"Yeah, I haven't heard about this!" Reese chimed in.

Jack laughed out loud. "Hmmm, I am not sure. Probably something fluffy. What do you think?"

"I love poodles!" I cheered.

"Then a poodle it will be!"

I scrunched my face together, looking confused. "Well, okay!" I felt this weird combination of delight and concern. *Was he really getting the dog I wanted? This dog wasn't for me... right?*

I sat next to Reese at the kitchen table.

"Well, kiddo, Blair and I are gonna do some math practice. You're welcome to stay if you want," Jack babbled to Reese.

"Okay, I think I'll go home now." Reese jumped up onto his chair dramatically and then hopped down. "See ya, suckers!" he snapped and then darted out of the house. I was still thinking about the fact that Jack was all set to buy a poodle after I suggested it.

Jack came around the table and sat at the bench with me. He scooted close and gently rubbed my back. "I cannot wait to get you a dog," he gushed.

My thoughts came to a halt. I was utterly stunned. I wanted to feel good and happy, *I was getting what I wanted…right*?

I giggled a little bit and smiled. "What is our project today?" I looked at him and changed the subject.

* * *

Jack: Kiddo! I just got a little poodle!

I felt excitement run through me…yessss, I wanted to meet this dog! I could not wait to get to play with it.

Blair: Wow! What is its name? Can I come meet it?

I was surprised he already had it ready…I had only mentioned it a couple of weeks ago and now he had a dog!

Jack: Haven't named him yet. But whenever you are free, I am around tonight!

Tonight? I was going to get to meet the dog tonight? I was anxious to see it and to get my hands on it.

Blair: Can I come by before gymnastics class? Around 4?

Jack: Yeah, sounds good. I'll see you then!

It was pretty normal now for Jack to text me random things. Sometimes he would see if I was going to be over at Marissa's when he was visiting the family; other times he would just check in with me to see how my week was going, and other times he would ask me to schedule tutoring. Mrs. Campbell would still call my mom to ask about tutoring although it seemed unnecessary. I was unsure if Mrs. Campbell knew that Jack texted me too. At this point, I felt like I was learning so much from Mr. Campbell. He also loved to give me things when I came over. He usually had sweets, and sometimes I got to pick out hand-me-down clothes from Danielle. I loved looking at her clothes; one time I brought home a cute tennis visor. I did feel a little strange about accepting gifts, but I liked tutoring…and I could always give the stuff back too, just like borrowing.

Before gymnastics class that night, I bundled up in an oversized hoodie to run to my mom's warm car. I could see my breath in the air as I ran over. It was so cold.

"Don't forget we are stopping at Jack's to meet his new dog before class."

"Oh right," she hesitated. "Are you sure he is okay with that? I didn't check with Mrs. Campbell about it…"

"No, no, it's fine. He has more tutoring worksheets for me anyway… remember? And I told him we were coming."

"Okay honey," she huffed, seeming somehow nervous.

I turned up the radio to Lady Gaga's new song and giggled. I started to sing the lyrics "I am on the edge of glory" and giggled, embracing my terrible singing voice. My mom chimed in and started to sing along too. I loved hearing my mom laugh. In those moments when we were both laughing, it felt like nothing else mattered; it was just us.

When we arrived at Jack's house, it was still light, but the kind of light that was short and fading, cold and bitter. Luckily, Jack had a driveway we could pull into, so I did not have to walk very far to get to the door. I had texted him on our way to his house that we were coming and ran out of the car and up to the door to meet the precious pup. I knew my mom did not want me to be long. She stayed in the car. I knocked on the door softly because I did not want to wake Lizzy or Elena up if they were napping. I could see Jack through the big glass window; he was coming to the front door and holding a little curly haired puppy bouncing up and down in his arms.

"Hey," Jack whispered as he opened the door. "Danielle is putting Elena to nap. Let's go outside."

I was hoping he wouldn't say that. It was so cold, and he was not even wearing a jacket or shoes. He had the precious pup in his hands.

"Okay," I whispered back.

"I want to talk to your mom really quickly," Jack said and motioned for me to follow him over to the car. He tiptoed barefoot over to the car…like a kid who forgot their shoes, with the tiny white pup in his arms.

"Hey, Mrs. Beam," Jack said and grinned ear to ear. It was weird seeing him talk to my mom; they had only ever met once before when my mom was picking me up from his house a couple of months ago. It made me nervous. I had this fear that she would see Jack, and the way he looks at me, and know that something was strange. But I could not pinpoint what was strange. I mean Jack had a wife and children. It's not like he could actually have feelings for me. But maybe I liked him too much… maybe it was my fault I was afraid. He hadn't done anything wrong…goodness…he got a puppy… what I had desperately wanted.

"Oh, you can call me Cathy!" my mom said, her face cheering up instantly in response to Jack's energetic greeting. She laughed. She liked him…that made me happy… *score!* I thought…if she's not suspicious, nothing must be awry here. "Oh, your dog is so precious! What is its name?"

"I don't know yet!" Jack bubbled. "What do you think?" Jack looked and me and winked.

"Snowflake," I smiled, looking at the white ball of curly locks.

"Snowflake is so fitting considering this weather! That makes perfect sense. Snowflake it is!"

"Hi, Snowflake!" I said, petting her gently. I was standing next to Jack. "I am going to go in the car now. I am so so so so cold." I ran around the car and hopped in the passenger seat next to my mom.

My mom laughed. "Oh, Blair, look at you going and taking over people's homes! I am sure Jack wants Lizzy and Elena to help name the dog!"

"Oh Lizzy wants to call it puppy forever and Elena can't talk! I needed an expert's advice, and Blair has made so much progress in our tutoring sessions."

"I don't know where she got the brains from...it wasn't me!" my mom laughed. She continued, "Thank you for all your help with tutoring and stuff. I feel like I must owe you more money than you have charged us."

Jack handed my mom the puppy through the window. "Blair is welcome here any time. She is really great to have around with the kids too. She is welcome to come play with Snowflake whenever she wants...I don't want to overstep, though.

You let me know if she is over here too much," Jack said as his face got more serious.

"Oh?" my mom looked surprised. "Well thank you, but I don't think Blair is going to let this thing out of her sight," she said, handing the dog back to Jack.

"Well, have a good night, guys, and Cathy, we should have you and Blair over soon! It's so good to see you!" Jack cheered. He was visibly cold now. "I am going to head in before I freeze to death out here," he said and tiptoed back in the house.

"Well, I see you've gotten what you wanted," my mom raised her eyebrows and laughed. She started to pull the car out of the driveway.

I felt anxious. I even got to name the dog. WOW. I wished the dog lived with me at my house and could cuddle with me when I wanted, but it was a dog and it was mine… well almost mine.

* * *

Red flag!

- **Gift Giving**

Cards, cell phones, athletic gear, clothing, school supplies, books, money, movie/event tickets, jewelry, etc. can be used to make children feel like they owe an adult something. Remember, a gift or an act of kindness is only kind when nothing is expected in return. In this story, Blair's feelings of answerability toward Jack are masked by the enthusiasm she has for the iPad and for the dog. Although the dog was not a direct gift to her, the fact that he got the dog she wanted makes Blair feel like she owes something to Jack.

YOU ALWAYS HAVE THE RIGHT TO REFUSE A GIFT WHEN IT FEELS UNCOMFORTABLE OR TO REFUSE A FAVOR IN RETURN FOR A GIFT.

Let the adults in your children's life know that the children only accept gifts on holidays or special occasions, and ask them to inform you of the gift they are giving before they offer it to the child.

LOVE IS UNCONDITIONAL;
IT DOES NOT DEPEND ON FAVORS.

IT IS A BOND OF MUTUAL LOVE AND RESPECT.

Signs that gift giving may be reason for concern:

- an adult favors one child over others

- **an adult who gives gifts to children without acquiring permission from parents**

- **a child becomes secretive about gifts or cannot explain where they got items**

- **the gift has been prohibited by the parent[35]**

* * *

Jack's name appeared on my phone. He texted me. Shivers danced down my spine and into my tummy. I closed my phone, waited a moment… and then opened the message.

Jack: Is that iPad still treating you well?

Blair: Yes, thank you, I love it! Thank you sooooooo much!

Jack: Do you still want to see a different way to communicate on there since you don't have texting on the iPad?

Last weekend I was over Jack's house with Marissa's family; we had gone over for a Christmas cookie exchange and Reese had been over. It was pretty common for Reese to walk over

35 "An Adult Who Gives Gifts without Permission." www.dioceseofbmt.org. http://www.dioceseofbmt.org/wp-content/uploads/2015/05/ParentTraining28.pdf. (May 2019).

when there were people over at the Campbells'. Jack had been showing him how to use his iPad. Marissa and I heard them talking and were fascinated.

"Yeah, dude, just use this address and you can text people back and forth. You just need an Internet connection," Jack explained.

We learned that part of Jack's job involved using computers to communicate with his students, so he could talk to them whenever they needed help with assignments. He said it was so helpful. That was so cool... Jack had offered to sometime show Marissa and me how it worked.

Blair: Yeah! I really want to learn about it!

Jack: Can I call you? I can walk you through it!

I had never really talked to Jack on the phone before. I had seen Marissa talk to him sometimes though. He would call her if her dad didn't pick up and he would ask about plans. But he was going to teach me something... And I had nothing better to do. I had just gotten home from school and hopped on the instant messenger from my iPad. It was the latest and greatest invention. My username was gymnasticsxgirl07, and I loved going on and talking to all the boys I was too nervous to talk to in person. I had the biggest crush on Lance Miller.

Marissa said that our friend Olivia told her that he liked me too, but we only ever talked on instant messenger. I exited out of IM for now.

Blair: Yeah!

I texted him back and then dialed Jack's number.

"Hey, trouble maker! What are you up to?" Jack's cheerful voice came through. It was like I could feel his words in my stomach. I didn't like that his voice had that effect on me.

"I am just messing around on instant messenger, but nothing much really," I said and smiled to myself.

"Oh, I bet you've got a ton of boys messaging you on there," Jack cooed. "You're the hottest girl in the sixth grade."

My jaw dropped and my eyes widened. I froze for a moment and giggled. My open mouth turned into a smile. I felt giddy. I looked around to make sure no one could see me or hear the phone. I was alone. Good. I moved to the corner of my room away from the door and brought my iPad.

"You know, that's what all the dads say about you," Jack said. "They all think you are hot; you're hotter than Marissa."

Me? Prettier than Marissa? But I always knew she was way prettier than me... she was skinner and had reddish blonde hair. My petite frame and long brunette hair had nothing on Marissa. Marissa didn't even have to wear makeup to look nice. I always had to put on powder to cover my red cheeks and some mascara before I went out.

"They do? They say that?" I said. I didn't really know what to say. Was I supposed to thank him? It was a compliment, after all. I had this nervous excitement filling my body, and I did not know what to do with it. I was not going to tell Marissa this. This was my secret. This was between me and Jack only.

"Hell yeah! The dads talk about how pretty the daughters are all the time. We need a break from our wives sometimes... we need a fantasy."

First Jack told me that the all these couples were unfaithful to each other and now he was telling they talk about young girls... *Was this really normal?*

"Really, is that true? I can't believe that," I said, trying to stay hushed in my room.

"Oh my god yeah! You wouldn't believe what Marissa's dad said about her the other day..."

"He was talking about his daughter? Has he ever said anything about me?" I wasn't sure if I wanted to know. I wasn't sure what I wanted the answer to be.

"Oh yeah...all the time... it's just guy talk though, Blair. It's nothing personal...you'll understand one day."

I didn't like that he said one day. I wanted to understand more; I wanted to be an adult now. I had always felt more mature than most people my age, and sometimes it was hard to fit in when Marissa wasn't around. I had always loved talking to my mom's friends from the hospital when they came over. I loved listening to their stories and hearing about their lives. It felt good when they talked to me like I was on their level. I liked when Jack did it too. I felt like I was learning about a whole new world. A secret world. It was thrilling. I started to feel a little guilty...something was off here. I changed the topic.

"Yeah, I guess...one day," I muttered. My feelings were confusing me. "What about this iPad stuff...what were you going to show me?"

"Oh yeah, sorry. You distract me sometimes," Jack said.

I ignored the comment, unsure what he meant by it.

"But yeah, why don't we set you up with a Chatty account. It makes it so that we can text on your iPad and then it instantly disappears. I will show you."

"What do you mean disappears?"

"I will show you," Jack said. "Go to the app store on your iPad and search Chatty."

I looked at my iPad screen, pressed my finger on the app store, and opened a search window. C-h-a-t-t-y I typed.

"Okay, I found it," I said, hitting download.

"Awesome! Now I already made you an account, so you can just log on as tennisPro, and your password is snowflake," he paused for a moment. "Try it. Try logging in."

"Okayyyy..." I said and typed in the information. I was intoxicated by this idea that I could talk to people and then have the messages erased forever. It would be like a secret world.

"It's as simple as that. You'll save so much storage on your iPad now too. More room for games!" Jack said.

I heard my mom call down, "Blair! What are you up to? Come hang out!" I could hear her coming down the stairs toward my door.

I did not want her to know about this. I didn't think she'd understand; she hated technology. "One sec!" I yelled.

"I've got to go. My mom is calling," I said to Jack and hung up quickly. I am not sure why I hung up so quickly, but it just seemed easier than having to explain why I was talking to Jack. I left my iPad on my bed and went upstairs to hang out with my mom.

* * *

The winter dragged on. The long, cold New Jersey winter sank in and put me in hibernation mode. I spent a lot of time on the iPad using Chatty with Jack...we learned we could talk this way without anyone ever knowing...unlike phone calls that leave a trace. He often popped up on my screen while I was on AIM with my friends and asked me about Lance, the boy that often messaged me. I have had a crush on Lance since the fourth grade, but we have never had a conversation in person. We awkwardly look at each other in the hallway and smile. I giggle when someone points him out to me. The one time he said my name on the playground, I got butterflies and ran away. Jack asked me if I have ever kissed a boy. This question sent nervous vibrations down my back. "No," I said.

Marissa too talked to Jack often; we talked to him together a lot, at family gatherings and parties. Sometimes Jack would find us when we were by ourselves and chatted with us alone. It often became sexual. He told us about who is cheating on whom, and we relished in the neighborhood gossip. He told us about his first kiss with an older girl when he was our age. He even made sexual jokes about his beautiful wife.

I felt like it was normal for me to talk to Jack alone sometimes. I mean, we talked when people were around too, and no one thought that was weird… what was the difference? And I liked talking to him. He treated me like an adult, he asked me questions, he complimented me. I started to feel different when I was with Marissa. His eyes always lingered on me for a little longer than they did on anyone else. I also had not disclosed this to Marissa… how much Jack and I actually talked. I could have told her, but I wouldn't have wanted her to tell anyone.

It started to become my little secret. I couldn't help but feel Jack and I had a special connection, one that we both were fighting but couldn't help. It scared me. It intrigued me. Jack confirmed to me that he spent so much time with Marissa's family because he wanted an excuse to see me. My eleven year old heart was vulnerable; it was open; it was told to trust adults; it loved the thrill that cannot be considered wrong because, of course, Jack was a trusted adult. He had never actually touched me or kissed me or even tried to. It was all totally innocent.

The one person who knew we talked a lot was Reese, Jack's neighbor who was my age. Reese was like a son to Jack, or rather Jack was like a father to Reese. They practiced baseball, they talked about girls and played video games together. They were family. Reese was on my bus, and we would pass by Jack's house every morning on the way to school. Reese and I would talk about Jack all the time. Reese idolized him. Jack was the best at baseball, at video gaming, at talking to girls and tutoring. Jack told Reese he could help him become a professor one day too.

"You know, Jack likes you a lot, Blair," Reese said to me one February day on the bus.

"What?" I winced, my eyes wide, checking to make sure no one else heard that. I could not believe he just said that out loud, on the bus.

"He thinks you're really cool. He talks about you a lot to me," Reese said. "You know he is just like a big kid. I swear he is like an older brother to me."

"Yeah, we talk on the phone and on the Chatty app," I said nervously, and it felt weird saying it out loud.

"Yeah, I know. Jack tells me about it," Reese said. I was shocked. *He does?* I thought. I did not think he would want anyone to know.

When I talked to Reese, I was reassured that it was normal, that other kids were close to Jack, that I wasn't really alone in this.

* * *

OFFENDERS MAY USE OTHER KIDS TO NORMALIZE THE RELATIONSHIP.

Sex counselor Marlowe Garrison said that offenders "Insert themselves into the daily life of the victim."[36] They may attend a family function of the child's or a child's friend to normalize their appearance in the child's life.

Here, Reese is groomed just like Blair into thinking that adults are just big kids and there is no reason age should come between Blair and Jack's relationship. This dangerous idea establishes normalcy for Blair in her relationship with Jack and squashes any feelings of doubt in their relationship.

---

36 Webster, Emma. "What Is Sexual Grooming?" www.allure.com. https://www.allure.com/story/what-is-sexual-grooming-abuse. (May 2019).

PART 3

FILLING A NEED

MARCH 2015.

THREE MONTHS BEFORE FIRST SEXUAL ENCOUNTER.

"OUCH!" Marissa yelped. I could see the tears filling her eyeballs. She was hurting. My heart ached for her.

It was a normal Friday night. Marissa was sleeping over at my house. We had our pajamas on. I was wearing light pink and blue plaid pajama bottoms and an oversized t-shirt. Marissa had on a pair of athletic shorts and one of her dad's old hospital t-shirts. We were lying in my double-sized bed watching TV when Marissa sat up. "I want ice cream," she said before she abruptly stood up and slipped. Down she went, falling into my white plastic hamper that was right behind her. Her arms went up and her butt landed at the bottom of the basket, hitting its hard bottom.

"Are you okay, Maris?" I responded to her cry.

"I hit my tailbone," she wailed; she was not trying to hide the tears.

Oh no, I thought. *What could I do to help her?*

"Do you want some ice?" I asked, worried. I hated to see her in pain. I reached down and pulled her out of the now-mis-shapen hamper and sat her on my bed.

I could hear my mom coming around the corner. She'd heard us making a commotion. My mom knocked at the door. "Can I come in, girls? Is something wrong?" she said, obviously sounding concerned.

"Yeah, come in," I said, still in panic.

Marissa looked at my mom and smiled. "I fell on my butt," she said, starting to crack up laughing.

I looked at her now hysterical face and started to laugh.

"I think I broke my tailbone," she burst out, unable to hold back laughter.

We were both now hysterically laughing on my bed. My mom looked at the two of us and shook her head, laughing along with us.

"Well, Marissa, can I get you anything? Do you think you'll need an ambulance ride?" my mom joked.

"No, that just really hurt for a second." She smiled, and we looked at each other.

"You girls are too much sometimes! Now go to bed. I know I am!" She closed the door behind her and returned to her room.

Marissa and I looked at each other and laughed again. I lay back on my bed to catch my breath.

"My abs hurt, Maris. You made me laugh too much," I giggled.

"Mine too…and my butt!" she snickered.

I loved being friends with Marissa. We got along so well; she was funny and silly and never took things too seriously.

She helped me lighten up, and we always had a good time together. We were a duo, and everyone knew it.

The weather had finally started to make a turn. There was no longer frost on the ground when I left to get on the bus in the morning. I could smell it in the air. Spring was coming. It was March 2015. I had been doing a good job of staying friends with Marissa and keeping my one-on-one conversations with Jack to myself and to Reese. It felt kind of nice to have something of my own. Something that wasn't mine and Marissa's. It was just mine.

Marissa got a text from Jack.

Jack: I am at your house. Where are you?

Marissa read the text to me. She was pretty casual about it. "What should I say?" she asked.

I knew that Jack knew she was at my house; we had talked on Chatty earlier, and I told him she was coming over. He suggested we go to Marissa's since he would be over after their adult league football practice. I told him we already made plans.

"Tell him you're at my house." I shrugged.

"Okay," Marissa said as she looked down at her phone and started typing.

"He is calling me," Marissa said. Her eyes got wide and she looked up at me.

"I wonder why… answer!" I said.

"Hello," Marissa said with a little bit of attitude as usual.

"Hey, you two!" I could hear Jack's bouncing voice from where I was sitting across from Marissa on my bed.

"I am at your house, Maris. Actually, I am outside peeing right now…What are you guys up to?"

"Nothing…" Marissa said matter-of-factly. "We were just watching TV when I had an incident where I fell on my butt, all because I wanted ice cream."

"You guys want ice cream? Oh, that sounds good! What kind?"

"Mint chocolate chip is my favvvvvvvvorite," Marissa said.

"Oh well, no problem. I can bring some over. I am leaving your house anyway. I will just stop at Wawa on the way home."

"What? Jack, it's almost midnight...you can't come to the door. Blair's mom is asleep."

I was sitting on my bed in shock listening to this conversation. Jack, coming here...to my house... in the middle of the night? No. That was crossing the line. I could get in trouble for that... What if my mom found out? That would ruin everything.

"No worries. I will just come to Blair's window and drop it off really quick. No big deal!"

Blair's eyes widened again. "I mean, if you insist," Marissa said.

They hung up. I looked down at my phone. Jack had texted me.

Jack: I can't wait to see you ;)

I pretended I didn't see it. I did not answer. I did not want him to come to my window. Why did Marissa say that was okay? I was so nervous I was going to get in trouble. My mom would be so upset. I told Marissa I didn't think it was a good idea.

"But it will make my butt feel better and plus no one will know! And we will get ice cream...he is with my dad right now anyway…my dad probably knows he is coming…they always drink beer at my house after their football practices."

I took a deep breath in. Okay, he would just come to the window really quickly and we would get the ice cream and he'd leave. No harm in that…right? If my mom found out, we would just say we did not want to wake her.

Within minutes, Jack was calling me. "I am walking toward your house. Be ready to open the window for me," he said when I picked up.

Marissa and I looked at the window. My bedroom was on the first level of the house. My mom's bedroom was upstairs. The window to my room faced the side yard and was easy to walk up to. The bushes on the side of my window would mask Jack's appearance from the street. We tugged the window up. A loud creaking noise screeched out. We froze and looked at each other, hoping we did not wake my mom. No one stirred. We were silent. I could tell Marissa was nervous too.

We could hear footsteps, leaves crunching.

Oh no, I thought. *Just leave now.* I was so scared.

Jack appeared in front of us. He was smiling. All my fears washed away…how could I be scared? He looked so normal.

He was so comfortable, like he was supposed to be right there right then. Like he had nowhere better in the world to be. He held up a bag. "I brought you guys ice cream," he said and smiled his energetic smile. Marissa grabbed the bag.

"THANK YOU," she mouthed in all caps.

I looked at Jack. He was wearing a zip-up sweatshirt, and it was kind of a cold night. He didn't seem fazed. His eyes were a little red.

"What are you trouble makers up to?" he asked.

"Nothing," I said. "Just hanging out. Marissa is recovering from her butt injury," I laughed. "Thanks for the ice cream."

"Of course, guys," he said. "Now I better get out of here before someone calls the cops on me."

"Yeah, yeah, you better is right!" Marissa said.

With that, Jack raced away and we closed the window. Marissa and I tiptoed upstairs to the kitchen to get spoons. We were eating ice cream straight from the carton tonight.

* * *

Stories like Blair's highlight the power that grooming has over a person's mind and the lasting effects of manipulation that survivors face. Trauma, whether it is one-time, multiple, or long-lasting repetitive events, affects everyone differently.[37] Once they experience trauma, they may be forever changed. Trauma at its core is defined by the American Psychological Association as an "emotional response to a terrible event like an accident, rape or natural disaster." Consequently, most people who experience such traumatic and terrible events do everything in their power to drive this experience out of their minds. The highly acclaimed book *The Body Keeps the Score* explains that it is immensely easier for the body to try and forget the trauma than it is to relive it. Our bodies use up so much energy trying to continue living while also trying to mask this pain we endured.[38] Many survivors live on, carrying on their backs the shame and guilt that come along with their trauma.

They keep trying to push past the trauma they lived through, but their bodies remember. They cannot forget the pain; they live on edge, waiting to protect themselves from the next traumatic experience that might strike. They

---

37 *Trauma-Informed Care in Behavioral Health Services*. Substance Abuse and Mental Health Services Administration (US); 2014. (Treatment Improvement Protocol (TIP) Series, No. 57.) Chapter 3, Understanding the Impact of Trauma. https://www.ncbi.nlm.nih.gov/books/NBK207191/

38 van der Kolk, Bessel A. *The Body Keeps the Score*: Brain, Mind and Body in the Healing of Trauma. Viking, 2014.

feel out of control long after the traumatic event has ceased. Those who have experienced grooming are confused; they are infatuated with the offender and have trouble distinguishing the good from the bad. They have learned that they themselves are not trustworthy, that they cannot use their intuition to make decisions. They turn to other ways to cope, to regain control. These survivors, who are overwhelmingly women, fail to reach their full potential because they have wounds that have not healed. Those who do soar above and achieve their dreams are working extraordinarily harder than their counterparts.

Research actually shows that the human body physiologically changes after experiencing trauma. The brain's "alarm system" increases stress hormone activity. Every day, some survivors of trauma walk around hyper-vigilant, waiting for the next trauma to occur. Some experience other symptoms of PTSD or none at all. This reaction makes it hard for the brain to decide what information coming in is relevant and what is not. Trauma has been shown to weaken the part of the brain that makes a person feel fully alive.[39]

However, recent research on the emotion, biology and mind-set around trauma also shows there are ways to reverse the damage. Human connection is one way,

---

39 Courtois, Christine A. *It's Not You, It's What Happened to You.* Telemachus Press, 2014.

allowing survivors to reconnect with other people in order to look inside themselves and fathom their experience and their emotions. We need to start hearing survivors in order to heal them.[40]

We need to listen and support survivors' healing so they can rise up and live lives with less depression, anxiety, shame and guilt.

Let people be vulnerable, show their true selves with their real experiences, and be heard.

* * *

The next morning, I woke up, warmly cuddled in my blanket. The sun was peering through the window. I was happy I had no reason to get out of bed yet. Marissa was on the other side of the bed, still sleeping. Then I remembered last night. Jack had been there. My stomach dropped. I wished it were a dream. It was too real for him to have come to my bedroom window in the middle of the night. I felt guilty. In my head, I could rationalize it because Marissa had been here, so it could not have been all my fault. It could not have been about me liking Jack. I didn't ask him to come here; I didn't even say

40 Ibid

yes. Ugh, and I hadn't faced my mom yet. *What if she knew everything and was waiting until we got up to confront us?*

I hoped that wasn't the case. I squished my eyes shut, pulled the covers over my head and hoped for the best.

When Marissa woke up a little bit later, we didn't talk about the night before. We just rolled out of bed at the smell of pancakes and walked, like zombies, to fill our bellies. My mom was in her bathrobe, smiling and flipping pancakes on the griddle.

"Morning, girls!" she said with a smile as we sat down to enjoy some delicious pancakes.

*Phew...*I thought, *we got away with that one... everything was okay... everything seemed normal...*

That day, Marissa and I would end up going over to her house to spend the day. We would run into Jack there; he was hanging out with Marissa's dad.

"Hey, guys," he said, walking by us. Marissa and I were sitting at her kitchen table.

I felt uncomfortable knowing what had happened last night. *Why was no one else weirded out? Was something wrong with me?* Everything seemed to continue on as normal...it just didn't feel right. But Marissa was my best friend. She would never let anything bad happen to us.

* * *

Marissa and I sat in the lunchroom. We sat with the so-called "cool" crowd at lunch. I had always kind of looked up to these girls and also kind of been afraid of them. I didn't really consider myself friends with those girls; they kind of intimidated me, but I was friends with Marissa, so I could sit there. Marissa was much more outspoken than I was. She was so good at making friends. Her mom was also good friends with the other moms, which helped her make friends... I thought. The girls were making plans to go to the movies tonight. We wanted to see the new *Coco* movie that just came out in theaters. I texted my mom to see if I could go.

Blair: Can I go to the movies tonight with Marissa and friends?

Mom: Of course. What time is the movie? Who else is going?

Blair: It's at 7:05 at AMC. Marissa and some girls from school you don't know yet, Kylie, Amanda and Jessica.

Mom: Oh, that sounds great. Yeah you can go!

Blair: And can Marissa sleep over afterward?

Mom: I would not expect anything less! Marissa is always welcome.

Blair: Okay, thanks!

"Marissa, my mom can bring us to the movies tonight, and you can sleep over after," I said to her.

"Thanks, Blair!" she said and turned back to the gaggle of girls.

* * *

The movie night was so fun! My mom was reluctant to drop us off alone at the movies. She was worried that someone might "steal us." Marissa and I laughed at her. "We are meeting friends here!" Marissa said. "And we both have phones."

"Okay, okay, dears. Text when you're inside!" my mom said and then looked at me and made me confirm I would text her. I gave her a kiss goodbye.

Movies usually bored me, but I was glad I wouldn't have to manage any conversations with all the girls that night; I could just sit back and watch the movie. Afterward, Marissa and I ended up back at our usual spot on my bed. Tonight, we were gossiping about the girls we were hanging out with.

"Can you believe Kylie and Ben are dating now?" Marissa asked.

"I know...it's crazy!"

Boys were such a curious concept to me. I really liked the idea of talking to boys, but I was so nervous to talk to them in person. I still messaged Lance Miller online.

It was now approaching midnight, and I was starting to get tired. I looked at my phone. Jack texted me.

I wanted to ignore it, to not look at it, but I couldn't...I wanted to know what he had to say. I normally wouldn't tell Marissa he texted, but since he had called Marissa that other time, I didn't think she would judge.

I looked at the message. Jack was at Marissa's house again after football practice. He wanted to know if we needed anything tonight.

"Yes! Let's get more ice cream," Marissa pleaded. My stomach was going to fall out of my body. N*ononononononooooo*, I thought. I did not want to get in trouble. I felt a little angry with Marissa for wanting him to come to my house. She was not the one who was going to get in trouble if her mom found out.

Before I knew it, Jack was on the phone. He was bringing us ice cream, what did I want…

"Anything Snickers," I rolled my eyes, wishing I could prevent him from coming over. It felt out of my control.

Marissa smiled. I tried to relax. We were just having fun, getting a snack; this was no big deal.

"Remember when I broke my butt last week?" Marissa bubbled.

We both burst out laughing.

Then we heard a knock. We froze, staring at each other. I felt a rush of adrenaline shoot up my core. I started to sweat. Jack was here. We hadn't opened the creaky window yet. Together we carefully pushed the window and the screen up to see Jack.

"Look what I got," Jack said. He was holding a bag full of everything Snickers had ever made… my favorite candy. *YUM*, I thought. I took out a fun-sized Snickers and popped it into my mouth. It was so good, so sweet. I let it melt on my tongue.

"What are you guys up to?" Jack beamed. Again, his smile and ease made me feel at ease, like I had no reason to worry. His eyes were kind of red again, like they were last time when he stopped by. It was a little warmer this time, so he was wearing just a t-shirt.

"We went to the movies tonight," I told him. "We saw *Coco*."

"Ohhhhhhh, was it a date?" Jack asked.

"No!" I said obviously, my face in a frown.

"We went with some girls from school," Marissa chimed in.

"Well you two are going to be turning those boys down left and right. You let me know if I need to beat anyone up," Jack said.

He had already been standing at my window longer than last week. He seemed like he was ready to stay and chat.

"Have you guys ever orgasmed?" he asked. Marissa and I were at this point sitting on my bed, eating candy looking up at him. I had never heard that word before. It made me uncomfortable.

"Ewwww," Marissa said. I wanted to pretend like I knew what that meant, but I had no idea. I didn't say anything.

"It's the best feeling ever! You know, sometimes, girls that are good friends will practice kissing and stuff on each other before they get boyfriends, ya know… to make sure they are good at it…" I froze. I looked down at my bed. I giggled a little. Marissa laughed and continued talking to Jack. I don't remember what she said.

"Blair, how are those Snickers?"

"Good. Thanks, Jack, for getting them."

"Anytime! I am going to get going now. You two stay out of trouble."

Finally, I thought. These feelings were so confusing. I was so interested in being an adult and learning all the adult things. I wanted to be like a grownup. I liked feeling special… the thrill was kind of fun sometimes…but then why did I feel like I couldn't tell my mom?

Marissa and I closed the window behind him and went to bed. We did not talk about what Jack had said. I didn't want her to know that I had no idea what that word "orgasm" was. Turns out these window visits would become a weekly event.

* * *

The scars that grooming carves into survivors' souls are not always defined by rape or physical abuse. The wounds left by a groomer are real, no matter the extent to which a groomer progresses sexually. Here, Blair and Marissa are both being taken advantage of because they are children, and an adult is crossing boundaries of what is okay and what is inappropriate. The groomer is normalizing sexual language to prepare the child for abuse and normalize secrecy. Again, trauma is trauma and abuse is abuse. The body responds to the betrayal of the senses oftentimes by staying silent and finding ways to push down emotions and find control in outside of themselves. Groomers prey on the feelings of young people. Specifically, those that are vulnerable in some way. Shame and guilt seep into the young person's mind when they are confused by the feelings of pleasure, filling a void in their life mixed with a sense that something is wrong. Be the light for a child or friend; let the people in your life know they are worthy of love and connection.

Take an interest. Ask questions and share your own truth.

Give people, especially children, the opportunity to do the same.

Tips for learning how to talk to children about grooming:

- **Start early and have a continuous, open conversation**
- **Use the news/TV to prompt a conversation. If it comes up, ask the child if they know what child sexual abuse is and how they can prevent it**

Read books on these topics. Some good ones are:

- **School aged:**
  - ***Where Did I Come From?* by Peter Mayle and Authur Robbins**
  - ***What Is Happening to Me?* by Peter Mayle and Arthur Robins**
  - ***My Body Belongs to Me* by Jill Starishevsky**
- **Older-children:**
  - ***It's so Amazing: A Book About Eggs, Sperm, Birth, Babies and Families* by Robie Harris and Michael Emberley**[41]

---

41 McCall, Catherine. "How and When to Talk to Your Child about Sexual Abuse" www.psychologytoday.com. https://www.psychologytoday.com/us/blog/overcoming-child-abuse/201006/how-and-when-talk-your-child-about-sexual-abuse. (May 2019).

APRIL 2015.

TWO MONTHS BEFORE FIRST SEXUAL ENCOUNTER.

My mom and I paraded up to the pretty, red, ranch-style home. I knocked three times and took a step back. Within seconds, we could hear a dog scampering around and the door rattling. A tall red-haired woman opened the door. She was probably in her sixties and had a big white smile. "Hello!" she exclaimed.

I had gotten new neighbors across the street. My mom had always wanted me to have neighborhood friends, and she had hoped they had a kid for me to play with. We hadn't seen new kids get on the bus, though, so we predicted they did not have any children. My mom talked about baking cookies and bringing them over to introduce ourselves, but we had not gotten around to it. One day, their mail showed up in our mail box. The two of us had walked over to deliver it to them.

"You must be the neighbors! Come in, come in, come in." She motioned for us to come inside, and a small, curly-brown-haired dog came running out. "Oh, that's Max! Don't mind him… Off Max, OFF!" she directed the dog away from us.

"Oh no, we don't want to intrude. We are just stopping by to drop off some mail," my mom said and held up the envelopes.

"Oh my god, you are kidding!" she said as she retrieved the envelopes from my mom. "And what are your names?" the woman said, looking at me and my mom.

"I am Blair!" I said smiling big. Adults were so much fun to talk to; they were always so interested. "And this is my mom, Nurse Cathy," I said and looked over at my mom. She was wearing a black cardigan and jeans with her dark brown hair was blown smooth.

"I take it from your mail that your name is Ann and your husband is Richard," my mom said, smiling and pulling me in for a tight side hug.

"Yup, that's us, and our dog Max, of course," Ann smiled.

"Well if you are looking for a job, honey, I work for a real estate company, and they are looking for kids to help out delivering magazine to homes in the afternoons," Ann said, looking at me.

"I would LOVE to! Yes!" I said.

"Well, here, I will give you all my number, and you guys can come over soon. We will chat about taking a route throughout the day. The schedule is different every week, so I would just text you on Sunday the days I would need you that week...sound good, honey? Here is my number!" she said and handed a piece of paper to my mom.

I had a job! Score!

That next week, I would start going over to Ann's a few days a week after school. She'd give me a bunch of magazines, and I would put them in the front basket of my bike and drop them off at houses on a couple of streets for her. Afterward, if it was a nice day, I usually rode down the trails off the beach that led into the woods. My mom used to walk our dog down there when I was little. Ruby, her name was. She was a German Shepard. I missed walking Ruby down there. Sometimes people were fishing in the lake, but it was mostly quiet.

I was excited to have something new going on. It was just mine. It was not Marissa's or anyone else's. AND I got paid to take rides on my bike. *What could be better?*

One afternoon, I had just gotten back from doing my magazine route. I had extended my route a little bit afterward by taking a ride along the beach boardwalk, which was pretty well traveled. I walked into my room and opened up my iPad. Jack was active on Chatty. I could see him starting to type to me.

"Hi," appeared on my screen. That was usually how he started conversations.

"Hi," I typed back. I had seen Jack the past three Fridays now. Of course, I had seen him secretly at my window when Marissa came over. I had also been over for tutoring like normal. We had been talking pretty much every day using the Chatty app. Jack said it was the easiest way for him to talk.

"I drove by you riding your bike today! SO FUN! What were you up to?" he typed.

"My neighbors are paying me to deliver magazines for a real estate agent. Isn't that awesome?" I typed my message and within one minute it disappeared from the conversation history.

"So cute! I want to see your magazines!"

"lol...yeah, it's a lot of fun delivering them, especially now that the weather is nice."

"I liked seeing you riding your bike. You looked good." *He was looking at me?* I thought. I had stopped trying to fight my feelings. I accepted that I liked when Jack complimented me. I knew I couldn't tell anyone that, but I couldn't stop myself from feeling it. Jack told me it was natural for men to like younger women and for women to like older men. "It's Mother Nature" he always said.

"Maybe I can meet you and grab a magazine soon, on one of your rides?"

"Yeah I guess..."

"I could meet you down in the trails off the beach...we could go for a ride together."

My stomach turned. Another secret meeting. I was just getting comfortable with the idea of Jack coming to my window. I was convinced that because Marissa was there nothing was wrong with it. It was innocent and he was Marissa's dad's friend, so it was okay... this seemed like another line that was about to be crossed.

"Okay," I typed.

"When are you doing another delivery?"

"Tomorrow, after school."

"I'll see you then :) I will bring Snowflake. You haven't seen the doggy in a while," appeared on my screen before being erased forever.

* * *

Blair is alone with her confusion. She is unsure whether this meeting is crossing a boundary or simply an innocent meeting with her tutor and his dog. She also feels that she is in too deep; she could get in trouble now if she were to ask her mom or even Marissa, who might tell her mom. The previous time they have spent alone and talking has muddled her ideas of right and wrong. Her feelings of admiration toward Jack further confuse the situation; she is terrified to lose him or upset the balance. This relationship thrives in secrecy.

"They first rape the child's mind in order to rape their body,"[42] a convicted child sexual offender said in an

42 Huffman, Charlotte. "Two Child Sex Offenders Explain How They Picked Their Targets." www.wfaa.com. https://www.wfaa.com/article/features/originals/two-child-sex-offenders-explain-how-they-picked-their-targets/287-434667495. (May 2019).

interview. He discussed how he would create opportunities to be alone with the victim. "You become the child's confidante,"[43] he said. "You become the one they look to as the one that is going to provide their answers and give them their guidance. You supersede the other really necessary and powerful relationships in their lives. In fact, you discount them. You find ways in the things you say and do to discount those relationships."[44]

As caretakers, you can shine a light on the relationships your children have; bring them out of secrecy and talk about them.

* * *

I could not sleep last night knowing I was going to break another unspoken rule. No one had ever told me that I couldn't go on a bike ride with Jack and Snowflake... I wasn't lying to anyone by doing it...I wasn't stealing or drinking... I wasn't hurting anyone...and besides, Jack was nice to me. He just wanted me to hang out with Snowflake. I thought about not going...about just riding my regular route down the main road and telling Jack I forgot about our plan to meet on the trails. But I knew he would be there waiting for

43 Ibid
44 Ibid

me. I could not keep him waiting. After all, he had done so many nice things for me: spent way too many hours tutoring me, given me an iPad, brought Marissa and me ice cream. I settled myself on my bike after school, rode my regular route and headed down toward the trails.

Sure enough, Jack was there…waiting. He was on a beach cruiser, too, and had a bag and a blanket in his basket. When he saw me, his face lit up. He was so happy to see me. I released the shame and guilt I had and embraced how happy he made me feel. I smiled. Snowflake was so little and fluffy standing next to Jack's bike on a leash. I felt like I looked funny with my reflective vest on that Ann made me wear when I was doing my route. But my eyes were set on Jack, and no one else was around.

When I finally reached him, I hopped off my bike and steadied my kickstand. He—without hesitation—wrapped his arms around my waist and pulled me in for a hug. His warm embrace felt good in the cool spring air. My body heated up from the inside out. I felt warm inside. I felt liked. Snowflake tugged on his leash, and I was pulled deeper into the hug. I did not want to be caught in my daze. I regained my footing and looked up, trying to remain unfazed. "This is the magazine," I said, grabbing an extra copy from the basket of my bike and handing it to him.

"Wow, you are so beautiful, Blair," Jack said while looking at me. In the eyes. But it was more like he was looking past my eyes and into my heart and soul. He would not look away. He was mesmerized…by me?

"Thanks," I giggled nervously.

"I brought your favorite beachside sub, and I got the same one for myself. I was hungry and I thought we could have a picnic because it is so nice out."

I was hungry…although I was always hungry…and I did love my beachside sub. I got ham, American cheese, cheddar cheese, lettuce, tomato, onion, mayo, salt and pepper. It was DELICIOUS. I couldn't say no… plus he'd already bought the sandwiches…they couldn't go to waste.

We rode together alone on the trail, with Snowflake scampering along, for a few minutes before sitting down. Jack lay out the picnic blanket and commented on how romantic the scene was.

"Does Danielle know you are here?" I asked.

"Oh yeah," Jack said. "She knows all about you."

"She does?"

"Yeah, she has known for a long time that I am not in love with her. She understands that I need to find it somewhere."

Was he talking about being in love with me?

"She is okay with it because she knows I will have to wait a long time to be with you. She still has time to live her perfect life in our house."

He was talking about being in love with me.

"Oh, I can't believe she is okay with that." I didn't know how to respond.

"Yeah, it's nothing really," he said causally. I took a bite of my sandwich.

"Thanks for the sandwich," I said.

"Oh my god," Jack said after biting into the sandwich. "This is amazing! How did you come up with this combination? It is the best sandwich I've ever had!"

He made me feel so good, so liked, so appreciated. I smiled so big when he said that. I loved the sandwich too.

"It's pretty good, isn't it?" I smiled. Snowflake was tied up on a tree and starting to get anxious.

"You had better get him back now," I said, looking at Snowflake.

"Okay," Jack said but looked disappointed. I had never seen him look disappointed before—ever. He was always so happy. We packed up the picnic and headed out toward the main trail. There was still no one around. Before we reached the head of the trail, he stopped. He looked at me with that intense look again. I felt like he could read my mind. He knew how I was feeling, even if I didn't say it. He knew I felt good, he knew I lit up when he complimented me, he knew I thought about him when he wasn't around, and he knew I wanted to tell him I felt the same way. But I didn't tell him that.

"Look, I got you something," Jack said. He got up and reached into the bag in the basket of his bike and pulled out a stuffed dog; it looked just like Snowflake. "Here, so you can always have Snowflake with you, even when you are home in your bedroom."

"Oh, Jack, you didn't have to do that. Really, I like coming to visit him. It isn't a big deal."

"No, I want you have this, to remind you of my pup. Just put it on your bed and you can cuddle it just like a real dog."

That was so nice of him, but I did not want the stuffed animal. *What would my mom say? What would I tell her? Could I tell her the truth?*

"Can I kiss you, Blair?"

I looked away. I could not handle that intense stare anymore. I felt guilty for looking away, after all the nice things he had done for me…I couldn't even give him a kiss…

"I want to kiss you, Jack…but I don't want you to be my first kiss, you know? You are married, you have children and a family…I want to kiss someone my own age."

"Lance," Jack said, rolling his eyes. He seemed mad. I had never seen him angry. Instantly, the anger turned to sadness. "I wish you did want to kiss me, but it's okay. I'll wait for you, however long it takes, however many boys your own age you need to kiss. I will wait…until then…will you kiss me on the cheek?"

I couldn't stand to look at him…his face was too sad. It made me feel so guilty. I felt so intensely guilty. I could not physically walk away…my body was planted there alone in the woods with him. "No," I shook my head. It was involuntary. I couldn't. I didn't want to kiss him. I knew I felt good around him, maybe I even had a crush on him…but I did not want to kiss him. All I wanted in that moment was to curl up in my bed, crawl under the covers, and hide. I looked up at his unbearable face. I couldn't tell if he was mad at me or sad with me. I extended my neck up and got on my tiptoes. I puckered my lips and they grazed his prickly skin. He smiled. I could tell he wasn't satisfied, but it was enough to know he wasn't mad.

"Bye. Thanks again for the sandwich," I said. My feet felt like giant weights that I had to lift up for every step I took toward my bike to ride home. My face stayed squinted in disgust and shame the whole bike ride home.

It felt like it took years for me to pedal my way home. I felt my legs pulling up and pushing down on the pedals trying to carry the weight of my embarrassment. When I walked in the door, I was greeted by my mom.

"How was your day, honey?"

I was happy to see my mom. I was also happy she couldn't read my thoughts; I could keep them secret from her.

"Great, Mom, really good." I smiled and plopped myself on the couch.

"I've got gymnastics tonight, Mom. Remember?"

"Yup, at six o'clock," she answered.

"Okay, sounds good. Anything good for dinner?" I asked even though I was full of my beachside sub.

* * *

Keeping a secret wasn't as hard as it might have seemed, which was surprising…especially for me. I was terrible at keeping secrets. Every year when my mom's birthday came around, I would make my mom the prettiest card, draw her something special or pick out a lipstick for her when I was at the mall with my grandma. I was always SO excited to give her my extraordinary gift that I could not stop thinking about it. I wanted so badly to see her face light up when she saw I had gotten her something, so every year I ended up spilling the beans and telling her what I had gotten before the big day arrived.

My grandma will never let me forget the time we went to the mall to pick out a present for my mom. We found the perfect bracelet for her. My grandma and I were so excited to give it to her, but her birthday had still been a week away. That night at dinner, I sat with my chin resting on my hand, daydreaming into the distance and wistfully said, "Ahhh, such a pretty bracelet…" My mom looked at me, confused, and my eyes got wide. I had once again spilled the beans on another birthday present.

Secrets were just not my thing. But this thing that had happened with Jack, this instance where I had kissed him on the cheek… that was not something I was proud of, like all the gifts I picked out for my mom. In fact, I felt quite shameful and confused about it. I was shameful because Jack was married, he was thirty-seven years old and I kissed him. I was confused because, even though I did not want to kiss him, I still liked him. I still wanted to go to tutoring with him and hang out with him and Marissa and Marissa's family. I liked the attention he gave me. I liked the things he gave me. He was so good to me.

After that day in the woods with Snowflake, Jack became a lot more open about his feelings for me. The next Thursday night, I got a text from him as I was going to bed.

Jack: Hey, Blair, are you up?

Blair: Yes, why?

I wanted to tell him I was going to bed soon, but I did not want him to think I was lame.

Blair: Can I see you tonight? Bring you ice cream?

I knew that was code for coming to my window. Jack had never come to my window without Marissa here. I was kind of desensitized to it by now. He came almost every Friday after football practice. Each time he seemed to stay for a bit longer. He always brought us snacks and talked to us about taboo topics. He would tell us about the different kinds of porn that existed and that all men had fantasies. He would joke with us. Marissa and I didn't talk much about Jack, though, outside of our sleepovers. It was like an unspoken rule that those visits never happened.

My heart pounded. I was afraid to have him over without Marissa, especially after what happened the other day in the woods. But I did not want him to get mad or disappointed again; he didn't deserve that.

Within minutes, I was opening the window for Jack. He told me he was coming from the bar with his friends. He smelled kind of funny. My knees were planted onto my bed, and my body was pressed against the wall and window sill. Just my shoulders and head were visible to him. Jack's face was in front of mine. He stood outside, his body pressed against my house and his head above my window. He was looking me in the eyes.

"Miss Blair Beam," he said. He was looking at me intensely again. "You are so beautiful. You need to stop being so beautiful. You make me want you so badly, but I will wait for you. I will wait as long as you need."

No one ever called me Miss Blair Beam. I was Blair…or Bee… It made my chest contract a little when he said my full name "Blair Beam" out loud. It sounded so mature. So, adult-like.

"I like you, Jack, I do. But I feel confused. I feel like this isn't normal. You're married, you're twenty-five years older than me…"

"It's forbidden love, Blair, just like Jack and Rose. Or Romeo and Juliet. The Capulets and Montagues. Society doesn't want us to be together because there is an age difference, but age is really just a number, Blair. I mean, look at you and the other kids I teach. Most of them are way older than you and in college, but you are so much wiser than all of them. Age doesn't mean anything. But, love, love means something, and I love you."

He was pouring his heart out to me at my bedroom window. It really was like Romeo and Juliet. I had read that book in school. Everyone wanted Romeo and Juliet to be together. It was so silly that their families hated each other. Romeo and Juliet were meant to be together.

"Wow, I never thought of it that way," I said, still processing all the words that were just said to me.

"I know you don't want to kiss me, Blair, and that is okay. But for now, can I just feel your face?" Jack asked with a pleading look in his eyes.

He was asking me for permission. He was so sweet. I wanted to kiss him to satisfy him, but just the thought of our lips touching made my head want to burst with guilt. That feeling of shame was an entire body feeling. It racked my head; it was a constant thought. I woke up and went to bed with a shameful conscience. It was in my chest and prevented me from breathing deeply and fully. It was in the pit of my stomach when the idea of kissing came up. My body did not want to kiss him. My body knew it was wrong. My mind and my heart were conflicted.

"Yes," I said. And I could feel Jack's prickly cheeks brush up against mine. He nuzzled his face into mine.

"You just tell me when you are ready, Miss Blair Beam."

He didn't seem angry tonight. He seemed loving and understanding. He cared about me and he knew I wasn't ready. I didn't know if I would ever be ready, but I was not ready to give this up. He left my window, and I closed the screen and window and lay down on my bed. My brain was going a mile and minute, and I could not keep up. I just kept thinking about what Jack said about Romeo and Juliet. I dreamt about us being together and running away together; it would be like a fantasy, I thought, and drifted into sleep.

* * *

"Hey, Blair, do you want to go to tutoring tonight? Jack has an opening..." my mom called down from upstairs.

"Yeah, sure," I said right away, as I already knew my mom was going to ask me that. Jack had told me on the Chatty app that he had asked Danielle to have me over tonight. He was using this method of communication more and more. He told me it was safer. He still texted me sometimes, but he said if his number started to show up too much on my phone bill, my mom might think something was up. He said they wouldn't understand our love. They were part of the problem in the world that believed that age mattered.

I started to feel more and more resentment toward my mom, but I kept cool for now because she didn't know about us, and she was not trying to stop it. Yet. Sometimes, I daydreamed about telling my mom all about my feelings for Jack and fantasized her support and what that would look like for me. Sometimes, I pretended she knew, and we just didn't talk about it. It was easier to think she had a clue. The truth was, she didn't. She had no clue. Not yet, anyway. She was just as charmed as I was by Jack's good looks, his energy, his positivity and the big house he lived in.

I got ready, and my mom dropped me off at Jack's house. Danielle sped out the door as soon as Jack's car and my mom's car were pulling into the driveway. I was excited to see him, but also nervous. I did not like the pressure Jack had been putting on me to kiss him, but he made me feel so good. My body was fighting these urges to kiss him because the thought of kissing him made me want to never face my friends and family again. Because it felt wrong. Some part of me knew that if I kissed him, I would forever regret making him my very first kiss.

I got out of the car and went to the front door. My mom waved goodbye and drove away. He came waltzing to the door. "Hey, guys!" Lizzy said as she opened the door. She rushed over to her father. Danielle left her behind but was taking Elena to a doctor's visit. Jack picked Lizzy up and spun her around. Lizzy's soft locks flew through the air and she beamed.

"I am so happy you are home, Daddy!" Lizzy giggled.

"I am so happy to see you, Lizzy. Give me a high-five!" Jack said and smiled at his daughter.

Lizzy wound up her hand and gave her daddy the hardest high-five she could.

"Blair!" Jack said to me with excitement. He was staring at me intensely. "What's up?" he asked with a big grin. He was looking at me in a way that indicated he knew "what was up." It was like he was just asking to seem normal. He squinted his eyes a little bit, prompting me to go along with normal conversation.

"Oh nothing, lots of homework these days, and gymnastics class, but that's all," I replied.

"Lizzy, do you want to watch *Happy Feet*?" Jack asked his daughter.

"YES!" she replied eagerly.

We all moved to the living where Jack set up a movie for Lizzy before he and I would sit down in the office for tutoring. There was a clear door, so Jack could always keep an eye on her.

Jack got to work setting up the movie On Demand. "Lizzy loves this movie," Jack explained as he hit play. I was sitting in the middle of the couch, next to Lizzy, who had her head on my shoulder and was cuddled up next to me. She was so affectionate, and I loved knowing that she trusted me. Jack turned the lights down and sat down on the other side of me. He was sitting close to me; the left side of my body was touching his, awkwardly at first, but Jack loosened up quickly and tried to cuddle me. He looked at me and smiled innocently, as if to indicate that it was okay. I liked feeling the warmth of his body. I trusted him. He put his hand on my left thigh, as if it were nothing but just a casual touch. I liked this; I did not need anything more than his comfort. This felt good, and Jack said he would wait for me. *This could work*, I thought. *I want it to work.*

After five minutes, Jack wiggled away and stood up. "Ready to get to work, kiddo?"

"Yes, let's go," I whispered, trying not to upset Lizzy, who was almost asleep on the couch.

We moved to the office and closed the glass door.

* * *

Do you know a child/anyone who is already a victim?

Survivors, we know this is not an exhaustive list of the warning signs we begin to show when the abuse begins.

We also know we are really good at masking our pain, so do take these cues with a grain of salt:

- Secretiveness
- Anxiety/panic attacks
- Nervousness
- Depression
- Euphoria
- Anger
- Fearfulness
- Absenteeism
- Weight fluctuations due to eating disorders/drug/alcohol use
- Sudden disinterest in school, appearance, socializing, extracurricular activities

- **Familial/friend conflict**
  - **this is related to the wedge that offenders will drive between victims and their friends and family in order to isolate them; victims may begin to fight more with their parents and distrust people close to them**
- **Disassociation from friendships**
  - **social isolation is a huge red flag; groomers are experts in segregating the child from other children45**

Again, many children will do a good job of hiding the relationship, so it may be difficult to detect. Being educated about grooming and developing a healthy curiosity about adults in a child's life will go a long way in keeping children and our community safe. Remember to encourage open communication and remove shame around talking about bodies and touching. Children who are educated and have language for unsafe relationships are more likely to speak up when they are feeling confused.

45 Huffman, Charlotte. "Two Child Sex Offenders Explain How They Picked Their Targets." www.wfaa.com. https://www.wfaa.com/article/features/originals/two-child-sex-offenders-explain-how-they-picked-their-targets/287-434667495. (May 2019).

APRIL 29, 2015.

SIX WEEKS BEFORE FIRST SEXUAL ENCOUNTER

It was Saturday morning now. Yesterday was my twelfth birthday. I had gone out to dinner with my family, and Marissa had come with us. Marissa couldn't sleep over last night, though, because she had to stay at her grandma's. We had gone to the local Red Lobster because I had recently discovered that I loved seafood, and this was my new favorite spot. *I mean, who could pass up the cheddar bay biscuits?* Right now, though, I was sitting in my pajamas on my bed with the TV on. I was tired. I was getting a phone call. It was from Jack. This was strange. He never called me; he always used the Chatty app he taught me to use because he said no one could trace it. *It must be important*, I thought. "Hello," I answered.

"Hi Blair," he said. I knew Jack was in Florida with Danielle this weekend. They had a wedding to go to, and Danielle was the bride's maid of honor.

"How is Florida going?" I asked. I knew he wasn't looking forward to going. He told me he didn't really like Florida, but Danielle did, and it was her friend's wedding, so he put up with it for her.

"I feel so guilty, Blair, and I miss you," he mumbled. "I am standing on the balcony of our hotel room. Danielle went to go get a pedicure in the spa downstairs with the bridal party, and I wanted to call. I cannot stop thinking about you. Danielle knows too..."

Wow, Jack is with his beautiful wife for the weekend in Florida, and he cannot stop thinking about me? How could that be possible? I felt so special.

"I am feeling so guilty, Blair. I have to tell you, I had sex with Danielle last night. We had gone to dinner and smoked some weed on the balcony, and it happened. I am so sorry. We never have sex anymore, and I wanted to wait to ever have sex again until you're ready, but I said your name out loud during it, and now Danielle really knows about us."

"You did?" I said, totally stunned by his confession. "I'm not mad at you or anything. She is your wife… what did she say when you said my name?"

"She told me afterward that she knew something was up and that she wasn't surprised because of how pretty you are."

I felt a tingling sensation in my stomach whenever he called me pretty. "Pretty" made me feel like an innocent princess that could do no wrong… a princess waiting for her prince, like princess Rapunzel or Ariel.

"Wow, I can't believe that," I said, trying to avoid the comment he made. I never knew how to respond to compliments, and Jack was constantly giving them to me.

"I just miss you so much. Last night, I just wished I was at your window, hanging out rather than here," he continued. His tone of voice seemed distraught.

"Yeah, it was weird that you didn't stop by since last night was Friday, but I understood, and it was my birthday."

"I know it was your birthday and don't worry. I got you something. I can't wait to give it to you," he gushed.

"Oh, Jack, you give me so much. You didn't have to do that," I said and felt uncomfortable. I did not want a gift from him. He really did tutor me so much that my grades were improving, and I didn't have to get pulled out of class anymore. He gave me that Snowflake stuffed toy. Taking more from him felt so wrong, but he always told me I deserved it.

"Well, I have to go, Blair. Danielle will be back soon, but I will see you soon. I miss you," he said as if I were his wife and he was away on business.

"I miss you, too," I said and hung up as fast as I could. *What just happened?* My mind and my body needed a moment to recover from that conversation. I was getting deeper and deeper into this tale of forbidden love. Poor us. I thought the world was against us. It still felt so wrong, but knowing that Danielle knew, and was not stopping it, made me feel better. It had to be normal if Jack's wife was okay with it... right? We had someone on our side.

PART 4

ISOLATING THE VICTIM

MAY 2015.

ONE MONTH BEFORE THE FIRST SEXUAL ENCOUNTER.

I was so bad at basketball. Reese passed the ball to me. It bounced right past me. I turned around, bent over to pick it up and shot it into the hoop. Andddddd I missed again. I was never any good at sports. Reese, Marissa and I were outside of Jack's house, playing basketball with Ryan, another one of Jack's students. Jack had invited the Martins over so, of course, I tagged along. Their families had been becoming better and better friends. Mrs. Campbell and Mrs. Martin had become tight pals because they both had one-year-olds, but Jack also told me that he invited them over whenever he knew I was around. Soon, Jack came outside with a two-liter

Diet Coke and a pack of Mentos. It was a warm spring afternoon, and the sun was shining down on us.

"Hey, guys, check this out," Jack called everyone over. We all hurried over to where he was standing in the driveway. He opened the Diet Coke bottle and dropped the Mentos candies inside. He quickly closed the lid. The Diet Coke started spurting up and out of the bottle, erupting like a volcano.

"Whoa!" Ryan exclaimed

"How did you do that?" Reese asked with excitement and wonder.

"Ahhhh," Marissa shrieked, hopping away from the explosive soda bottle.

I stood with Marissa, staring in amazement at the bottle. Everyone loved Jack. *He always did such cool things. How in the world did he like me?* I thought. Once the bottle calmed down, I excused myself to the bathroom while everyone else went back to basketball. Jack followed me inside; I started toward the bathroom. The rest of the parents were all out on the back porch gossiping about town drama with Danielle. Jack and I were alone in the house. I went into the bathroom and when I came out, Jack stood outside the door.

"Hey, Blair," he said and smiled, all the while touching the back of my arm. I felt his light touch throughout my whole body. It made me feel like it was just the two of us in the world and no one else mattered in the moment. "Let me show you something," he walked toward his daughter Elena's room. I followed behind him. We entered the room together. I felt a sense of adrenaline running through me because we were kind of alone, but other people were so close to coming in and finding us together. He sat on the bench in the nursery and pulled a small jewelry box out of his pocket. It was a long, white, rectangular box. He motioned for me to sit next to him. I sat in my short denim shorts and a new navy blue Hollister t-shirt I had gotten for my birthday. I looked over at the crib for Elena. He put his hand on my bare leg. "Happy Birthday, Blair," he said and handed me the box with a folded-up piece of paper.

His touch sent me into a daze. I honestly felt a little lightheaded and overwhelmed in that moment. I didn't know what to say. I wanted to reject the gift, but he looked so happy to give it to me. I avoided the jewelry box by opening up the folded piece of paper.

Dear Blair,

Happy Birthday, my love. I am sorry this is late. Words cannot describe the love I feel for you. I am a married man and I have never felt this way about anyone before. Our love is magical. I can't wait until I can share my love for you with the world. Until then, wear this to remind you how I feel about you every day.

XOXO

I wanted to cry; it was so sweet and so sad. I wanted to tell him I felt the same way, but I also did not want to commit myself to this. It seemed like the choice had already been made. I looked at him. Looking at him hurt. So many conflicted feelings paralyzed my mind.

"It's okay," he said. "You don't need to say anything. Just wear the bracelet."

I opened the box. Inside of it, a delicate silver bracelet gently hung. There were small hearts filled with diamonds attached by silver chains. "Just tell anyone who asks that a boy at school got it for you. They won't know the diamonds are real. Plus, I am a boy who has been to your school, so it isn't even a lie."

Wow, they were real? This was too beautiful and expensive for my twelfth birthday.

"I got it for you in Florida when Danielle was off with the bridal party. I saw the sweet little hearts, and I couldn't stop thinking of you. I had to buy it," he gushed.

"Thank you, Jack," I said. My eyes were having a hard time focusing on him. It almost hurt to look at him sometimes. It felt like every time I focused on his face, I dug myself deeper into this black hole of forbidden love. He put the bracelet on my wrist.

"I can keep the box for now so you don't have to carry it," he said, pulling my sleeve over the bracelet. I put the note in my pocket and stood up.

"We should probably go… before someone finds us," I said, looking down at my wrist and then around the room to make sure no one was looking.

"You are right. I just can't stand to be in the same room as you and have to stay away. I just want to tell everyone how I feel. Why don't they understand?"

"I don't know, but maybe one day they will. Right?" I said. I hoped there would be a day when I wouldn't have to feel so guilty for my emotions.

"One day they will, when you are eighteen." He looked hopeful. "You know that Reese knows about us, right?" he added.

"No. He does?" I was surprised. Reese hadn't said anything about it to me on the bus.

"Oh yeah, I told him all about us. I told him he will be the best man in our wedding someday. He is so excited."

"Wow, I had no idea." *Another person knew and thought it was okay?* I thought.

"I have one more thing for you," Jack said and looked at me. He pulled a flip phone out of his pocket.

"I got you this pay-as-you-go phone. I put a ton of minutes on it, so we can talk on the phone without anyone knowing. Just hide it in your room. We can talk on the phone at night when no one is around."

He handed me the phone. I stuffed it in my pocket for now. I would put it in my purse that was outside when no one was looking. It felt like I was holding a bomb that could go off at any moment. This phone made our relationships so real. So did the bracelet and the note. It was physical, tangible proof that he loved me. He really loved me. It made my insides squirm. I wished I could wake up from this dream. I wished I didn't have these feelings. These good feelings. I wished I could walk away from this. I wished I had never met Jack, but now that I had, and now that he loved me, I couldn't control myself. I was out of control.

We exited his daughter's bedroom; he went to the back porch to join the parents, and I went out the front door to rejoin the basketball game.

"What took you so long?" Marissa asked when I exited. I felt the bracelet on my wrist that no one else could see under my sleeve.

"Oh, ya know, I just have a stomach ache. I feel better now," I lied and picked up the basketball to pass to Reese.

* * *

Again and again, in grooming relationships, the grooming sex offender takes advantage of the special bond with the child to create opportunities for alone time between the two of them. This reinforces the bond and normalizes the one-on-one relationship. Babysitting, tutoring, mentoring, private coaching are all examples of situations that enable this special individual bond. Many times, a groomer continues to take advantage of this relationship as they begin to establish the impression that they, the groomer, are the only one who is able to genuinely provide love and attention to the child, as Jack does with Blair. The groomer begins to point out, or prey upon, flaws in the other people who love the child in order to further isolate them, even when the groomer is not present. The

child begins to trust or believe *only* in the groomer. This is why groomers typically target vulnerable children who have challenges in their lives. It is easy for the groomer to blame these challenges on everyone in the child's life and act as the hero to the child.46

In this scene, Blair and Jack find themselves "alone" while other adults are present in the home, making the interaction seem normal and okay because they are not technically "alone." Jack plants a seed of hope of them being able to be together in the future and not have to hide their feelings for each other, like Jack and Rose from *Titanic* or *Romeo and Juliet*. This comparison glamorizes the forbiddenness of their feelings and the lies that Blair is forced to tell. Her lies become heroic and brave in this context.

---

46 "Grooming and Red Flag Behaviors." www.d2l.org. https://www.d2l.org/child-grooming-signs-behavior-awareness/. (May 2019).

JUNE 2015.

ZERO MONTHS BEFORE THE FIRST SEXUAL ENCOUNTER.

School was almost over, and I had almost officially survived the 6th grade. This year had been kind of a crazy one. My uncle had died, I had tried tennis for the first time, I continued my gymnastics lessons, and Marissa and I were closer than ever. However, now that my gymnastics season was over, I didn't have a formal way to exercise anymore, so I rediscovered the trampoline I had in my backyard. On this warm June afternoon, I wandered back to the corner of my yard. My modest home's greatest asset was that it had a cute yard and trees behind it. The trampoline was set all the way in the back corner. It could be seen from the front yard, but only because some bushes had recently been cut back.

I climbed up onto the trampoline. We had taken the netting down because it kept falling down. Marissa and I thought the netting had been annoying anyway, so the trampoline was open air. I plopped down onto the warm black mesh netting and looked at my phone for a few minutes. Then I got up and started walking around in circles, jumping up and down and trying to perfect my front flip. I was enjoying being by myself for a few moments.

Lately, I was feeling a little bombarded by being with Marissa all the time, and then in my free time talking to Jack on the phone he had gotten me before facing my mom. I needed space to just think, and it felt so good to be back here alone. Jumping up and down released so much of the tension I had been feeling. I had been fighting feelings for Jack, giving in to them and trying to hide them from everyone in my life, trying to appear normal, trying to rationalize the relationship and focus on school. Luckily, my grades hadn't been affected, but I was exhausted.

After a few minutes of bouncing, I saw Jack's car drive by my front yard. The pang of guilt I had exhausted on the trampoline now encompassed my mind, my chest, my stomach and I froze. *It was probably a coincidence,* I thought. Part of me hoped it was, and part of me liked the idea that Jack was driving by to check on me. Either way, I was done on the trampoline. I put my bottom on the black mesh and scooted off the side. I slid my flip-flops back on and walked back to my house.

When I entered my room, I went straight for my secret phone. I had hidden it in my bedside table drawer, inside an old jewelry box, and put it inside a black silk jewelry bag. My mom was not one to go through my stuff, so I knew as long as it wasn't where she put clothes away or out in the open, she wouldn't find it. I opened the phone up.

Jack: I saw you jumping on the trampoline… you are such a tease…you look so good.

It was *Jack that drove by.*

Blair: I thought I saw you drive by. lol.

Jack: I miss you. I want to see you. Can you go back out on the trampoline? I want to come visit.

Blair: But my mom is home. You can't come over… I'm sorry.

Jack: It's okay. I will hide in the bushes. I just want to be close to you.

My chest contracted. I did not want him in my space. I had one space that I could go on my own, and it was being taken from me. I also did not want Jack in my yard. My mom would be so angry and scared if she found out someone was sneaking around in our bushes.

Jack: Please, just for a few minutes.

Blair: Okay.

I tucked my phone in my pocket and walked back to the trampoline tucked away in the corner of my yard. I was nervous. I wanted to get this over with. I hopped up onto my trampoline. I didn't want to jump anymore, especially knowing someone was watching me. Suddenly, I heard a rustling in the bushes next to me. My house was located next to another home, but there were woods behind it. Jack must have parked on the other side of the woods at a trailhead and walked through the woods. There was no way anyone could see him from my back deck.

"Hey," Jack loudly whispered to get my attention.

Nononono. I thought. Jack being here felt so wrong.

"Hi," I said, trying not to look at him just in case my mom could see him from the window.

"Can I see you jump around some more?" Jack asked. "You looked so good from the street."

The street was so far away; I knew I was only a small speck from the road.

"Mmmmm, I don't wanna," I said. I was nervous. I did not want to be his show. I was having fun when I thought I was alone, but I did not want someone staring at me.

"Please, just for a couple of minutes, I swear, and I will leave. I just can't stand not being around you."

"Okay," I stood up and jumped around awkwardly. I didn't know exactly what I was supposed to be doing. Jack seemed to like it. I could only see the top half of his body from behind the fence, but he seemed to be enjoying himself.

After a minute or two of awkwardly walking and bouncing, I fell back on my butt and sat down. I was uncomfortable and wanted him to leave. But I also did not want him to notice my discomfort. I was a big girl, and I could handle whatever he threw at me. Plus… he was waiting for me, so I owed him the world. He talked to me about my day for a minute, but I couldn't stop thinking about whether or not my mom was staring at me through the window, wondering who I was talking to behind the fence. So I lay on my back and looked up at the sky when I spoke.

Finally, Jack said he was leaving. I was so relieved.

I hopped off the trampoline and ran inside. I felt this sort of rush when I made my dash back to my house. It was like I had just pulled off some magical deed. I didn't feel good about it necessarily, but it was an accomplishment.

"How are ya, honey?" my mom said as she came out from the living room, smiling and carrying with a pile of folded laundry. She handed the pile to me to put away.

"Good! I was just out on the trampoline. I forgot how much I liked it out there," I told her.

"Yeah, but you better be careful. You know I want to put that netting back up. I hate the idea of you flying off that thing. It gives me nightmares."

"No, Mom, it's fine! It is funnier that way!" I told her, remembering when Marissa insisted we take it down.

"Okay, dear," she said and let a deep breath out.

“Thanks for folding my clothes, Mom!” I said and walked into my room and shut the door behind me so I could make sure my secret phone was tucked away.

JUNE 2015.

ZERO MONTHS BEFORE THE FIRST SEXUAL ENCOUNTER.

Summertime had officially set in with my first trip to the boardwalk. Marissa's family was headed down to Point Pleasant, New Jersey, for the day to visit Jack's family. He had rented a house down there for the week, and we were driving there for the day. Point Pleasant was a more kid-friendly beach town than Glenvale. It had a boardwalk, amusement park and lots of funnel cake. Marissa and I sat in the backseat of the car, squished together with her baby sister for the hour car ride. I was so excited to get to see the amusement park for the first time since last summer. We pulled up to the beach-front house that Jack was staying in for the week. It was beautiful. The house was huge, and we could already see kids running around outside. There were so many cars in the driveway. This was definitely a party. Marissa and I all filed out of the car and grabbed our drawstring bags filled with our towel and change of clothes for later. I had my bathing suit on already with a white cover-up dress over top.

I wasn't too nervous about today. I was mostly excited. I knew Jack was on his best behavior when Marissa and her family were around. I didn't think I would have to have any alone encounters with him where I would have to explain to him that I still was not ready to kiss him.

I had told him time and time again I still wanted to be with someone my own age first. I had still been texting Lance on my normal phone, but we were too terrified to talk to each other in person, and it didn't seem real. Jack told me that was okay, and he would wait as long as I wanted, but he didn't seem to stop asking. I wanted him to stop asking. I liked it when he gave me attention, but more and more often, I was starting to feel uncomfortable. The problem was, I trusted Jack; he made me feel so good. I liked his hugs... a lot. I liked the way he talked to me like I was an adult and made me feel special. When he looked at me, it was like no one else in the world existed. He told me he had never felt this way before. This was love, he said.

Marissa and I ran away from the car and sprinted up the beach, bypassing the beautiful house. We laid our towels down, away from the gaggle of kids playing football on the sand, and went down to the water to dip our toes in.

"Hey, guys! I am teaching Reese how to surf. Do you guys want to learn?" Jack came out of the house with Reese. They were both shirtless and carrying surfboards. Jack's six-pack abs and strong arms were visible. He looked good.

"Yes! I have always wanted to learn to surf!" Marissa exclaimed and ran toward the house to grab another board. I followed behind her. Jack followed us to the line of surfboards leaning against the house.

"I rented a bunch so we'd all be able to try it out," he explained as he picked up a board and handed it to me. "This one is perfect for you," Jack said, handing a board to me. "Marissa, you can pick whichever one you want," he told her.

We all ran toward the ocean. The hot sand burned my toes as we made our way to the icy water. The boys, Reese and his two friends, dove right in, and Marissa and I followed. Jack hopped up on his surfboard and immediately started riding waves. *Wow, he is so good at that.* Everyone was impressed. Marissa and I spent the next half hour trying to get up on our boards but failing miserably.

We laughed and splashed around in the water. Jack kept coming over and pretending to be a shark and flipping our boards over. This was the Jack I was so captivated by. He was athletic and good at everything; he made everyone laugh; everyone liked him and wanted to be around him. He kept giving me subtle looks that he wasn't giving anyone else. I knew he was watching me in an extra special way.

Finally, Marissa and I decided we were freezing and were going to go back to the beach. We lay out on our towels to warm up until the ice cream man came, and we rose to go ask her mom for money for some Choco Tacos. Before we could even ask, Jack came down and paid for all the kids' ice creams. There had to have been at least twelve kids at the house and parents wandering around everywhere.

Marissa and I sat together on the bench outside the house, gossiping and eating our Choco Tacos. I was having such a great day. Marissa and I were having a blast together. It was hot and sunny and wet. We were eating ice cream. It was summertime. I also had this sense of power in the secret I held. I was starting to crave the adrenaline I felt when Jack and I were alone. Even though it was scary thinking we could get caught, it was exciting. I finished up my ice cream and felt my sticky hands getting sand stuck to them. *Eww, I need a shower,* I thought.

"Marissa, I think I wanna shower," I said. Danielle was walking by with another mother. I wasn't sure who the other mom was, but I recognized her from other parties at the Campbells' house.

"Oh, girls, you are welcome to any shower! We have two outside showers and a shower inside downstairs as well. They all have shampoo, conditioner and soap in them, and we have plenty of towels in each, so feel free."

"Thanks, Mrs. Campbell!" Marissa and I said in unison.

"I want to use the inside shower," Marissa said. "You can go after me."

"Nah, that's okay. I've never used an outside shower before. I will meet you inside when I am done."

"Okay," Marissa said and grabbed her bag with a change of clothes and went inside. I grabbed my bag and walked over to the shower stall. I opened the door and set my stuff down on the dry bench behind the curtain. I was reaching for a towel to lay out when I heard footsteps coming down the stairs. It didn't faze me. I proceeded to organize myself in the small shower stall when I heard a knock. "Anyone in there?" Jack said and pushed the door open before I could respond. He quickly shut the door behind him and locked it. Suddenly, we were alone in the shower stall. I still had my bikini on, which I was thankful for.

"Hi," Jack whispered. A flood of warmth penetrated my body. He took my hand gently. I breathed in deeply and quickly.

"Someone could find us," I whispered back, looking down at the gap under the shower stall door. Someone could easily bend over and see that two people were inside.

"Exactly," Jack smiled. "Isn't this exciting?"

I looked up at him, scared. I did not want to get in trouble. I did not want Marissa to come outside and find us, or worse—her parents. The worst possible scenarios kept playing in my head.

"It's okay, Blair. I promise, I would never do anything to hurt you or get you in trouble."

I let a deep sigh out. He was right. He was the adult here, and I trusted him. He had never lied to me before. The look on his face made me relax. My body wanted him to come closer, but my head wanted him to stay away. My mind was disturbed with the contradiction. He took a step closer to me. My back was pressed against the wooden shower stall door. His sandy chest was pressed against my bikini top. The weight of his body felt good. He took my hands and gently lifted them, pressing them against the wall. He looked at me, and my whole body was on fire. I was powerless to control it. I just knew I had to be quiet or someone would find us. "Are you ready?" Jack whispered softly into my ear and then looked at me so genuinely.

I squinted my eyes and forced a smile. I shook my head no from side to side because I couldn't formulate words, and I was terrified of someone hearing us. I was so confused. Why did my body like feeling his body pressed against mine?

"Does this feel good?" Jack put my arms down and reached around my waist pulling me in for a hug. I felt so comforted. So loved. So safe. I dug my head into his chest to avoid his lips.

He moved his hands gently to my hips and pushed me back against the shower stall door. He lightly touched my face, which was looking down, and lifted my gaze to meet his. I took another breath in. His face started to come in to kiss me, and I continued to shake my head from side to side. My jaw clamped shut. I pressed my lips together as hard as I could. I felt Jack's lips press against mine. *It's not my first kiss if I don't kiss him back*, I thought. I felt his tongue brush against my lips that were sealed shut. We heard footsteps. Jack backed away from me. "I'll go out first. You stay here for a few minutes and then leave," he urged in the barest whisper.

Jack was gone. I stood alone in the shower stall. My body was sandy and my knotted hair was a mess. I heard the crowd of people walk by, and Jack engaged in conversation with them. *We are safe*, I thought.

When they passed by, I turned on the shower water and cleaned up fast so I could meet Marissa inside in a timely manner.

* * *

Blair has been selected; she has been groomed, and now, she has been physically assaulted. We can look at the characteristics that made her vulnerable: her divorced parents, the death in her family and her lack of confidence.

Consider, though, that most everyone faces challenges and can be considered vulnerable in some way.

LET THAT SINK IN.

ANYONE CAN BE A VICTIM.

No person is off limits when it comes to child sexual abuse. Let that fact remove the blame from parents or caretakers who have lost their job, work long hours, have fallen ill, need to care for elders or siblings, etc. No one is to blame for child sexual abuse except the perpetrator. You can, however, do your duty to educate yourself on this epidemic of mass proportions. We can learn about the problem and try to prevent it like we would any other epidemic. We would never let our children skip basic hygiene or miss a doctor's visit, so why would we fail to speak up when it comes to something as pervasive as child sexual assault?

* * *

Jack: Are you going out on your trampoline today? It's such a nice day out, and I would love to see you.

Jack was back from his trip at the beach, and I hadn't seen him in a few days. We had been talking on the go-phone late at night, and he apologized for being so forward in the shower stall. He was just really excited about me. He always called me a tease. He asked me if it felt good. I told him yes because, in a lot of ways, it did.

Blair: I can…I am home.

I did want to see Jack. I was used to seeing him all the time. It was weird that he was away for the past week.

Jack: Great! I have something for you.

I read the text message. *What could he have for me?* I thought. I closed the phone and started back toward my trampoline. I started to feel the nervous excitement I always felt when I was going to see Jack alone. I hopped up on the trampoline and started to jump around until I heard rustling in the bushes. I could see Jack's face sticking up over the fence.

"Hey, Blair," he whispered. "I haven't been able to stop thinking about the shower stall all week, and I got something for you."

Jack held up a small little pink striped bag with tissue paper coming out the top. It was a Victoria's Secret bag. He reached in, crinkled the paper around and pulled out a fancy sparkly pink and black lace bra. It was huge. My insides quivered. I would not wear that…my boobs would not even fit into that… I barely had boobs… I laughed nervously.

"Now you don't have to wear it. I just thought you might want it. You know, because you are a turning into a woman now. You are such a beautiful woman."

"I don't know. I don't think I want it," I said nervously. I felt bad that he had bought it, but there was no way it would fit me, and I did not want it.

"That's okay, but I will leave it here for you." He tucked the bag into the fence behind a bush.

"Hey, Blair! Dinner is done!" my mom called, popping her head out of the deck door. She definitely could not see him in the bushes.

"Okay!" I responded loudly. I hopped off the trampoline and started to walk inside without saying goodbye to Jack. I was a little angry. *Why would he buy that for me? He knew I didn't want to even kiss him*...but I also felt bad. I did not know what I felt.

I went inside and quickly sent Jack a text. I did not want to be rude.

Blair: Sorry, gtg.

I am never picking up that bag, I thought. *I wonder if anyone will ever find it...*

I raced upstairs and joined my mom for chicken parmesan and spaghetti. My favorite!

To this day, I don't know if anyone ever found the bag.

JULY 2015.

ONE MONTH AFTER FIRST SEXUAL ENCOUNTER

Marissa and my weekly Friday night sleepovers had been interrupted for a few weeks because of summertime week-end trips and a cross-country sleepaway camp. But here we sat this Friday night in July, on my bed just as usual, gos-siping, laughing and texting. My grandma was staying over tonight because my mom had a night shift at the hospital. I was so grateful to have Marissa as a friend. We got on each other's nerves sometimes, but she was really like family to me. Since the second grade, she knew everything about me and my family. She was there for the yummy Italian dinners my mom made. She was there when my uncle passed away.

She challenged me to do tennis. We took gymnastics lessons together and slept at each other's houses practically every weekend. She really was like a sister to me.

"Jack just texted me, asking to come over like he used to," Marissa said and suddenly looked up from her phone. It was about 10:30 p.m., a little bit earlier than usual. It was odd thinking about Jack coming to my window to visit both Marissa and me now. Jack had been making almost daily visits to my house this summer, without Marissa. He either would stop by late at night and stand at my window and talk to me about how the world was against us, or sneak through the woods and talk to me while I jumped on the trampoline.

"Oh, okay... I guess he hasn't done that in a while," I lied to Marissa. In my head, I was able to rationalize the lie because Jack had told me Marissa would never understand us, and that she might be jealous. She might tell her parents. And that would end us.

I had been lying to Marissa more and more. But in reality, she hadn't asked me if Jack had been coming to my window without her. She hadn't asked me if Jack loved me, or if he was visiting me on the trampoline. But I also hadn't told her or anyone. *So, was I really lying about it?* It felt like a lie.

Jack made it very clear that everyone was against us. Forbidden love, he called it. We listened to the song "Dirty Little Secret," and he told me it was about couples like us. That so many people have the same problem because the world thinks age matters too much. I started to feel a little bit more distant from everyone in my life because I knew they couldn't possibly understand the feelings I had for Jack. Even though he made me feel so uncomfortable sometimes when he touched me too much, he was the only person I could talk to about it. Only his words validated my feelings for him as natural, and only his apology for pushing my boundaries would comfort me.

"He is at my house right now, and he has my phone charger that I forgot. He is going to drop it off," Marissa said, after texting him back and forth for a while. She must have asked for the phone charger, I guessed.

Perfect way to rationalize Jack's visit, I thought. We could always just say Jack was dropping off Marissa's phone charger.

"Okay, that's fine."

I wanted to text Jack on my secret phone, but Marissa did not know about it, so I wouldn't risk taking it out. She still texted him on her regular phone. They didn't talk as much, and it was usually related to the family plans.

"Do you want ice cream?" Marissa asked, smiling widely and raising her eyebrows.

"Of course!" I smiled back. So many thoughts were running through my head.

Marissa and I were in our baggy pajama pants and t-shirts. We lay on my bed watching a Hallmark movie until Jack appeared at the window. I began my routine of slowly and carefully opening up the window, being careful not to make a sound. It was only 10:30 p.m., so we had to be extra quiet. Jack handed over the phone charger to Marissa.

"I snuck into your room to grab this from the wall," Jack laughed quietly. I felt so intense sitting there with Marissa. Jack looked at me, and I could feel the passion between us. I wondered if Marissa noticed. Jack then handed over a pint of Oreo ice cream with some plastic spoons. I handed a spoon to Marissa, and we started eating out of the cartoon.

"I could stare at you two all day," Jack said.

The comments started to seem normal to me. It also didn't bother me when he told other people they looked good because the way he looked at me told me I was the only girl he really saw.

"Tell me about the boys at school, Marissa. Who is hitting on Blair these days? I hear there is a certain someone who likes her," he raised his eyebrows. Jack never got mad that boys at school liked me. He just told me I was way too mature for them. He told me I was ready for more. I still told him I did not want him to be my first kiss. I hadn't counted what happened in the shower stall as a first kiss.

All of a sudden, I saw headlights turn into the side driveway of my house.

My mom.

No.

My mom was home from work. She worked the 3 p.m. to 11 p.m. shift at the hospital tonight and was arriving home just a tad early. In the flash, Jack was gone. Nervous energy surged within me. I was scared. It felt like I went into autopilot. I quickly pulled down my window without caring if I was making any noise, threw the ice cream carton in my drawer, shut the lights out and Marissa and I got under the covers. I thought I was going to throw up. *Is this the end?* I thought.

Marissa and I lay silently in bed for a few minutes. We heard my mom enter the house. She came down the stairs and opened the door to my room, but she never came into my room. This felt so strange. She looked enraged, even in the weak light coming in from the hallway. "Blair, who was underneath your bedroom window?" she sounded less angry than I expected.

"What are you talking about?" I didn't know what to say. I hated lying, outright lying no less, but I didn't have a choice... did I? I couldn't get Jack in trouble...I loved him. That's right, I definitely loved him.

"No one was here, Mrs. Beam," Marissa chimed in.

"Well I just saw someone in the bushes underneath the window, and I called the police. If there is anything you want to tell me, you better start talking," she looked at us in the dark. "So... anything you want to say?"

"No," Marissa and I said in unison.

I was glad Marissa was here; we could figure this out together.

Within minutes, there were three police cars outside my house. My grandma came down in her robe. I had never seen her face so distraught and confused. Even after my uncle died, she didn't look like this. They found Jack's car key under the window. It must have fallen out of his pocket. They knew it was him. My mom took my hand and asked to talk to me alone. Without Marissa, I was nervous. I did not want to lie to my mom. "Blair, honey, what is going on here? You know you can tell me anything...You know I love you no matter what, and I would never be mad at you... you're my baby, Blair..." she was rambling. *You wouldn't support my love for Jack,* I thought. *I had to protect him.*

"It was nothing, Mom. I promise. Jack was over at Marissa's house and she forgot her charger... he just stopped by to drop it off, and we told him to come to the window so he wouldn't wake grandma up. Really! He also brought us ice cream...I can show you. It's in my drawer."

My mom let out of sigh of relief, but she still looked skeptical. "Okay, honey, I believe you."

A wave of relief swept through me. She believed me, thank god.

The next thing I knew, Jack was in my front yard. He had walked back after fleeing quickly through the back yard and into the woods. He ran home because he was scared. We found out his wife and kids were away for the weekend, and he told the police what I had told my mom. Then Marissa's parents showed up.

"I don't know what to say," Marissa's mom said to my mom. "I am sure this is a big misunderstanding. Let me talk to my husband about this."

"Okay, let me know what he says. I can file trespassing charges right now, but I don't want to start any drama unnecessarily. You know you guys are my friends, and I trust your judgement with this guy," my mom told her friend.

* * *

I know what you are thinking: "It could never be my kid *or* my student *or* my sister" and "Not in *my* town."

Rethink.

What is most alarming about childhood sexual assault is that groomers build the community's trust. Offenders slowly reduce boundaries before the assault ever happens.

We must become in tune with our own internal alarm bells and put the voices of others aside. The more you ignore your body's internal cues, the easier it will be to turn your back when something just "feels wrong." It is called trusting your gut. Listen to your intuition. You don't need more reason to respond to it. You are not obligated to justify your feelings.

Now what do you do with that feeling?

- **Be an active bystander. Let the adult know they crossed a boundary, what the boundary is and that you are vigilant.**

- **Give the adults clear limits. Be composed and stern.**

- **Give intervention in front of others so they also become aware of the limits.**

- **If boundaries continue to be crossed, it's time to report the behavior.**[47]

* * *

The rest of that night is a blur to me. I know that Marissa's mom took her home that night, and I went to sleep alone. I remember texting Jack on the secret phone, and he was relieved I texted him and they hadn't found the phone. Part of me hoped this incident would put an end to us. Part of me wished Jack and I could remain my special secret.

The next day, my mom would talk to Marissa's mom, who reassured her that Jack's misbehavior was yet another

47 "Trust Your Gut." www.d2l.com. https://www.d2l.org/trustyourgut/. (May 2019).

example of how much of a big kid he was and that we had nothing to worry about. My parents, both my mom and my dad, were still skeptical and began asking around to more people. My mom had called my dad and told him what happened. My dad's neighbor went to high school with Jack and so did my mom's good friend. Everyone spoke so highly of Jack. They all said he was the nicest guy who would do anything for anyone. My parents reluctantly decided not to press charges. But I was not to see Jack any longer or get tutored by him.

That would prove a challenge to enforce.

My friendship with Marissa quickly dwindled. It was the summertime; we didn't see each other at school every day, and her family was constantly hanging out with Jack. My mom was adamant that I was not to hang out with them. I was still talking to Jack on my secret phone, but he told me we should take a break from him coming to my house. I was relieved to hear him say that. He told me not to worry, that we would have our time… as soon as I turned eighteen. We had seven years to wait.

The less I was hanging out with Marissa, the more she started to hang out with other friends and leave me behind because I was not allowed to go if Jack's family was involved. I asked my mom on a daily basis if I could please go.

"It's not fair, Mom. I didn't do anything wrong. It was all a misunderstanding like Marissa's mom said, and now I can't hang out with my best friend," I said. I could tell I was wearing on her. She'd cave eventually.

Finally, she talked to Marissa's mom, and again she was convinced. I could go over to the Campbells' again and even start to go back to tutoring. Since it was summertime, I didn't want to fall behind. It was all a big misunderstanding.

Blair: I am coming to Six Flags with Marissa's family and you guys today!

Jack: No way! Really? I have missed you so much! That is so great! I cannot wait to see you, Blair. The past couple of weeks have been torture without you.

It was true—not seeing Jack meant that he was all I thought about.

Blair: I can't wait to see you too.

When we arrived at Six Flags and I saw Jack for the first time in weeks, I was elated. I tried to hold back my happiness when he came bouncing out of his Jeep with Lizzy in his arms. I had to hide it. People were suspicious now. We had to be extra careful. Jack was wearing khaki shorts, aviator sunglasses and a white active-wear polo. His muscles bulged out of his sleeves.

"Hey, guys!" he said and waved, but he didn't look at me directly. He was careful today: no intense stares, no private conversations, no whispers of how pretty I looked. I missed it. I missed the way he made me feel. I missed the rush of adrenaline I felt whenever he looked at me for too long and played footsie with me under the table. *Today was so ordinary*, I thought.

PART 5

SEXUALIZING THE RELATIONSHIP

AUGUST 2015.

TWO MONTHS AFTER FIRST SEXUAL ENCOUNTER

"Manhunt!" Reese screamed. It was Labor Day weekend. The official end to summer. Marissa and I would start the seventh grade next week. I was hoping once school started, we would get as close as we used to be, but I was also nervous to spend too much time with her. My life was becoming increasingly private. Ever since I was allowed to see Jack again, our nightly phone calls turned into impassioned conversations about our future together.

"I am obsessed with you, Blair. I cannot get you out of my head," Jack would tell me. My stomach seemed to be lined with goose bumps. I could feel the bottom of my tummy shiver whenever he told me he loved me. It felt good to be so important to someone else.

I had done it again. I got lost in my own head. "Blair," Marissa snapped. I had completely zoned out.

"Yeah, sorry, I'm just tired," I answered quickly. "Let's play!"

There were probably about fifteen kids over at Jack's house. A bunch of parents were hanging out in the backyard as it got dark. They were drinking beer and eating the leftover burgers from earlier. Jack was in the front yard with us about to commission a game of manhunt.

"Alright, everyone, here are the rules," he said, sounding enthused and ready to play. All the kids looked up at Jack, eager to get started. I had never played manhunt before. From what I understood, it was basically hide and go seek in the dark. "We are allowed to hide in my yard and Reese's yard and anywhere in between. Any other place is out of bounds. Got it, you guys?" Jack rallied the troop of children.

There was a crowd consensus.

"Now…who wants to be the hunter?" Jack asked the group.

A neighborhood boy who was a year younger than me, Henry, raised his hand impatiently.

"Alright settled! Henry, go wait inside for two minutes, and then try to come find us," Jack directed.

The restless crowd of kids started to scramble. Marissa and I took off in the same direction. We crouched down behind a bush and looked at each other. "Shhhh," Marissa said, index finger to her lips.

"Boo!" A faceless person spooked us from the side. Jack suddenly appeared in front of us. It was so dark now, though, it was hard to tell who it was.

"Guys, you have to spilt up. Henry is going to find you! Three, two, one, run!" Jack provoked us.

Marissa ran in one direction, and I moved in another. I felt nervous. I did not want to be without Marissa.

I nestled in behind a new bush on the side of Jack's house. Honestly, it was a little spooky to be alone in the dark.

I wasn't alone for long. Jack creeped in next to me. He didn't say anything at first; he just gently lingered his fingers on the top of my hand. I looked over at this dark outline. He then interlaced his fingers with mine and gave my hand a gentle squeeze. "Thank you for letting me be yours," Jack whispered softly in my ear. "I can't stop thinking about you, Blair. Ever," he said while giving me that deep look again. He had on a navy-blue sweatshirt with the hood up. He squeezed my hand again and whispered into my ear, "Follow me."

Jack got up, and together we ran into his neighbor's front yard. We sat plainly in the middle of their small yard. It was dark enough that no one could see us. We were out of bounds now too. He took his sweat shirt off and laid it on the cool summer ground and gestured for me to sit on it. *How sweet,* I thought.

"Blair, the two weeks we were not allowed to see each other, I almost lost my mind," Jack sounded so emotional… *is he going to cry?* His passionate energy was consuming my body. His voice was cracking, and his grasp on me seemed desperate. I felt an intensity I had never felt. "I don't know what I would do without you, but I also don't know what I would do if we were ever caught. For real…ya know…" He looked away.

My heart ached for him because I knew he had a greater risk in this relationship than I did. He had to have been serious about us or why would he take the risk? I wanted to comfort him; I wanted to make him feel better. "Actually, I know what I would do… I would hang myself on the swing set in the backyard if we ever got caught," he said and paused. "My children would find me." A tear rolled down his face.

We sat silently for a moment. In this moment, I knew I was in over my head. I had someone's life in my hands. I could not take that lightly. Jack pulled me in for a tight embrace. My shoulders caved inward, and my body let go to him. I let myself fully enjoy this embrace without worrying that someone would come home or see us. I was melting into him, sitting there on the ground in the darkness of the summer night. He realized his grip and held my face in his hands. His touch was so gentle. He touched me tenderly like a set of fine china, like I was delicate and precious, to be handled with care. His eyes admired mine. He leaned toward me and kissed my lips. And I let him. I completely surrendered to him for those moments. My lifeless limbs lay there. I did nothing to stop him. I had officially given away my first kiss.

* * *

So, the big question is, why doesn't Blair just leave? Why does the child continue to subject themselves to the abuse? The answer is, children are trapped in these relationships. They are confused; they see all the positive aspects of the groomer and all the love, support and gifts they get from them. They blame themselves for the abuse. Maybe they wonder when they were supposed to have shouted, "NO!"

to claim rape. The child has worked so hard to keep this relationship secret and fear they would be blamed if they were to come forward. They have become reliant on the relationship to fill their needs and fear life without the abuser. They have come to see themselves as unwanted outside the relationship and believe if their relationship came out, they would be even more unlovable.

Abusers will use threats, intimidation or blackmail to keep the child quiet. Many abusers will remind the child that they will go to jail or kill themselves if anyone finds out about their relationship and that it would destroy their life.[48]

The good news is, we can stop these cycles of abuse. We can start small, in our homes, in our workplaces, in our playgrounds, in our communities by coming together to heal survivors through listening and connecting. We can be educated and empowered bystanders by speaking up when something seems amiss. We can encourage people to share their stories to find solidarity and hope. We can move away from anger and toward love to change the culture around sexual violence.

---

48 "Grooming: What it is, signs and how to protect children." www.nspcc.org.uk. https://www.nspcc.org.uk/preventing-abuse/child-abuse-and-neglect/grooming/. (May 2019).

Red flag

- **Secret keeping!**

Avoid secret keeping in your home, classroom, camp, team, etc. Be open and honest with the children in your life and explain that if you are asked to keep a secret, something is probably wrong!

SEPTEMBER 2015.

THREE MONTHS AFTER FIRST SEXUAL ENCOUNTER

"My daddy needs you in my room," Lizzy nudged me. I was sitting on Jack's couch with his daughter. We were watching TV. I came over for tutoring and was waiting for Jack to be ready. Danielle was at the Martins' house with Elena. It was just Lizzy, Jack and me in the house. Jack had been calling my name from the other side of the house. I ignored his call.

"My daddy needs you, Blair!" Lizzy said again.

"Okay, okay, Lizzy…I'll be RIGHT back…okay?" I looked at the little girl wishing she hadn't noticed her father's call.

I stood up. Breathing in through my nose deeply, I walked over to Jack. He was in Lizzy's room. He was sitting on the edge of her bed and patted the spot next to him, motioning for me to sit beside him. I obeyed. He looked at me with his agonizing stare. He extended his arm around my back and pulled me in close to him. He kissed the top of my head. "I love seeing you in my house."

My guard was back up…I hated when he did this. His kid was home, his wife could walk in any second, and I was terrified. Why couldn't we just talk on the phone? Why couldn't he wait for me to get older…when it was allowed. The way he caressed me was so wrong in my head, but my body couldn't help but crave the contact.

He rubbed the side of me. It felt warm and snug for a moment, until my mind reminded me all the ways this could go wrong.

"Come with me," he urged and stood up, taking my hand in his. He walked into his bedroom. "I have always wanted to see you in my bed," he said, looking at me.

My insides cringed. *Noooooooo. This is where he and his wife sleep.*

"I don't want to do this," I said and looked down at the ground. "Not here, ya know?" I was trying to sound casual. I glanced up and saw the swing set in the backyard through his bedroom window.

"Please," he begged, sitting down on the bed and looking up at me.

His eyes trespassed into my heart, and I surrendered once again. He took my little body in his arms and kissed it all over. My senses were in flames; my heart was breaking with conflict... *What did I want? What was I supposed to want? Why was my mind not in sync with my body? Was this what love felt like? Why didn't I have the courage to leave and never come back?* My body was inert as I slowly lay down and surrendered myself to him.

* * *

Slowly and continuously, once the groomer has isolated the child, they begin to introduce sexual activity. Grooming sexual offenders were asked how they kept parents from suspecting there was a sexual relationship between the child and the groomer. The former child supervisor pointedly replied, "Lied. Continually," he said. "We would sneak around and find ways to meet at the mall or meet at the movie theater... When we became sexual... that's when everything went into protection mode. Our mission became 'We've got to hide this, keep this secret.'"[49] To protect your child, the offender offers, "If a parent sees

49 Huffman, Charlotte. "Two Child Sex Offenders Explain How They Picked Their Targets." www.wfaa.com. https://www.wfaa.com/article/features/originals/two-child-sex-offenders-explain-how-they-picked-their-targets/287-434667495. (May 2019).

their child spending an inordinate amount of time with a significant adult that is outside the family, that is something to really spend some time looking at," he said. "If your child starts talking about another significant adult in ways that you are going, 'I didn't realize you guys were that close,' then there could be a problem,"[50] he said.

Sexualizing the relationship may begin early in the relationship, as the groomer begins to desensitize the child to physical touch with "accidental" brushes, hugs, pats on the back, etc.[51] Playing hide-and-go-seek-like games, tag and other touch games, with other kids and adults around helps normalize the touch to the child. The groomer may show the child pornography, have them sit on their lap and/or hold their hand. Sexual content begins to become a topic of conversation. They create situations where the offender and the child are naked. Whether they are swimming or sending photos on the phone, the offender exploits the child's human desire to learn about their body and uses pleasure to develop the sexual relationship. The offender is usually in a position to teach the child about their body and control what the child finds arousing.

---

50 Ibid

51 Georgia M. Winters & Elizabeth L. Jeglic. "Stages of Sexual Grooming: Recognizing Potentially Predatory Behaviors of Child Molesters," Deviant Behavior, 38:6, 724-733, https://www.tandfonline.com/doi/full/10.1080/01639625.2016.1197656

Likewise, media mogul Oprah Winfrey (herself a victim of sexual abuse from the ages of ten to fourteen) hosted a show where she interviewed child molesters and commented that,

***"If an abuser does his or her job well, the abuse feels good."*[52]**

This can add to a victim's feelings of shame and confusion, she said. This can be true for many victims who experience sexual abuse at an early age.[53] However, it is important to note that this does not mean all children feel positive sensations throughout the abuse. Many groomers use intimidation, fear and guilt to get children to allow the sexual relations, and it may *not* feel good. Still, the traumatic effects of the abuse remain the same. Survivors of child sexual violence of all kinds face body issues, eating disorders, low self-esteem, anxiety, PTSD and difficulty developing intimate relationships.

Let's empower survivors through acceptance, validation, self-disclosure, connection and encouragement.

Support them in quieting their shame and promoting resilience.

---

52 Sands, Nicole. "Months Before Interviewing Michael Jackson Accusers, Oprah Winfery Opened Up About Her Own Abuse." people.com. https://people.com/tv/oprah-winfrey-details-own-abuse-months-before-interviewing-michael-jackson-accusers/. (May 2019).

53 Ibid

OCTOBER 2015.

FOUR MONTHS AFTER FIRST SEXUAL ENCOUNTER

Up until I was eleven, I never had a paid job. I had an allowance, and I never needed or longed for anything. To be honest, I was pretty spoiled. But that didn't mean that when I started to get paid for delivering magazines I wasn't thrilled by the idea of independence and earning my own money. It made me feel more grown up. So now that I was twelve and was juggling school, my friendship with Marissa, tutoring, my relationship with Jack and magazine delivery...I really thought I was a full-blown grown up. Not only did I have a source of income, but I also had a relationship, a man who loved me. Not just a boy, a man.

Today was a cool October day. This fall was settling in faster than last year's. "Global warming," my mom would blame. I just got home from school and set my backpack down in my room. I'd retreat upstairs and have my normal "How did your day go?" conversation with my mom, who would offer me a snack and a hug. My head was spinning with secrets. Some days, I had to hide feelings of guilt. These sprang on me especially when my mom did extra special things for me, like buy us show tickets or make me a separate pot of angel hair pasta because I hated spaghetti noodles and they were her favorite. Those times were hard. Those were the times I wanted to spill the beans of my secret love life to my mom. I wanted to tell her I was in love, that I found the love of my life. I wanted for her to jump for joy with me. But I knew better; Jack made sure.

I threw on a warmer jacket than I wore to school that day to walk over to my neighbor's house to pick up magazines to deliver. I quickly ran into my room to grab my secret phone before running out the door and slamming it closed behind me. I knew I was probably going to see Jack today. He synced up his schedule with mine each week so he could have picnics with me whenever I delivered magazines. Every Sunday, he would ask me what days I was delivering magazines, and he always made it work with his schedule. He was so sweet; he always wanted to spend time with me and go on romantic dates. He always told me about the romantic dates he would take me on when we could be seen in public together.

I jogged across my lawn, looked both ways and crossed the street over to my neighbor's house. They made me a key to the front door, and I let my myself in. "Max!" I exclaimed, and the floppy dog came fumbling toward me. I picked up the magazines Ann left for me, remembering to grab some extras, and out the door I went. I hopped on my bike and rode down and around Glenvale, dropping off Ann's real estate books and waving to the neighbors. I then made my way to the wooded trailhead around the corner. Jack texted me that he would meet me down there. He parked on the other side of the park so we entered from opposite directions, and he was now walking toward me. There was no one else around.

I smiled when I saw him. It was an automatic response to light up when Jack was around. He made everyone smile and laugh and feel comfortable. It was his gift. He radiated this positive energy that people, including me, could not stay away from.

He opened his arms wide, and I walked toward him for a hug. "Hi, Blair," he said. "You look so beautiful. Your skin is so smooth and white." He touched my face and sent a tingly sensation through my shoulders, down my arms and into the pit of my stomach. I looked up at him. "And your eyes… they are like a rainbow. You have a little yellow ring around your pupil and green and blue emerging outward. They are so magical," he said, his gentle words piercing through my chest and landing deep within my heart.

"Thanks, Jack. You have pretty eyes too," I said and looked up at his own pale skin and defined chin. He had a slender face and light hair that was perfectly tossed around and contrasted his light blue eyes. "Your eyes are like an ocean," I said to him. "They are so blue."

Together we walked hand in hand through the trail. There was a lake back in the woods, and we eventually set up the blanket he brought back there. He pulled out the beachside subs, and he sat next to me as we ate together. We looked at birds and watched the squirrels go by. Jack even joked that he would throw me into the lake at one point. I laughed out loud and told him he better not dare.

Then Jack brought up us being together in the future…how different things would be, how much better things would be. I could have whatever I wanted: a house, a dog, clothes, a car… and one day, we'd have our own kids together. I would be a mom. But not just any mom, a mother to his children.

"You are so special, Blair. There isn't anyone else I would want to spend the rest of my life with," he told me and leaned in to kiss me. My mind told me to jerk backward and resist. My body told me to lean closer, to let go. I kissed him. A part of me still said this was good practice for when I had to kiss a boy my own age for real. His hands were on me. They lingered on my face as he pulled me in close to kiss his lips. Then his fingers moved down onto my neck, and slowly they trickled over my chest and down my tummy that was full of the sandwiches he bought. I felt his cold fingers on my warm belly where the edge of my shirt met my low-rise jean button. I moved his hand away cautiously. He had done this before, in his bedroom while I was babysitting, and I had been too nervous to make any noise. He took my hand gently and placed it on his crotch. He rubbed my hand around, and I could feel hardness underneath his jeans. I opened my eyes. He opened his. We started kissing. I shook my head no and wrinkled my face.

He unzipped his jeans. He guided my hand to gently stroke him. "You're almost there," he said. "Please, Blair, please," he begged. My hand was limp. I let him guide my hand on himself until he was out of breath and satisfied. He leaned forward and put his body on top of mine. "Oh Blair, you are incredible," he said finally. "Well, you better get home," he said next.

I don't remember what we talked about on the walk back to the road.

* * *

Blair is not alone.

Victims of any sort of trauma often have trouble remembering what happened to them and specific details about their trauma. They may not remember any of their assault at all. James Hopper, PhD explains in *Time Magazine* that the brain is simply reacting to a dangerous situation the way it is supposed to. Apparently, in times of stress, the human brain's pre-frontal cortex is impaired or even shut off. This is the executive functioning center of the brain, and without it, we cannot control what we focus on, we cannot make sense of what we are experiencing and thus, we cannot remember all the details the way we remember most events.[54]

Hopper also explains that when fear kicks in, the brain's amygdala takes over and tells the brain to focus on small details, instead of the horrible sensations it is feeling. Fear also prevents the brain from coding and storing contextual and time-sequencing information.[55]

---

54 "Why Rape and Trauma Survivors have Fragmented and Incomplete Memories." www.time.com. http://time.com/3625414/rape-trauma-brain-memory/. (May 2019).

55 Ibid

These advancements in research on trauma suggest that it is erroneous for people, law enforcement included, to expect survivors to remember details of a traumatic event as they do any other event.

Some may remember everything perfectly; others may not, which is totally normal.

OCTOBER 2015.

FOUR MONTHS AFTER FIRST SEXUAL ENCOUNTER

I could hear my mom on the phone upstairs. It was Danielle.

"Oh, hi, Danielle," my mom said, using the voice she always used when she spoke to most other moms in town. It was a pretend happy voice. It's not that my mom wasn't happy; she was, but that was not how she talked to everyone. There was definitely something special about the Campbell family that made people want to be liked by them. Hence the high-pitched cheer my mom used on the phone.

"Oh, thank you for the invitation for tonight. I will be working tonight, but I believe Blair will be joining you with the Martins."

Danielle was inviting my family over for the Halloween party. That was surprising. We mostly kept to ourselves. We gathered with our extended family nearby, but we weren't much of party goers unless I was tagging along with Marissa.

"Oh well, I'll have to see if Blair is free for a few hours…let me ask her…just a moment."

My mom called my name, and I came galloping up the stairs.

"Yes, Mom?" I said when I reached the top of the stairs.

"Danielle Campbell wants to know if you could keep an eye on Lizzy and Elena while they get ready for the party tonight? Do you feel like going over or are you feeling tired?" she asked, giving me an out. My mom knew me well enough to know that if I didn't want to go, I might not want to say it outright. Knowing Danielle was on the phone, she knew to give me the option to say no.

"Yeah sure, I am not doing anything," I answered.

My mom put the phone back to her ear. "Of course, Danielle, I'll bring her over in an hour or so."

* * *

I arrived at Jack's house that afternoon, and Jack and Danielle were both at home. This was the first time I had seen them interact as a couple in a while. They mostly appeared for social gatherings with a smile, or I saw Danielle when I arrived and left tutoring. Today was the first time I was there by myself for something other than tutoring. Jack and Danielle were busy arguing over how much money to spend on the party, where to put decorations and who to invite, while I kept Lizzy and Elena occupied.

After a few hours of reading books, coloring pictures, molding play dough and playing Barbies, I took Lizzy, who was already dressed in her ladybug costume, outside for some photos. Danielle and Jack were outside hanging decorations. I carried Elena out in my arms; she hadn't been dressed for Halloween yet. Being in the presence of Jack and Danielle as a couple was a weird experience. Jack said that Danielle knew all about us and was only with him for his money, so I did not feel bad for Danielle, but I did feel jealous. I wanted to be her in more ways than one. She was athletic, beautiful, kind, had a successful tennis career and two precious children. I envied her, and oddly enough, I wanted her to like me too.

Once they were done hanging decorations, Lizzy ran over to her mom.

"Mommy, Mommy, look at my ladybug costume. Blair helped me put it on!" Lizzy shouted. I tried to stop her from running over to her mom because I felt that was the reason I was there, but Danielle waved her hand, indicating it was okay for Lizzy to come over.

"Blair, let me get your opinion on where to put the chocolate fountain," Jack said to me as he walked inside.

Danielle was making a fuss over Lizzy and had taken Elena in her arms, so I followed him inside. He was walking toward Lizzy's room. *Was he putting a fountain in his daughter's room? No way that is what we are going to talk about...*

We entered Lizzy's room, and he sat down on the bed.

"I have something for you, Blair," he said and held out a bag that was hidden under Lizzy's bed.

"Jack, no, you don't need to give me anything... really...it's not my birthday or anything,"

"But it's Halloween, and Halloween is my favorite holiday. It always has been, plus I want you to have this. Open it," he quietly said, eyeing the bag.

My eyes scanned the bag, and I tried to predict what was inside. I reached my hand into the orange tissue paper and pulled out a small black velvet jewelry box.

"Please, Jack no, I don't deserve this," I said and looked up at him, feeling guilty for taking this gift, feeling like I was wrong for accepting it.

"Open it, Blair. I bought it especially for you. I want you to have it."

I opened the box, and a heart shaped pendant appeared before me. I touched the diamonds that lined one side of the heart shape. It was a stunning necklace. I had always wanted one like it. My mom wore a necklace with three hearts on it, and she always said they represented me, my grandma and her.

"You stole my heart, Blair," he said and looked at me intensely. "Now let me put it on you and remember, if anyone asks, I didn't buy it for you."

He took the box from me and removed the necklace with care. Jack pulled my hair away from my face and pushed it gently behind my shoulders. He opened the clasp and put the necklace around my neck. I looked up at him as he stood in front of me.

"You are the most beautiful creature on this Earth," he said and kissed me on the forehead. "There is a note in the bag too. Please make sure you read it before you come over tonight. But come on, let's get you home."

We exited Lizzy's room, and Jack told Danielle he'd drive me home. I was surprised. Danielle always drove me home, no matter what. But she said okay. I hopped in the front seat of the Jeep and buckled in.

"I am so excited to see you in your costume tonight," Jack said, putting his hand on my thigh.

"I am wearing an old dance costume tonight and throwing a headband on to be a flapper," I laughed, nervously avoiding the fact that his hand was moving up my thigh and making me more and more anxious. He took me straight home, though.

"I wish I could kiss you goodbye, but they would see," he said, as we pulled into the driveway.

"I know, we better not. But, Jack, thank you for the necklace and note… They are so special and generous. And the necklace is beautiful. I am so grateful for you." I hopped out of the car and ran inside to read my love note.

* * *

Marissa and I arrived at the tennis match late, after taking extra-long in the locker room to get our uniforms on and ponytails perfected. This was the fall tennis "practice" season, and I still hated the matches. Last year, they hadn't let me play on the competitive team in the spring…so I really had to get better this year. I still had anxiety about people watching me play. I didn't have to beg my mom anymore not to come, though. She understood my fears because she hated people watching her as well. I rubbed my arms quickly and took a deep breath waiting for the match to start. *Man, it is cold out…*

Halloween had now come and gone. I had a new necklace from Jack, which I had to take off for the match, but I would put it right back on afterward. When my mom asked where I got it, I told her I got it at a gift shop after school with my magazine delivery money. She said it was pretty.

Standing in the cold, waiting for the practice match to start, I couldn't stop thinking about the Halloween party this past weekend. It was the most fun I'd had in a long time. Marissa and I ran around the house as if we owned the place, took Lizzy trick or treating and got to talk to a tarot card reader that Jack hired for the party. I had always wanted to talk to a psychic. What she told me was racking my brain.

"You have already met the love of your life, Blair. You better not let him go," the older Middle-Eastern woman dressed as a witch told me after consulting the cards I had shuffled. She wore a black dress with a subtle purple print. Her hair was black, and she had a big nose. I nodded my head knowingly.

"Remember, Blair, some secrets are best kept as secrets," she said, before asking me if I had any specific questions. She seemed too spot-on with my life; I was scared to ask her any more questions. Afterward, I went immediately to Jack and told him what she had told me.

"Well...I think she is right," he said and smiled. "I got a good psychic...huh?" he said, before we had to walk away from each other or risk people getting suspicious.

The ball pounced on the ground. I had been too distracted to pay attention to the coin toss, and the match was starting. Marissa was my partner again, and I looked to her for comfort. I felt relieved because I didn't see anyone in the crowd I knew. Now I could just play at my pace and not worry about what other people were doing. *Phew.*

After the first set, I turned, glanced over my shoulder and found parents were lined up. I tried to avoid the crowd and pretend I did not see them. I heard my name. Jack was calling my name. I looked up quickly and saw Jack and Marissa's father cheering us on. My adrenaline kicked in, and I began to focus in on the game, but I couldn't stop thinking about being watched. Jack just always seemed to be around.

When we finally finished the match with a losing score, I was greeted by Jack and Marissa's father with water and congratulations.

"Give me a high-five, kiddo," Jack said to me standing next to Marissa's dad. I gave him a high-five, still too out of breath to respond.

"You keep getting better and better," Marissa's dad chimed in.

"Thanks," I smiled.

"Blair, you have got goosebumps all over you. Let me give you my jacket," Jack said and took off his zip-up hoodie and placed it around my shoulders. I was cold, and it did feel good to have an extra layer.

"Thanks, Jack," I said, putting my arms through the sleeves and zipping up the jacket that was at-least three sizes too big for me.

"Anytime, kiddo," he smiled.

NOVEMBER 2015.

FIVE MONTHS AFTER FIRST SEXUAL ENCOUNTER

"Yes, Mom, okay," I answered my mom into my cell phone. I was pedaling my bike into the wooded trail after my magazine route. My mom had been feeling sick for days, and she was finally going to the doctor. She had left a note on the front door, letting me know she'd be gone when I got home, but she had to call too.

"Alright, sweetie. I'll see ya soon…I love you," she said in her congested tone. *Poor mom,* I thought.

"I love you too," I said and hung up the phone. Now I was halfway down the trail, and Jack was up ahead. I passed a lonely man walking and smiled as I put away the phone in my pocket.

Picnics were a regular thing now. I looked forward to getting my favorite beachside sub and getting to hang out with Jack after school. He didn't always make me do sexual stuff...and it only lasted a couple of minutes... I figured I owed him for all the stuff he had given me over the past year... plus, if we were going to be together one day, I had better get used to the things adults do.

Jack waited at the head of the trail for me and then came out to give me a hug. We walked back to our normal spot in the woods next to the lake. It was pretty cold out today, and I sat extra close to Jack to share his body heat. He stroked my hair.

"I am so lucky to have you," Jack said and smiled. "I don't know what I would do without you."

He turned my head. I inhaled deeply, bracing myself for what was to come. Jack began kissing me and touching me, and I was cold and I let him take my hand and touch himself. I felt awkward and didn't know what to do.

We heard footsteps.

Instantly, Jack sprung from the ground, zipped his pants and snatched the blanket from under me.

"We are not together," he hissed. "I am going to head out. You wait here and leave in a couple of minutes." I looked over, stood up and grabbed my bike leaned up against the tree.

"Okay," I said, feeling scared and nervous and alone.

The footsteps were multiplying and moving toward me.

Police.

Three uniformed police officers and the man I had walked past earlier appeared before me. A woman police officer asked me my name.

"Blair," I said. "I am just going home now. I was on a bike ride."

"Blair, honey, can you stay with me for a minute and answer a few questions," the lady asked me.

I wanted to run, to just take off. I mean, I hadn't done anything wrong, right? Why was I being questioned? My stomach contracted. I wished in that moment that I had superpowers. That I could make myself so small that no one would see me or notice me—ever, except for Jack, because he knew how to make me feel special and good inside.

"Okay," I started to sweat and my mind was racing.

The officers took me over to their police cars and asked me to get in. I stepped into the back seat of the police car, and the tall, thin black woman squatted down outside the car next to me. The door was open. The officer was very gentle when she spoke.

"Now, Blair, tell me again what you were doing in the woods."

"I was just taking a bike ride, and I wanted to venture off the trail along the lake a little bit. I deliver magazines in the neighborhood a couple of days a week when I get home from school, and then I like to come back here," I said. My bike was outside the police car; I stared at it, wondering if I could hop on it and escape this scene.

"Okay, and do you know Jack Campbell?" she asked. I could see Jack standing with two other police officers in the distance. Jack was pacing around. He looked frustrated.

"Yeah," I said.

"How you know him?" she prompted.

"He is my tutor," I answered.

"Were you meeting him in the woods today?" she asked.

"No," I answered.

"Do you know what he was doing back there?"

"No, but I know he lives around here."

"Has Jack ever touched you, your hair, given you a hug… anything?" she asked. She was still squatted on the ground, looking up at me.

"NO," I responded. She could tell I was getting frustrated.

"Alright, sweetie, do you have a parent I could talk to? We are going to take you home."

"No really, it's fine. I can ride my bike home. You couldn't fit this in the police car anyway," I said, looking over at my pastel pink beach cruiser.

"That's okay, honey, we'll get someone with a bigger vehicle to carry your bike. How about we call your mom or dad."

What was going on? Was Jack going to be okay? What did I do? What was happening? Were my parents going to be mad at me? Was Jack going to kill himself?

I dialed my mom. It rang and rang. She didn't pick up. She was at doctor's; I knew this.

Another police officer had arrived. She was also a woman, and she told me her name was Detective Ryder. She scared me. She had big red hair and was definitely older than my mom. She looked like a no-nonsense kind of woman. She came over to me and introduced herself. She asked me to get out of the cop car and come into her car. She said it was a police car too, but it didn't look like one. She drove a baby blue sedan.

She and the other police officer got in the car and had me direct them to my house. They pulled into the driveway. I could see my grandma was home. That was strange; she usually only came over to watch me for overnights. My mom still wasn't home.

My heart was beating so fast. My body was sweating and my hands were shaking and I was still planning escape routes in my head. It was too late now; they knew where I lived.

"Blair, can you go get a parent for us?" Detective Ryder said and turned around and looked at me.

"Okay, my mom isn't home, but I can see what my grandma is doing."

With each painful step I took up the driveway, I felt more shame and fear and guilt seep into my pores. These were all the feelings I had pushed away for so long, the feelings I let Jack numb with kindness. I finally reached my front door. It was locked. I had my key. I turned the key and opened the door. I could feel the police watching me. I heard the shower running. *Oh right, my grandma's water was off. She was using our shower...*

I walked up the stairs and knocked on the bathroom door. *I just have to say it. The police are here, and they want to talk to you. Just rip the Band-Aid off...* I thought. I said it.

"What?" my grandma responded.

Now I had to say it again? The words "the police are here" hurt to come out of my mouth.

"What's going on?" she asked.

"I don't know, Grandma. They just want to talk to you, okay?" I was frustrated and upset. *Don't make me say it again...*

When my grandma got out of the shower, she invited the officers in, and I was told to go to my room. My grandma and the officers sat upstairs at the kitchen table, talking until I heard my mom come in and join them. I sat in agony, alone in my room.

What could they be talking about? No one saw anything... I did not dare take out my secret phone while the police were in my house. They finally came down to retrieve me.

I was wrong about thinking I had never seen my mom as distraught as she had been the night Jack was at my window. The look on my mom's face now seemed as if she had died. Like she was gone and she stood in a shell of herself. "Blair, honey, baby, dear," she touched my arm like I was a china doll. "Please just tell the truth, honey. You've done nothing wrong, my sweet girl. You always have been and you always will be," she said, as a tear streamed down her face. I could tell she was about to explode with tears, but she was standing strong.

"The police want to take you down to the station and talk to you some more... can you do that for me, baby? Can you please just talk to them and tell them the truth? No one is mad, honey."

My body was paralyzed with confusion. My heart ached for my mother. I loved my mom and hated seeing her this way. My heart also ached for Jack, the man who loved me and just wanted to be allowed to love me. I wanted him to be allowed to love me. The thought of telling the police was terrifying to me. Not only because I knew the consequences, but also because the words were painful to speak. I could not utter the words penis, vagina or sex. I could not utter the things he had done to me. I felt like my mouth literally could not form those words. It was easier to say no. That those things had not happened. And that is what I did.

I told the police no again and again. They asked again and again. Finally, after sitting in a small, cold and uncomfortable room at the police station for an hour, they told me they had seen us hug. I told them he kissed me once. But nothing else ever happened. Finally, I shut down. I was tired, hungry, emotional. I wanted my mom, but I also wanted to be far from her. I didn't want to hurt her with my lies or hurt her with the truth. The only person to turn to was Jack.

When I got home, there was a man in sitting in my room. All I wanted was to text Jack and make sure he was okay. The man had my iPad and the plush dog, the one Jack had given me.

My grandma came down into my room. "Please just talk to this man quickly, and then you can go to bed, and Blair please, just tell the truth."

"I am not a liar," I lied.

I sat across from the man. He was a middle-aged man and wasn't wearing a police uniform. I wondered if he had any kids my age. He looked at me desperately. "Blair," he said, "please tell me if you have ever taken photos of yourself without clothes on and sent them anywhere or received any photos of children without clothes on."

What was he talking about? I would never do that...

"No," I answered truthfully.

He went on, again and again asking the same question in different ways. I felt like he wanted my response to change, like he wanted me to have sent nude photos or to have received them. My response remained the same until he finally left.

My mom came down and sat with me. She hugged me, and we cried. I didn't know why we were crying, but we cried. All I could think about was the secret phone in my drawer; I needed to find a better hiding spot for that.

* * *

I sat on the edge of my bed alone. I was wearing hand-me-down sweatpants from my cousin and a Glenvale Middle School t-shirt that I had put on late the night before, once I was done being questioned. It was morning now. I had been so tired, but I could not sleep. My mind kept racing, trying to rationalize the lies I had told, worrying about Jack, but also wondering if I should have told more of the truth. I was scared to turn my secret phone on, but I had to know that he was okay. I turned it on. There were no messages… I was surprised, but then I wondered if Jack was in jail. I was so curious… *But what could they have arrested him for?* I wondered.

I looked at the phone—the phone that once seemed like a simple secret now seemed like a weapon, a bomb waiting to go off. I dialed Jack. He picked up immediately, but did not say hello. "Hello?" I whispered and moved into my closet and shut the door so no one could hear me. "Blair," Jack responded. "Is it safe for us to talk?" he asked. He sounded scared.

"Yes, I am hiding in my closet," I reassured him.

"Is your bedroom door locked?" Jack asked.

"No, but that is a good idea," I responded and tiptoed over to lock my door before returning to my closet.

"It's locked," I told him.

"Okay good. Blair, that was so scary. I almost lost everything today, my freedom, my house, my kids and worst of all...you," he said. He was crying.

"I know. I was so scared too," I tried to sympathize.

"Yeah, Blair, but you have nothing to lose. I have everything to lose..." There was a silence. "What did you tell the police?"

"Ah..." *Oh no...I had told the police we kissed... he would not like that...* My stomach turned inside out and my head pounded...I had to tell him the truth. "I told them nothing happened except that you kissed me once... I figured they'd get off my back if I gave them something...it was like they wanted more to have happened, and I didn't know what they saw."

"Okay, Blair, they did not see a thing... they might have told you they did, but they didn't. Now, this is very important...I need you to call that detective back and ask to speak with her again. I need you to tell her that kiss did *not* happen." The inside of my stomach now just physically hurt. I could not go back to the police station with those people. It was hard enough to lie to them the first time... *Now I have to go back and tell another lie?*

I was quiet on the other end of the phone.

"Blair, I need you to do this. For me, for my kids, my family... If you don't do this, I don't think I can live any longer."

Agony took over my senses. It was painful to think about my options. Calling back the detective made me want to vomit because it made me so nervous, but the thought of not calling and losing Jack made me want to crawl into a hole and never come out. I had to call.

"Okay, Jack...but give me a few days, okay? I don't think I can go back there quite yet."

"Okay, Blair... you take your time...I love you, and I know you will always protect me...that is just the kind of person you are."

"Yea..." I said. He made me feel proud to further this little secret into an enormous deception from my parents and the police.

* * *

I don't know how to describe the following week, except for weird. The police had instructed my mom not to tell a soul about what had happened and that meant Marissa and her parents. So I could not talk to Marissa about it, and I was banned from spending any time at her house in case Jack were to come over. My mom was extra nice to me, which was confusing because I was feeling increasingly angry with the fact that she did not like the man I loved. She also did not know I loved him… *Would that make things different?* I wondered. But I was a terrific actor. I was good at smiling, keeping my grades up and making small talk. I finally picked up my phone…my real non-secret phone… the following Tuesday after school and dialed the number on the detective's business card. She had given it to me in case I "remembered" anything else.

"Yes of course, why don't you come in this afternoon, Blair. I would love to speak with you more," the scary red-haired lady said.

She is not going to like what I have to say, I thought.

"Okay, let me just check with my mom," I hadn't mentioned to her that I was calling. "HEY, MOM," I yelled upstairs. "Can you take me to the police station again? I have to talk to Detective Ryder again!" I tried to make this request as causal sounding as possible.

"You what? Yeah okay, honey… when?" She was coming down the stairs now.

"When would you like me to come in?" I directed her questions back at the phone.

"How about four o'clock?" It was three o'clock now.

"Okay."

"Alright, I will see you then. Thanks for calling, Blair."

My shoulders turned inward as my stomach got heavier. My body felt like it was caving in to the weight of this massive lie. I straightened myself. *I can do this*, I thought. *For Jack.*

* * *

The police station was still as cold and stuffy as it was the week before. I got chills the moment I entered. My mom and I sat on hard chairs in the waiting room, waiting for Detective Ryder to come out.

"Now, honey, I am proud of you for calling the detective back. I want you to know you are safe, and you can tell her anything. You know you can talk to me too, but I know I am your mom, and you may not want to tell me everything. That is okay, though," she said and looked me in the eyes. She had been holding up a brave face, but in this moment, I could see the worry in her eyes.

"I know, Mom," I said, looking down at my jeans.

I did it; I went in and talked to Detective Ryder. I told her I was wrong last week and nothing had ever happened. He had never kissed me, and I had made that up. She looked disappointed. Before I left, she asked if she could show me something, but she wanted my mom to see this too. I said okay.

Detective Ryder left the room and came back with my mom and my iPad and my plush dog. She lifted up the iPad and said, "Our tech guy did some investigating on this iPad and found some startling things. Now I am going to hit play, and you tell me what you hear," she said and hit the play button.

First a conversation of me on the phone with Jack started to play. Only my voice was audible, but I was laughing and giggling, and only I knew who I was talking to. Then, my mom's voice started to play. She was on the phone too and talking to her own mom on the phone.

I couldn't bear look at my mom. I was so confused. *What exactly is going on here?*

"Blair, these recordings were recorded by someone else remotely and then sent directly to an email address. She showed me the email address. That was clearly Jack's email. *How could this be...this must be some sort of mistake...Jack would never record me.* "That is not all, Blair. There are recordings of all your iPad activity, and they have been sent to this email address," she said, calmly looking at me directly. "And this dog here, its eyeball is a voice recorder. It has been collecting activity of you as well," she said and looked at me with sad, but stern eyes. "I know this may seem overwhelming… but Blair, if anything changes with your statement and the information you want to give me, I will be here waiting to listen to you. Do you mind if I talk to your mother alone?"

I got up and went to sit in the waiting room. My mom began the process of pressing charges against Jack for stalking that day. She told me that on the car ride home. This did not go as planned. I was scared to talk to Jack. I knew he'd have a perfect explanation for the recordings, and there was no reason to press charges. *Why would my mom do this?*

* * *

The discovery of Blair being stalked from the comfort of her home reminds us of the danger of online grooming. Today, more and more stories are surfacing of children taking to offenders online; it could be someone they know or a stranger. They may pretend to be the same age as the child. These perpetrators are using the same tactics, identifying vulnerable victims, manipulating them with

compliments and praise, sexualizing the relationship and guilting them into silence.

Young people may be forced to send explicit images of themselves, take part in sexual activities on a webcam or have sexual conversations online.

How do we use the Internet for all the good it offers?

- **Talk to children about their online world, just like you would about any other part of their world**

- **Use the same social media that your child does so you can understand it better**

- **Have conversations about online safety and talk about what is appropriate to share online and what is not[56]**

56 "Share Aware." www.nspcc.org. https://www.nspcc.org.uk/preventing-abuse/keeping-children-safe/share-aware/. (May 2019).

DECEMBER 2015.

SIX MONTHS AFTER FIRST SEXUAL ENCOUNTER

Over the next few weeks, winter set in. It was dark when I woke up, and it was dark again by five o'clock in the afternoon. Days were short, but they felt long. I waited all day to call Jack on my secret phone at night. I had been locking my door at 10 p.m. and crawling into my closet to hear Jack tell me he loved me, that we only had seven more years to wait. He promised me he'd wait.

I had asked him about the spyware that Detective Ryder had showed me. As I predicted, he had a perfectly reasonable explanation. He explained that it was parents' protection, and he had no idea what was still on it. He had been using it for Lizzy to make sure no weirdos were getting into her iPad, but he never disabled the feature. That made total sense; Jack was innocent. Of course, this information added fuel to the rage I felt against my mother for pressing charges. She told me I would understand one day. I did not think so. I was also distraught that I was no longer allowed to see Marissa unless it was at my house. And I couldn't even explain to her why I wasn't allowed over because the police told us to keep this information quiet.

Marissa had started having other girls over to her house. I understandably stopped getting invited. I can remember sitting at the lunch table and feeling like I was sitting alone. I never knew what the conversation was about anymore, and I didn't care. None of them knew about my sad story of forbidden love, and none of them would ever understand. How in the world could I sit and giggle with them about boys and videos on YouTube when I was trying to save someone's life? I began to live in my head. My life became a fantasy world that lived on my secret phone, was locked up in my closet, and occupied my head. It was the only world that mattered to me.

It was almost Christmas now. I arrived at school and hurried inside because it was so cold out. The foyer to the school was decorated with a Christmas tree and an oversized Menorah for Hanukkah. The halls were plastered with string lights, garland and bows. I had talked to Jack the night before, and he had told me he was at the school with Lizzy for the Reindeer Ball, a fundraiser for the school. *How sweet was he?*

When I reached my locker, I saw Marissa. I felt a little awkward. I could tell she felt awkward too. "Hi," I said.

"Hi," she answered, shut her locker door and walked away. My heart sank.

I took a deep breath. *It will all be worth it when I have Jack*, I reminded myself. I turned the code to open my locker. The red door creaked open, and I found a note hanging from the top shelf of my locker in Jack's handwriting and two wrapped gifts.

Oh my god. I had to hide these immediately. I stuffed the note and gifts in my bag and looked around to make sure no one saw. I shut my locker and headed into the bathroom.

I shut myself in a stall and dug through my messy schoolbag to retrieve the note.

Dear Blair,

I am so happy you are in my life. You are hands down the most beautiful human on this planet and I can't wait to make you my wife one day. We are going to have the most precious children together and make the best memories. I know that it is hard for us right now but the pain of not being with you ever is worse than the pain of waiting. I cannot wait until I can spoil you for the rest of your days. Until then, I got you some gifts and an extra sim card for your phone in case we ever get caught, you'll have another way to contact me. Please take these gifts and wear them. Know that it they are my promise to wait for you, for as long as it takes.

Merry Christmas.

XO

My mind drifted into my fantasy world for a moment, and my heart felt warm and fuzzy. I knew he loved me, like really loved me, and I loved him too. I reached into my bag and opened the first gift. Perfume. He got me perfume. WOW. This was fancy. He really was spoiling me. I checked to see if anyone else was in the bathroom and sprayed a little on myself. I breathed in and closed my eyes. It smelled so good. I smiled. I wanted to know what was in the smaller box. I peeled back the wrapping paper and discovered a little white jewelry box. I opened it up. Sitting on the Glenvale Middle School bathroom toilet, I stared at a simple diamond ring. It sparkled. I slipped it on my finger. It fit perfectly. I decided I would never take it off.

* * *

"Blair, you are going. End of story," my mom snapped. My mom never talked to me this way. My mom and I were pals; she was like a friend to me; we helped each other out. I never did anything wrong that warranted this kind of talk. I guess that had changed. I was a bad girl now. I had a secret. Now my punishment was to go and see a therapist. A THERAPIST? ME? A THERAPIST? I didn't need one. I had Jack to talk to.

"Mom, I don't need a therapist. Nothing happened! Oh my god, this is so ridiculous," I snapped back.

"So just talk to her about your day. I am sure she'll love to hear about it. Now get in the car." I knew this tone of voice and this face. My mom was serious. I was not getting out of this.

We sat silently in the car and in the waiting room. I decided that would be my tactic; I just wouldn't say a word. If I did that, I could not say anything wrong that might get Jack in trouble.

My mom took care of all kinds of paperwork in the waiting room. The place was filled with kids. Some had their mom or dad with them, but some didn't. There were small children, teenagers, people from all different races. I really did not feel like I belonged here. I did not have problems like all these other kids; I was the lucky one. I had a man who loved me.

Finally, after awkwardly waiting in the room for about fifteen minutes, the door to the front office opened, and a cheery woman with long brown hair said, "Blair!" I stood up. Immediately I liked her, but I could not let that show.

"Do you want me to come in with her?" my mom piped up quickly.

The woman let out a sigh and said, "Well normally, no, but since it's the first session, why don't you come on back?" My mom, the woman and I walked down a hallway full of closed doors and white noise machines until we reached the one open door and entered. We took seats around a small square table that was pushed up against the wall.

"Hello there, Blair. My name is Bella," the therapist said and looked at me, smiling. I really wanted to like her. She seemed to be the kind of person I would like. But I was careful; that is exactly what Jack said she would do. I had told Jack on the phone last night that my mom was making me go here, and he said the counselors were like the police's little detectives and that every session was recorded and sent to the police. He told me counselor's job was to trick kids into telling their secrets.

I said nothing and stared into my lap.

"This is Blair," my mom replied for me and introduced herself as well. "She does not want to be here today."

"That's okay, Blair. That is completely normal. It is hard to talk to a stranger, Blair. But we can start slow. Why don't I have your mom tell me why she thinks you need to be here, and then we can have some time to talk, just the two of us?"

I continued staring at my lap. I wanted to acknowledge the nice lady, but I couldn't give in. My mom sat and told Bella all that had happened with the police, very diplomatically as to not upset or blame me in any way. What my mom did not know was that I was still talking to Jack every day.

My mom left the room, and Bella got out a game. Chutes and Ladders. *My childhood favorite, of course.* I agreed to play with her, and we talked about the weather and TV shows. She finally asked me if I wanted to talk about what happened with the police and Jack. I told her it was all being exaggerated, nothing happened and that I wanted my family to drop the charges.

Bella and I would develop a good relationship. I would come in every week and mostly talk about how upset I was that Marissa and I were becoming more and more distant, how my uncle's death could sometimes be a stressor for my family. We kind of avoided the topic I was supposed to be talking about, but I secretly liked going. I had so many secrets. My trail of lies continued to get longer and longer. The more I told the lies, the deeper I got in it. The more confused my twelve-year-old brain became. No one truly knew the real Blair. My life seemed to be made of lies. I was a bad girl.

* * *

Blair is like many people; she is resistant to counseling. However, no matter the resistance at first, is it important for victims of assault to have a safe, nonbiased place to share their feelings. Benefits of therapy for victims of childhood sexual assault include the following:

- **Develop self-love practices to incorporate into your routine; this may help a survivor feel less overwhelmed and better about themselves again**
- **Helps survivor identify and validate feelings**
- **Support groups can build community so that the victims are not alone**
- **Gives survivors new and healthy ways to cope**

- **Opens the door to healing by processing emotions that have been silenced**[57]

* * *

It was the last match of the practice tennis season. I was so ready to be done for the season, but I also knew I would miss the exercise. It had become my outlet. My time on the court was my time to think. Being on the team with Marissa, however, was getting increasingly hard because we had to pretend to be best friends, but we really had drifted so far apart. I was still not allowed to talk to her about what was going on at home, but my mom had recently found out that Marissa's parents did know that we pressed charges against Jack for stalking. Apparently, Mrs. Martin asked why we hadn't reached out. Seems she had attended a dinner party over at the Campbells' where Jack had disclosed that we had pressed charges against him for stalking. He declared that I had a huge crush on him and that I was angry he did not act on it, so I made this all up.

I did not believe this. Jack would never tell people that; he loved me. My mom was lying to me. She just wanted something bad to have happened. My mom said she explained to Mrs. Martin that she was instructed not to tell anyone,

57 "Benefits of Sexual Abuse Counseling." www.betterhelp.com. https://www.betterhelp.com/advice/abuse/benefits-of-sexual-abuse-counseling/. (May 2019).

and that's why she hadn't mentioned it. Marissa's mom was shocked, but they continued to hang out with the Campbells, and I continued to be banned from their house. So I spent a lot of time in my closet, talking to Jack on the phone.

Today, though, was bittersweet. Saying goodbye to tennis for the season, I would miss being outside every day and running around the courts, but I couldn't help but be happy that I wouldn't be forced to pretend I was a normal kid every day after school anymore. And I knew I wouldn't be asked to join the real team in the spring. Now, I would only have to keep face during the school day, and I could come home and go back to my secret life.

I stood on the court. It was a particularly gross day for a match. I was surprised it was not canceled because the court was wet and slippery. Everyone had their warmest practice gear on, and some parents were huddled under umbrellas while others waited in their cars to shield themselves from the cold and wet weather.

I walked up to my opponent and participated in the coin toss. Marissa and I were serving first. Splashing through the court, we played. I was sad that Jack was not here to watch me. We finished the match, and I hurried inside to get home and shower the wet dirt and sweat off my body. When I made it to my room, I located my sim card, which was buried deep in my closet, and the actual phone, which was in a bag, in a jewelry box, inside my bedside table drawer. I had to separate the two now. In case my mom ever found one, she wouldn't be able to track my messages and calls without having the other half. I inserted the sim card into the phone and turned it on. A message from Jack.

Jack: You looked great at your match. You rock the wet hair look. Congrats on a great season.

He was there? I thought.

Blair: You were there????

Jack: Yes, I come to all of your matches. This time I just couldn't be seen. I wouldn't dream of missing one.

Blair: Wow, thanks!

I was so flattered he came. *I wonder where he was hiding... especially in the rain.*

This pattern would continue for the rest of my seventh grade school year. Every time I walked to the diner after school, Jack happened to be eating there too. I would get invited to a Valentine's Day party, and Jack would drive by. I would be sitting in my living room staring out the window, and I would see his car. When the weather was nice, I would go on a bike ride after school, and every day, the Jeep would follow me. I always knew he was watching.

* * *

I had sat down, but Marissa was still standing. She was looking around for someone. "What's up," I said to Marissa, opening the lid to my salad and dowsing it with dressing.

"Oh nothing," she grunted and sank into her seat. I could tell she was not satisfied with her company at lunch today. She opened up her lunch bag and pulled out her sandwich and chips. "I just don't know where all my friends are," she mumbled.

I was not surprised Marissa was feeling this way, but I was surprised she said it. The truth was, I was no fun to be around anymore, and we could not even hang out after school. Marissa was a good friend to me, but I wasn't being that great of a friend to her. I was all consumed in my relationship with Jack and could not talk to her about it. We both ate our lunches together in silence. After about ten minutes, Marissa spotted a table with some of her friends at it. "Oh, Blair, I'll be right back," she said, packing up her lunch bag and scurrying off to the other table.

I was now alone. I sat on the outskirts of the lunchroom at a table by myself. For some reason, I was more comfortable sitting alone with my secrets than I was sitting with others. A nice girl in my class with curly hair and glasses that I had never talked to before came up to me. "Hey, Blair, do you want to sit with us?" she asked politely. *Ugh, did I really look that pathetic?*

"No, I am good, but thanks anyway," I told her. I packed up my lunch and headed to the main office. The guidance counselor had reached out to me recently and told me I could come to her office any time to talk. Now seemed like a good time. Her office became my new lunch table. Every day, I would go get my chicken patty salad in the lunch line and make a bee line for Mrs. Clark's office. Adults just seemed to understand me better.

* * *

"Hello, Blair! What is my gorgeous girl up to?" Mrs. Clark would greet me every day. I would laugh and smile. I would talk to her about my annoyances with having to visit my dad on weekends and my mom making me go. I would tell her about Marissa and how we were drifting apart. I thought she knew what was going on with my mom pressing charges against Jack, but I wasn't sure. We didn't talk about it. She always welcomed me into her office, and sometimes I got the school gossip listening in on adult conversations. Lunch became my only reason to go to school.

PART 6

MAINTAINING CONTROL

MARCH 2016.

NINE MONTHS AFTER FIRST SEXUAL ENCOUNTER

"I miss you so much, Jack," I whispered into the phone. I was bold tonight. I was lying in my bed, getting ready to fall asleep. We talked every night on the phone, but I usually hid in my closet. This time of night was easily the highlight my entire day. I waited all day to call Jack and hear his comforting voice.

"You have no idea how much I miss you," Jack expressed. "I think about you every second of every day."

His words were always so intense. They always made me feel such overwhelming emotions. I was needed. If Jack did not have me, he would kill himself. Lizzy and Elena would lose their father. Danielle would lose her husband. And I would lose my best friend.

"I think about you—" My door knob twisted and my mother appeared as I stuffed my phone under my pillow.

"Who was that?" my mom asked, with apparent anxiety in her voice. I looked at her.

"What?"

"Don't you dare lie to me! I just saw you stuffing a phone underneath your pillow. Give it to me right now!" she demanded.

"No."

"Get up, Blair!" she shouted.

"No, I'm not," I half-yelled. I was scared; my heart was pounding; my palms were sweaty. I had failed. I had failed to protect the man I loved.

"GET UP!" she shouted louder.

I got out of bed and stood in my oversized t-shirt and striped PJ bottoms. She snatched the phone out from under my pillow and dialed Jack back. He answered.

"You scumbag!" my mom screeched into the phone. "Stay away from my daughter! You hear me, you asshole? DO YOU HEAR ME?" she continued to scream, spewing profuse language into the phone until he hung up.

"That's it!" she said and forcefully threw the phone to the ground and ran upstairs. "I am going over there. Right now! I am driving over there, and I am going to give him a piece of my mind!"

We were in the house alone, and I tried to calm my mother down. It was, however, of no use. She had her shoes on now and was headed out the door in total rage. Meanwhile, I had retrieved the sim card from the phone my mother threw on the ground and flushed it down the toilet. I left the phone there. That was irrelevant. I had another phone and another sim card to call Jack on. He had left them in my locker with my other Christmas gifts.

What I know now is that my mom stopped herself from reaching Jack's house. She called her sister on her way, who advised her to turn around and not get herself into any trouble. Before she could return, my aunt had called the police and told them my mother was on her way to Jack's. Her sister wanted to make sure no one got hurt.

On the way, the police began to follow my mom, who was speeding home. They turned their lights on for her to pull over. She was fed up with the police. She felt they were not doing enough, and she needed to be home now to protect her daughter. She did not stop when the police lights were on. She continued on her way home, which was a ninety-second drive. When she got out of the car in our driveway, she was slammed against the car, told to put her hands behind her back and cuffed for resisting the police.

Soon thereafter, the police burst into my room. I was now lying in bed, crying…hoping nothing bad had happened to Jack, having no idea that my mother had been arrested.

"You need to stop doing this," the male police officer stood over my bed and grunted at me. The guilt. The shame. I shut down, and I began to cry harder. I turned into my pillow. I did not want to be seen like this.

"This guy needs to get locked up. We can't do that without your help," he sternly said. But his words were lost on me. I don't remember what else he said, but I remember it felt like hours that he was in my room, standing over me. I was so scared of him. I wanted nothing to do with those mean police officers.

Upstairs, the chief of police sat in my living room with my mom, who was in hysterics. She told me she was so angry that night that no one could help her. The police agreed not to press charges against her that night. My mother sat there, crying and pleading with the chief, "What am I supposed to do? I cannot keep this man away from my daughter! Why is he still a free man?"

"My best advice to you, Mrs. Beam, is to put a 'For Sale' sign on this house and pack your bags. Outside of that, you can wait for trial."

AUGUST 2016.

FOURTEEN MONTHS AFTER FIRST SEXUAL ENCOUNTER

From then on out, I had to be more careful. I stopped talking to Jack for a while when I was in bed; I never forgot to lock my door; I always separated my sim card from the phone when I was done using it. My mom had taken away my real phone, and the police had my laptop, so I had no way to really contact friends anymore. That summer was long. My main focus was figuring out ways to keep my secret.

Luckily, my mom's love for me was unconditional. She told my dad what was going on, but he thought it was best that he stay out of all the drama. My aunt, uncle and cousin invited me on their family vacation down to Virginia Beach. My cousin was just three years older than me, and together we sang silly songs, made up our own songs, stayed up late in the hotel room and slept in late. We went to the beach and the pool and played mini golf. I felt like a kid with my cousin, but I still ended each night with a phone call to Jack, quietly when everyone was asleep while I was on the pull-out mattress. I hid the phone inside my pillow. I would unzipper my pillow case, and I had cut a hole just big enough for my phone to fit inside the pillow itself; that's where the phone stayed between our calls. I was more careful. It had been months since we had been caught. *I was getting pretty good at this.*

What I did not know at the time was that in August of 2016, my mom would begin to get phone calls from Danielle. Apparently, my mom, my grandma and I were out back-to-school shopping when Danielle called my mom for the first time. She had called from Reese's mother's phone so my mom might actually answer. Reese's mom explained to my mom that Danielle had something important to tell her. My mom said she would listen.

"They are still talking on the phone every night...Jack goes outside every night around eleven o'clock, and he has a different phone that he calls her on...I see it...I know it is happening," Danielle urged.

"That's impossible! Blair doesn't have a phone. We took it away from her. I can even check the phone records... she hasn't made a call in months."

"No, you're wrong. She has a different phone. They talk every night… I am sure of it," she insisted.

"Okay, okay, well listen, I am with Blair. I've got to go, but I will do my best," my mom said and hung up the phone without waiting for a goodbye. According to my mom, these phone calls from Danielle increased. She called every day to tell my mother, "You have to catch them." My mother was trying to listen outside my door, but never heard a thing. *That was because I had become so good at hiding and knowing when my mom was nearby… it had become a sort of a dreadful cat and mouse game.*

* * *

Even though Blair is physically surrounded by her mother and grandmother, she feels alone in her emotions. She is alone with Jack in the secret life she leads. Jack has tainted her image of her mother and anyone else who prevents her from being with him. Her secret disempowers her. It keeps her quiet. It allows the abuse to continue.

Just like coercive control often used in relationships with domestic violence, groomers are strategic and use ongoing techniques to limit a child's resources. Coercive control by definition violates the "rights and liberties including right to physical security; to live without fear; to dignity and respect; to social interaction and to autonomy, liberty and

personhood."[58] Over time, this this further deepens the complicated relationship between the victim and the groomers.

Now that Blair feels that the only person who has her best interests in mind is Jack, he has total control. Her world now revolves around keeping their relationship intact.

Blair is simply surviving.

* * *

It was late August. I was lying in my bed with the door locked, talking to Jack on the phone. I probably should not have been in my bed… that was my first mistake. It was about midnight now.

"Alright, Jack," I said, yawning. "I love you, but I need to go to sleep. I can't keep my eyes open any longer."

"Okay, my love, sleep tight," he gushed through the phone. It felt so good to have someone tell me goodnight.

"Goodnight, Jack," I said sleepily. With eyes almost closed, I got up while taking the phone apart so I could hide the pieces of it.

---

58 "Information for Professionals: Abusive Partners." www.opdv.ny.gov. https://www.opdv.ny.gov/professionals/abusers/coercivecontrol.html. (May 2019).

Something, though, caught my eye. It was a light, a green flashing light coming from underneath my dresser. *What in the world?*

I picked up the white plastic device with my hand and immediately wanted to smash it.

A baby monitor?

My mother was spying on me.

I quietly unplugged the monitor. Then I took the sim card in my hand that I was about to hide and put it in my mouth. I bit down hard on the piece of plastic and snapped it in half. I took the baby monitor and broken sim card to the bathroom. I spat the sim card out into the toilet and flushed. Well that shows her... any evidence is gone now! I plopped the baby monitor into the sink and turned the faucet on to drown out any chance of proof that Jack and I could be talking. When I was sure we were safe, I carried the dripping wet baby monitor upstairs and dramatically dropped it in front of my mom.

I don't think either one of us wanted to have this argument again.

"Where is the phone, Blair? Give it to me, and this is over...we can then both go to bed...we don't need to fight about this again."

"There is no phone," I looked her straight in the eyes and lied.

"Yes, there is, Blair. I heard you talking to him on the phone. This needs to end! I need my daughter back."

"Fine," I went down the stairs to my room. My mom trailed closely behind me. I handed her the phone without the sim card that had all the incriminating information, which had been flushed down the toilet.

"Thank you," she said stoically and marched upstairs. Within moments, she marched back down the stairs. "Where is the sim card, Blair?"

"Gone. I destroyed it," I told her with a smug look on my face.

"Get out of your room!" she screamed, as she came rushing into my room. One by one, she ripped out each drawer to my dresser and tore the contents apart. She searched under my bed, ripped my closet apart and turned my bed upside down looking for evidence. Finally, she turned around, looking shell-shocked.

"Fine! Get out! You are not allowed in your room until we get some evidence, and I can trust you again. We are sleeping on the couch! GO!"

It would be two months before I saw my room again. For the next sixty days, my mom and I shared the sectional in the living room. I stuck to my guns. There was no way I would break; I had to protect Jack.

* * *

Why are survivors like Blair so afraid to come forward?

- **All survivors, not just children, often feel the abuse is their fault and feel shameful about what happened; they are afraid of being blamed and judged**

- **People are afraid of a police investigation**

- **The abuser threatens to hurt themselves or others if the survivor comes forward**

- **The survivor is manipulated by the abuser and experiences positive feelings for their abuser**

- **Children often do not have the vocabulary to describe the abuse**

- **People do not want to disrupt the family or create stress, especially if the family is already under stress**

OCTOBER 2016.

SIXTEEN MONTHS AFTER FIRST SEXUAL ENCOUNTER

It had been months now since Jack and I had spoken. He still drove by my house regularly and made his presence known. He made sure I knew he still loved me, and he was still waiting for me. Every time I saw his Jeep drive past my house, I got butterflies in the pit of my stomach. To me, Jack driving by was like a big hug. My body warmed up knowing he was still there; he still loved me, and what I was doing was worth it. I was still sharing the sectional with my mom. I was still locked out of my bedroom, and I was still insistent that nothing was going on with Jack.

"I love you, Blair. I just cannot trust you right now. I need to protect my baby girl," she would say. It made me so angry to think that she thought she was protecting me. This man loved me; I just wished I could tell her the truth.

I had been telling more of the truth to my counselor Bella. Since my mom had caught us talking, I could not hide that from Bella any more, and I told her how much I loved Jack.

"We love each other, Bella. It's like Romeo and Juliet. We are forbidden from being together, and the world doesn't see how perfect we are together," my brainwashed mind insisted.

"So you love him. Okay. Well, it is also possible that Jack has told you this to try to keep you from telling anyone. Have you ever considered that?" Bella suggested.

"No, that's not Jack. And I… I know he loves me," I maintained. This sounded like the Oprah special my mom had made me watch recently. She plopped me in front of the TV to watch pedophiles talk to Oprah about how they "groomed" their victims. Oprah kept talking about being molested herself. I could not wrap my brain around that word. I could not have been "molested." What stuck with me from that talk was that Oprah had said, "If the molester is any good, he makes the child feel like they are a part of it…because it's a lure, it's a seduction… think it should be called child seduction and assault." These words conveyed a twinge of accuracy in my mind, but I blocked those thoughts and feelings out. At least until one day in late October.

I had known she was coming over. My mom told me that Reese's mother, Tina, had called and wanted to come over and talk to me. I said okay. I liked Tina, and Reese and I were still friends. Reese was one of my only friends at this point. Sometimes, Reese would pass along love notes to me from Jack. Reese still supported our relationship and that validated my feelings. At least one person understood.

The doorbell rang, and my mom instantly got up to let Tina in. I was sitting on the couch, which was also the bed my mom and I shared. I listened to their small talk in the distance. They then came up the stairs, and Tina suggested she and I go sit out on the deck. It was a warm fall day; the sun was shining. She wanted to talk to me alone.

I pulled myself up, walked through the kitchen and slid open the sliding glass door for Tina and me. I was nervous. *What is she here to talk to me about?* She started with the obvious. Small talk. We talked about how the sixth grade was going, cross country season, Reese's baseball, blah, blah, blah. I knew that wasn't why she came here.

Finally, she said, "Blair, there is something you need to hear. I know you love Jack, but I want you to know he is trying to get his wife back. Danielle wants to leave him, and he is on his hands and knees begging for her back. *That could not be true... Jack told me that Danielle was the one who wanted to stay married for the kids, that she knew about us and was okay with it...*

Tina reached into her purse and pulled out a small digital recorder that looked like a pen. There was a message Jack had left on Danielle's voicemail. Tina wanted me to hear it. She clicked the small on button on the recorder. "Danielle, please pick up," Jack was saying, sounding totally distraught and crying. "I love you, Danielle. I am so sorry. I don't know what I would do without you. You are the best thing that has ever happened to me...please don't leave me... I cannot go on without you." I listened to Jack beg and plead for his wife back. I sat still for a long moment. My silence was palpable. I did not react. Finally, I made eye contact with Tina. I began to bawl my eyes out. My heart was broken. I couldn't deny the truth any longer.

* * *

I stepped outside the doors of Glenvale Middle School, zipping up my brown Abercrombie puffer jacket. I saw Reese standing next to our bus. I was not allowed to ride the bus anymore because it passed Jack's house, and my mom was convinced he was sending me messages. And he was. But I would have never admitted that. I walked toward Reese. I was so still so upset by what his mom had showed me.

"How are you, Blair?" Reese said and looked at me genuinely.

"I'm okay. I think I'm just trying to move on. I don't know what to do, actually. I just cannot believe what your mom showed me."

"Blair, listen, he is a fucking asshole. This man needs to rot in prison. I was just as brainwashed as you. I never saw it either, but now I know everything he did was to trick us. Don't you see?"

Reese's words penetrated through my heart, my mind and my body. He was the last person on my side, and he had turned to the other side. I had no one left; I now knew I had been lied to. The ultimate betrayal had started to sink in.

"Yeah," I said, as I looked down and walked past Reese, heading toward my mom's car. I was quiet the whole ride home as usual. I could not stop thinking about what Reese had said. He had tricked us. That made me angry at Jack.

* * *

Sitting in the waiting room to go in to see Bella, my heart pounded. I knew what I had to do. Last week, she had told me that if there was anything about the abuse I wanted to disclose, all I had to say was that abuse happened. She would then right away call child protective services, and I would only have to tell them the details. I was immediately turned off by the idea and told her that was not something I was going to do. I just wanted to move on. I never wanted to see or hear of Jack again. I did not want anyone to know how much of myself I had given to him.

"Well," Bella said, "I must say I'm surprised that for such a persistent girl, you could really do something good here." She then dropped the subject.

Those words and Reese's words sat in the pit of my stomach that week. In this moment, sitting in the waiting room, I knew today was *the* day. The beginning of the end. I was going to tell Bella that I wanted to talk to child protective services. My hands were shaking. I knew in this moment it was right. I would not regret this, but I was still so scared my mind would be swept back into the hole it had been in for the past two years.

"Hello, Blair!" Bella said while waltzing through the door and motioning for me to come to the room. We walked back to the room, and Bella complimented my winter coat. I was not in the mood to talk about my coat or the weather or my Christmas plans. "So," I said as I sat down, taking the lead of the conversation. "I want to tell you about..." I said and stopped. I couldn't put my finger on the word to use. "But I am scared. I don't want to ruin his Christmas. It's only a week away..."

She knew exactly what I was talking about.

"Blair, I am proud of you for thinking more about this. I think you know what you have to do, know that there will be no perfect time to tell. There will always be a reason not to, but none of this is your fault. It may be hard, but you have to think about yourself at some point."

I let out a sigh. "Okay, I am telling you that..." I couldn't finish the sentence. I did not exactly know how to describe what I was telling her, and I definitely did not want to discuss details...my mouth simply could not form words...and my brain did not know what it was trying to say.

The word "abuse" hurt; it made my head and my heart hurt. I still was unsure if what happened was abuse. *I mean, I did love him...*

She took a breath in and nodded, giving me space to continue. When it was clear that I did not know where to go and what to say, she said, "Would it be easier if I asked you a question, and you just have to respond yes or no?"

I nodded.

"Okay, Blair, did Jack touch you inappropriately?"

I nodded once again. She looked at me. "Can you say yes or no?"

I was scared. The word hurt as it was coming out of my mouth. "Yes," I said and dropped my chin to my chest. I began to cry.

"It's okay. You've said a lot today. You don't need to say any more," Bella consoled me.

That day's session was short. She told me I would be asked for a statement in the coming days and told me how brave I was. I was in a daze. I just kept crying and breathing; it was all I could do.

* * *

SOMEONE DISCLOSES SEXUAL ABUSE TO YOU...NOW WHAT?

In a perfect world, every person would be trained on trauma-informed practices that ensure physical and emotional safety to the survivor. Some key take-aways we can all learn to best support survivors are:

- **Listen fully! That means try not to interrupt them, and sit with them in what may seem like uncomfortable silence. Take those silent moments to process what you are being told. The survivor is doing the same. Oftentimes, just being present and listening is comfort enough.**

- Thank them for sharing their story with you and remind them how brave they are. Let them know they are not alone.

- Resist feelings of anger and disbelief. In my life, many people I have shared my story with immediately resort to expressing anger toward my abuser. That has never made me feel better, but only angrier and less capable of protecting myself. Also, when I was still in love with my abuser, this made me shut down. Instead, show love and empathy for the survivor by letting them know you are listening and validating whatever they feel.

- Offer support! Make sure the survivor knows you believe them. Offer to provide resources for additional support.

- Let the child know you must report any suspected incidents of child sexual abuse. If it is not a child, let the person know your reporting obligations, if you have any. Always offer for the survivor to be a part of the reporting process. Give power back to the survivor, and let them make decisions surrounding police investigations.

- *Reminder: It is very rare for a report of child sexual abuse to be false.*

CONCLUSION

Christine Ford's testimony was published in *The Washington Post* in October 2018 when she made history and testified against a supreme court nominee. In the midst of my writing this book, she stood up to tell the country that this man sexually assaulted her as a girl. This testimony was different than that of most sexual assault survivors because she was not fighting for her own justice or trying to put her assailant behind bars; rather, she was hoping to simply prevent her assailant from holding a seat on the highest court in the United States and affect decades of rulings. In reality, Christine Ford's testimony meant much more for the unfortunate community of sexual assault survivors watching. Her treatment and the decision regarding her assailant would advise innumerous survivors around the globe on whether or not their assault mattered. It would signal survivors on whether or not they should come forward. Would speaking their truth be worth it? Would anyone believe them?

Children, young people and people of all sexual orientations have been told that their voices do not matter. High school girls who may be considering coming forward about their own sexual assault in hopes of getting justice, regaining control over their bodies and protecting others have been told their experiences are not important. The criminal justice system will ask them to retell their story again and again in police statements and testimony in order to seek rectitude. But people still do not believe survivors. Rape culture and our system of justice very often blames survivors for what is done to them.

Ford's testimony may not have been able to prevent her assailant from being nominated to the Supreme Court of the United States, and it may have sent a message that status and wealth override sexual assault; nevertheless, it did illuminate the injustices being done to survivors every day across the nation. The reality is that only 14 percent of sexual assault victims report to police. Only 12.5 percent of offenders are convicted of any offense, and only 6.5 percent of offenders are convicted of the original offense.

Ford's testimony shed a light on a dark space. Survivors let Ford's testimony and the stories of others be an invitation to speak up. There is a community of survivors and supporters out there listening, ready to hep you help others and yourself. The power and passion of survivors is enduring. This does not mean you need to be ready to make a police report, write a book or testify publicly. This simply means you deserve to be validated. What was done to you was *not okay.* You have the right to make choices about your body, and you are worthy of love and respect. You can turn to family, a friend, a counselor, and anyone you trust when you are ready to break free from the shame silencing you. Talking about what happened, when you are ready, will release you from the blame you place on yourself and remind you how courageous you are. Together, survivors and supporters alike have the power to change our communities, big and small, and to start to align themselves with genuine love and compassion. We together can change the culture around sexual violence.

DECEMBER 4, 2016.

EIGHTEEN MONTHS AFTER FIRST SEXUAL ENCOUNTER

I was sitting in seventh grade English class. I sat in the front row, by choice of course. I wanted my teacher, Ms. Gwen, to know that I was a good student. I always sat upright, or tried to. I would catch myself slouching often and remind myself the proper way to sit in a chair. I always had my eyes on the teacher. I asked questions often and usually did well in my classes. Grammar had always been tough for me and so was math. I just seemed to mix up the numbers and tiny details sometimes.

Ms. Gwen got a call. In the back of my head I wondered if it would be for me. If it was my time to make a statement.

Silly...I thought it the back of my head...not everything is about you, Blair...

"Blair," Ms. Gwen looked at me kindly. "Can you go down to Mrs. Clark's office?" Mrs. Clark was the guidance counselor I had been eating lunch with. "She asked if you could bring all your belongings with you too."

I knew what was about to happen. My stomach fell through the seat of my chair. I took a breath in and started to sweat a little bit. I hoped no one noticed. I collected my books on my desk into a pile. My hands were shaking. I hope no one noticed that either...I felt like everyone was watching me. I squatted down next to my desk to retrieve the books in the basket under my chair, stacked everything neatly together, and quickly exited the room. My heart was beating so fast.

I walked to my locker to get the rest of my belongings. I felt like every second that went by was a second wasted. I wanted to get this over with. I wanted it all to be over. I finally was on my way down to the main office where the guidance counselor's office was. I was wearing denim boot cut jeans, sneakers and a gray and purple striped shirt. I wished I had worn something nicer, but I did not know this was going to be such a big day.

When I finally arrived at the office, it was all I could do to smile at the secretaries and pretend I was totally fine. When I turned the corner to Mrs. Clark's office, I could see the police uniforms. Two police officers I had never seen were standing in her office. As I approached the door, I tried to smile, hiding my nerves, but tears began rolling down my face.

"Hey, Blair!" Mrs. Clark looked at me with a smirk on her face. She was clearly trying to make light of the heavy moment. "That's my girl!" she continued.

I looked around the room at the two male police officers standing in the corner of her small office; the room did not seem big enough for us all.

I smiled to acknowledge Mrs. Clark and the officers. Words were not coming to me.

"Now it's my understanding that you told your counselor you wanted to disclose some things to the police… the two of us are here to help you with that…"

I nodded my head.

"We think you are so brave, Blair," police officer number 1 said and looked at me. The words went in one ear and out the other… *let's get to the point,* I thought. "Now we are going to meet your mom at the station, and we are going to take you to our sex crimes unit location where you will be able to give your statement. How does that sound?"

I nodded my head again. The next couple of hours were a blur to me.

I remember walking out of my middle school, hoping no one could see me stroll into a cop car and ride off with the officers. I hoped no one wondered what I had done.

I remember waiting, and waiting and waiting. My mom and I waited at the police station, and we were finally driven to the sex crimes unit. Apparently, it was a secret location, and we did not get there until it was dark out. Darkness comes early in December. I am not sure what was taking them so long. I also was not sure why they were driving us there. Why couldn't my mom and I just meet the police officers there?

I remember it taking about twenty minutes to drive to the sex crimes office in a marked police SUV, and my stomach was already growling. It had been hours since I had lunch at school, and now my mom and I were without means to get any food. And to make matters worse, our car was back at the police station in Glenvale. I didn't really want food though; I wanted to get this over with.

I remember they turned the TV on for us in the family waiting room. After a while, we watched the news. It did not offer much comic relief. My mom tried to talk to me, but I did not have much to say.

After hours of waiting, a bald man, who introduced himself as Detective Walsh, told me they were ready for me and asked me to come into the office. He asked if I wanted my mom to come with me. I said no. I looked at her. She closed her eyes and nodded. She understood.

I walked into the office. A woman sat at a desk behind a computer. I sat at a table across from her. Detective Walsh smiled at me, "Do you want any soda or anything, kiddo?"

"No thank you, I am good," I said looking down.

"Okay, what about you?" he said, looking at the woman detective behind the desk. I forget her name. I would never see her again.

"No, Walsh," she answered.

"Okay, be right back."

He finally came back and placed a warm Diet Coke in front of me. My stomach growled. I didn't touch the Coke.

"Okay, let's get started," the detective said as he sat down and cracked open his soda. "Now, Blair, this nice detective over here is going to ask you questions and take down word for word on the computer everything you say. I am going to sit in on this, but if at any time you want me to leave, you just say so, okay? I know I am a man, and this may be awkward for you."

"Okay," I responded.

The two of them went on about how proud they were of me and how brave I was being. I really just wanted to get on with it. I had never ever told anyone the full truth before. I didn't know how it was going to sound coming out of my mouth.

She began asking me questions. It took forever for her to type out every word I said and then have me read it over to make sure it was all accurate. I began to tell her about how I met Jack and how our relationship progressed. Finally, the question I had been dreading.

"When did the relationship between you and Jack Campbell become sexual?" the woman detective asked.

I took a deep breath in through my nose and looked blindly at them both.

"Um, Detective Walsh, I am sorry, but could you step out now? I just am feeling a little uncomfortable. I am so sorry..."

"Say nothing more," the detective said and stood up. "Let me know when it is okay to reenter," he nodded and ducked out of the room. I hoped he was going to comfort my mom. *She must be going crazy in that waiting room by herself...*

I answered the detective's questions. I gave her every graphic detail of the sexual relationship between Jack and me. I told her about every time he touched me. In those moments, I had to just think of it as responding to her questions. I had to remove myself from the equation. I had to think I was talking about some other girl who had this relationship. Sometimes it felt that way. That I was separate from the girl who fell in love and was swept up in this charming man's game. I was no longer that girl. I was no longer under his spell.

Sometimes I still felt it calling me. When he continued to drive by. When I would worry about him going to jail. I just had to remember that I was no longer *that* girl any more.

It felt like days had gone by since the police officers picked me up from school that day. By the end of the woman's questions...I really just wanted to go home. When it was finally over, she had to print out the twenty-four-page document and have me read and initial every single page before they would drive us back to town. My eyes were puffy from crying, my emotions were drained, my body was tired, and I needed some food and some rest. I remember wondering if these detectives would ever stop talking...

Finally my mom and I made it back to our car late that night. We were finally alone. We walked back to the car together. I knew she wanted to hug me, but she knew I was not ready for that. Silently, we drove home. I knew she was proud of me.

That night, I would sleep in my own bed for the first time in months.

* * *

How can law enforcement better interact with survivors to avoid re-victimizing them?

- **Become trained on trauma-informed care**
    - **Know that every person will react differently to abuse and those reactions are valid**
    - **Some people may be upset, others may laugh when they recount their assault, still others may display no emotion at all**
    - **Know people often blame themselves for abuse**

- Learn how trauma affects the brain, a person's memory, reaction and behavior

- Understand the disclosure of sexual assault often occurs over time
  - Work to gain trust and communication with survivors by refraining from judgement
  - Acknowledge how hard it is for the victim to come forward, be empathetic
  - Pose simple questions
  - Avoid asking "what were you wearing?" "how much did you drink?"
  - Avoid "why" questions that could invoke victim blaming
  - Do not interrupt victim when they are speaking
- Express concern for the safety of the survivor and address that first and foremost
  - Let them know they are in a safe place

- **Empower the survivor with the choice to decide how to proceed**
  - **Inform them of what the next steps are, what their role is and what the role of the police officer is**

* * *

It was the Tuesday before Christmas when the police arrived at Jack's house, where his wife and children lived, and put him in handcuffs. I do not know what that scene looked like. I do remember my mom getting a phone call that day.

"Hello," she answered in her normal tone.

"Hi," she said after a brief pause and stood frozen in the middle of the kitchen. We had been on better terms since we were both back to sleeping in our own beds, and my mom felt like she could trust me again. I was amazed by her capacity to forgive me. Her love for me was unconditional. I could tell this was an important phone call. She nodded her head a few times and thanked the person on the other end of the phone profusely. Finally, she hung up.

"They got him," she announced. "Jack is in jail," she said, almost too calmly. I could tell my mom wanted to celebrate this moment but was afraid to show too much enthusiasm. She was still unsure how I would respond. I was unpredictable.

My body started to feel numb from head to toe. I felt an emptiness inside my chest. My heart was beating fast and big, and wet tears started to stream out of the corners of my eyes. It felt like something was tugging my stomach down. I felt terrible for ruining Jack's Christmas with his children, for betraying him and ruining what I thought we had. A part of me still adored this man. The man who was my first kiss, my first love, my first harsh taste at the evils of the world. Part of me missed the thrill of us. As I sat at my kitchen table, I felt alone.

Still, my chest felt a new and certain lightness to it. It was almost like armor had been broken off of me. I was no longer weighed down, but now I was empty. I had no friends, and I had some apologizes to make to my family.

Somewhere in the depths of my heart, I ached of happiness. This tiny inkling was enough to light me up and inspire me to continue to cooperate with police. This tiny sliver of bliss made me want to see Jack take responsibility for what he did to my mind, my body and my heart.

On this day, I had a false sense that this chapter of my life was ending. When I saw Jack's mug shot in the paper the next day, I was proud of myself, and I anticipated the end being near. I dreamed of reclaiming my friendship with Marissa and getting to be a normal teenager.

What I did not know was that this was just the very beginning. Little did I know the trial would not happen for another two years. Those two years would be filled with continued stalking by the man who had already taken so much from me.

* * *

"The defense argues the girl made up the charges" — read the headline of the news article the day after the arrest. I wanted to feel angry reading this statement, but I felt numb instead. I was tired of feeling. My heart was broken, and I had exhausted my capacity to talk about this situation any longer. Everyone in my family, my counselor Bella and my guidance counselor said they were proud; I had done the right thing. They called me brave. *Why would this lawyer say such a thing?* What made it all the more confusing was that this lawyer had his own children. *How could a parent defend a man like that?* My mind started to buzz until I shut it off. *I can't do this*, I told myself and let out a sigh.

* * *

Blair did it. She spoke out, BUT the shame continues.

I struggled getting to this part in the book where I would have to explain why it is important to speak out even when the culture we live in feeds on shaming others. So, I enlisted Brené Brown, a social worker, shame researcher and author for help. In her book *I Thought It Was Just Me (But It Isn't),* she writes about how survivors of trauma have to survive the traumatic event itself, and then they have to survive the stereotypes and shame that come along with it. These are two incredibly hard battles to endure, and it takes time to be ready to reach out to share your shame.[59]

People who have been sexually assaulted are usually dealing with two stereotypes: imperfection—the idea that they are damaged, and blame—the idea that they are at fault for what was done to them. The truth is, our culture will reinforce these stereotypes. These stereotypes will therefore continue to silence people. You may survive your trauma and have to continue to battle with shame and stereotypes. You may reach out to a person who will not know how to support you. But, like Brené Brown says, "It is hard to hate close up. Move in."[60] I am here to encourage survivors to

---

59 Brown, Brené. *I Thought It Was Just Me (But It Isn't) Telling the Truth about Perfectionism, Inadequacy, and Power.* Gotham Books, 2008.

60 Brown, Brené. *Braving the Wilderness: The Quest for True Belonging and the Courage to Stand Alone.* Random House, 2017.

find someone who can sit with you and your experience. Brené Brown says shame is fueled by isolation; reaching out is the way to demolish shame.

What happens when someone continues to shame you?

It will happen; people will say the wrong thing. I encourage you to ask for what you need. Let people know that you are not broken, you do not need fixing, you only need connection and someone to listen. You are still the same person you were before you shared this experience with them. Be the light for someone you know. Reinforce your family, friends, students, co-workers and communities. Work to create change by being empathic and simply being there.

* * *

Walking through the door, I felt the stark contrast between the frigid outside air and the warmth of my aunt's home. The smell of turkey and too many side dishes filled the air. *Christmas!* I thought and let out a sigh. I smiled. "Hello!" I said with cheer. I truly was excited to be at Christmas this year. To be here and fully present. To talk to people without fear of letting anyone know about my secret life. I knew everyone knew what I had just disclosed to the police, but they all knew better than to bring it up.

We ate, we laughed and enjoyed each other's company. I tried not to think about how Jack's Christmas would be compromised. After helping to clean up dinner and getting a slice of my homemade pecan pie, we made our way home, which was only five minutes away. Once left alone, my mind raced with thoughts of Jack. I Google-searched his name and read the article that had been released on him. I was so curious what other people thought. *Did everyone believe his lawyer that I made all this up?*

The comments brought me to tears.

"Apparently the girl has mental health problems."

"I know Jack and he would never do something like this."

"It is a shame she is ruining his life."

I sat in my room for a few minutes alone. Finally, I got up and found my mom, telling her what I had read. She had seen the comments too. "Come here," she said and pulled me in for a hug. "We saw the comments today and did not want to tell you. Your aunts are furious! Do you want to go back and talk to them?"

"Yeah," I nodded, tears streaming down my face. Finally, I could share this part of my life with the people I cared about the most. My two lives could finally come together.

My mom and I hopped back in the car on Christmas night. We drove back to my aunt's house; the rest of the family had left, but we women sat together. We were angry together. We pulled out the leftovers and talked and cried until there was nothing left to say.

* * *

Build support networks with your family and community.

Blair is lucky; she did not have to search far for a supportive network. She has embraced her fears. She has embraced what makes her vulnerable. Now she can finally start to heal.

It does not have to be your family that is your network. It may be a friend or a support group in the community. Or a therapist, for example. However, it is important to understand our fears and as Brené Brown says, "Build the kind of relationships we need to live full and connected lives."[61] This is where we can grow from our experiences.

* * *

I was slouched into my comfy couch that had been my bed for so many months with my mom, like I used to when I spent

61 Brown, Brené. *I Thought It Was Just Me (But It Isn't) Telling the Truth about Perfectionism, Inadequacy, and Power.* Gotham Books, 2008.

time with my family before this whole mess happened. I used to love sitting here and staring out the window, watching the world go by on the busy road in front of my home. I felt like a watchman sitting there, looking out the window into the bustling world, thinking about what other people have to celebrate or hurry off to. I wondered about Jack's children. *How were they? His family—did they believe he did this to me? His wife—did she really know what was going on? Would she defend him?*

Then it happened. It was less than a week since Jack was arrested. When it happened, I knew my nightmare was not over. I realized in that moment that my horrors were not over. Jack's Jeep drove past my home, honking his horn as loudly as he could as he drove past. As I watched it happen, it took a few long seconds for my mind and body to process what I had witnessed. I did not even know he was out of jail... *How could this happen? Why was he allowed to be near my house? Why did he want anything to do with me? Why didn't the police warn us that he had posted bail and been released?*

I was angry. I was hurt. I was confused. My heart hurt and confused my head and my thoughts. *When would this ever end? What did he want from me?*

* * *

I had a nasty habit of checking Jack's social media pages. He had been posting all sorts of suspicious things that I knew related to me. "Watching *Titanic*" was his status. Well, I knew *Titanic* reminded him of me and was him telling me to hang on to what we had... but I knew I would sound crazy if I told anyone he was trying to communicate with me.

The week after Christmas, I noticed a new friend request. I saw I had a bunch of mutual friends, so I accepted, without question. The profile photo looked like a blonde girl my age. I figured I must know her from school or dance class, but I did not recognize her. Within minutes, the account started posting weird status just like the ones Jack had been posting. The account started posting songs we had listened to together. "Dirty Little Secret" popped up. A Romeo and Juliet article popped up. Then a message to my inbox... "Hi."

There was a moment of weakness. A moment when I felt excited and flattered. He still wanted me even after I told the police. *It must be real love...* Fortunately, I was able to pull myself out of it before I could respond. I forced myself to block this person immediately. I told my mom, and together we filed a report with the police. They said they would "keep an eye on it." I still wasn't safe. Paranoia swept over me. I looked around my room that night... *Was he watching me?*

* * *

My time in the seventh grade passed slowly. I would eventually start to form friendships, but I was never sure if it was because their parents told them to be my friend because they felt bad for me or if it was because they truly liked me. Most things I did had me ponder that same thought. Did I get an A on my paper because I deserved it or because Mrs. Clark had talked to my teachers and told them what was going on in my life? That I had been molested years ago, and now the man stalked me while we awaited trial.

Two of the friends I had made, Maya and Layla, wanted to go to the high school play this weekend. They were showing *The Little Mermaid.* I LOVED that show, and I was excited to be in the high school, knowing that I would be a freshman soon. My mom offered to take us; she loved that show too. My mom, my grandma, my two girlfriends and I carpooled over to the show. We bought candy at the concessions, looked around the huge cafeteria that would soon be ours and took our seats in the back on the theater. *This is where the big kids go to school...* I remember thinking. I couldn't believe I would get to go to this school in just two short years. *WOW!*

"Blair, look at this kid!" Layla said while flipping through the show's program as we took our seats. She pointed at a boy's picture. "Isn't he cute?" she giggled. I looked at the photo. "Yeah!" I giggled. Sometimes I had a hard time relating to the people my age. I could not always get on their level with humor and laugh at the same things they did. I found it much more comforting hanging out with my mom, teachers, Mrs. Clark and other adults. I just thought they understood life better and they understood me. I tried hard to play along and join in on the small talk.

Minutes later, the lights would dim, the curtain would part and the first act of the show would begin. I loved listening to the music and watching the actors. I was also glad I had friends to sit with. I smiled. I felt good.

Intermission came, and I got up to use the bathroom. I was walking by myself across the cafeteria when I heard her say it.

"Tramp." I heard the word faintly... I wasn't sure where it was coming from. I minded my own business and kept walking toward the ladies room where the line had already begun. When I finally came out, I was rushing back into the auditorium to get back to the show. I saw one of the mothers of a girl in my class. She had been an outspoken PTA mom, so I quickly recognized her although I don't think I had spoken with her since kindergarten when I went to her daughter's birthday party.

"Tramp," the girl's mother whispered under her breath and looked at me as I walked by. We were both alone outside the auditorium itself. My body tensed immediately… *she knew how bad I was…*

The rest of the show was a daze. I could not stop thinking about what that mom had said to me, and when I got back to my seat, I realized she was actually sitting directly in front of me. I watched her discreetly lift her phone up and take a photo of me before the lights dimmed again. My eyes filled with tears. I was so thankful the room was dark.

* * *

I remember it was a chilly day because when the police came, I remember being cold, standing and talking to them about what happened. Other than that, though, the day had been ordinary. I went to school. Another day in the seventh grade at Glenvale Middle School. I exited the school at 2:30 p.m. after classes ended and walked past the buses out to the parking lot to look for my mom. My mom had to drive me to school every morning and pick me up every afternoon because my bus route passed Jack's house, and he had a habit of standing outside making googly eyes at me when I rode the bus.

I felt the brisk air on my hands and neck where my North Face jacket did not cover. I waved to Reese, who was getting on my bus—the bus I should be on, but could not be on—as

I headed toward my mom's car. I saw her, waiting patiently as she did every single day. Then Susie Guardsman's mother, the same mom from the play, stood up on the ledge of her truck and shouted, "Home wrecker!" across the middle school parking lot. I looked up at her. I had no idea how to respond. "Home wrecker!" she looked at me and screamed again. I looked around embarrassed. My body flooded with guilt. From my toes, all to the up to my eyeballs, feelings of shame took over. I quickly ducked into my mom's car. She was looking down at her phone. Tears started to stream down my face.

"What is wrong, Blair?" my mom said and looked over, suddenly very concerned. I looked at her, crying.

"That mom just called me a home wrecker," I said through tears, pointing to the woman.

"WHAT? WHO?" my mom said loudly, obviously very furious. I had told her about the incident at the high school play, and she was so upset I hadn't told her when it happened. I begged her not to say anything...the last thing I wanted was more attention.

"Call 9-1-1, call 9-1-1! This is harassment!" my mom yelled, her teeth clutched. She was angry. "Do you want me to?" she asked.

I pulled out my phone. It was a little easier to call 9-1-1 this time, now that I knew how it worked. I told the operator who I was and what had happened. They were on their way.

Hot, salty tears dripped down my checks as I watched the parking lot clear out. Susie's mom pulled away, the buses started their routes and my mom and I waited for the police to show up.

An hour and a half later, after documenting the incident and filing harassment charges, we would finally get to go home. I remember feeling so exhausted. Apparently, Jack's wife was leaving him because of my allegations against him…I guess I *was* a home wrecker…

MAY 2, 2017.

TWENTY THREE MONTHS AFTER FIRST SEXUAL ENCOUNTER

"Wait for me!" Jack called out the window. I was startled. Even though I was always on high alert, I had my headphones in and could barely hear the words. But I watched Jack shout the words out his window while I rode my bike on my daily ride, this regular Thursday after school.

I backpedaled, immediately hitting the brakes. There was a heart drawn in chalk underneath my feet. *What are the chances that is a coincidence?* Random chalk hearts had been showing up all along my usual route lately, but who would believe me that he had put them there? I shook my head and let out a sigh. My emotions had started to shift from the sadness of a broken heart to anger of betrayal and deceit. I dialed 9-1-1.

"9-1-1, what is your emergency?" the operator said.

"Hi, my name is Blair Beam. I have a restraining order against Jack Campbell, and he just shouted out the window of his car to me while I was on a bike ride," I said confidently. I had too much practice with this. I knew the operator would know who I was.

"Yeah, he said, 'Wait for me' out the window," I explained.

"Okay, Blair, we'll be right out," the operator assured me.

I asked the operator if I could hang up to call my mom since they usually liked to stay on the line until someone arrived. She let me call my mom, and soon my mother arrived at the scene. Here we would spend the next couple of hours trying to explain what happened, and I would sign a bunch of papers signing off on my statement. It seemed so routine at this point. I was shocked when the officer said they were going to arrest him for violating the restraining order. I was happy...but confused...*he had followed me so many times before, and I had reported it...* I was skeptical, but it felt good to have a win... I embraced it.

I would walk into school the next morning with my head held high. Smiling, I would walk into my guidance counselor's office and recount the day before. For once, I did not feel like I was being watched. I knew exactly where Jack was… he was sitting in a jail cell, and I did not have to worry about him following me or my friends if I wanted to go out with other people. *I actually can go out with other people if I want…* I felt free and alive for the first time in years. It was a good day.

That afternoon, I went on my usual bike ride. I felt so euphoric. Biking truly was my outlet—my way to escape my head and channel my feelings into my body; to release my sadness, anger, joy, fear, disappointment through sweat. I finally had my outlet back, back to myself. I was two blocks away from my house when I saw a newspaper lying on a neighbor's sidewalk. Glaring at me was a huge photo of Jack's face. "Jail Bait" the headline read. *This will never escape me*, I thought. But I kept on biking. At least it was only a photo…

* * *

Turns out, I would only have one weekend of peace. By the following Tuesday, Jack would be out on bail and driving past my house and my bike rides once again.

My mom would start tailing behind in the car while I rode to make sure I was safe.

* * *

Sometimes, I wondered if Jack had our family car bugged with a tracking device. *But that wouldn't explain how he always drove by when I went on jogs around the neighborhood… maybe there was some kind of device in my house, or outside my house, that indicated to him when I left, and he followed us places… maybe he had spies watching us…*

I concocted these stories in my head endlessly. Just as soon as I would start to think I was insane, Jack would prove more desperate to get my attention. It got to the point that every time I went on a bike ride around the neighborhood, I saw his car drive by me at least twice. Usually, but not always, this was accompanied by him honking at me or staring intensely at me when I looked up and saw his car waiting at the next corner or approaching as he passed in the opposite lane of traffic. I had been listening to the police and reporting every time I saw him. My family had fought hard to get a restraining order, which was difficult because Jack had not been convicted of anything. We were simply waiting to go to trial, and the had charges we had were only pending. We were told time and time again that all these incidents were coincidences. The police informed us that his lawyer had a record of getting criminals off on police technicalities, so they had to be careful in responding to my reports that Jack was stalking me. I got the sense that the police were quite scared of Jack's lawyer.

Tonight, I was in the car with my mom. I hadn't been over my father's home in a while. Whenever I did visit, we pretended everything was fine and kept the conversation surface level. It was easier that way. Silently, my mom drove to my gymnastics studio. We had a roller coaster of a relationship lately. I was unpredictable. I would go to school and act pleasant, but I resisted any form of love or support at home. We pulled up to my gymnastics studio door, and I got out of the car. Part of me really didn't want to go to class tonight, but I did want to get out of the house, so here I was. I still didn't really feel like I had many friends...

The studio was set in a standalone building, and the main entrance was on the side. One could see the studio from the street, and there was a parking lot directly behind it. My mom had pulled up out front to drop me off. I stared down at my phone that I had finally gotten back and walked up to the door. Before I could enter the studio, a girl, a young woman maybe in her late teens or early twenties, approached me.

"Blair," she whispered loudly. She was wearing a black zip-up sweatshirt and black yoga pants. Her dark hair was pulled back, and she was wearing glasses.

I looked up. She was standing in front of me and was next to the door to the gymnastics studio. *Did I know her?*

"Hi?" I said and looked at her confused. The January air was cold; I just wanted to get inside.

"Get in the car. Jack is in there. He wants to talk to you," she spat out quickly. I could see a sliver sedan that I did not recognize parked behind the gym.

"Blair...Blair... it's me..." I heard Jack's voice, loud and clear, coming from the car. It was dark. No one was around, and my mom had just pulled away.

"What?" I managed... My heart was racing. For a spilt second, I wanted to run up to the car and reunite with my love... take off with him and never have to deal with the outside world again...just me and him...we wouldn't need to worry about anything.

"Come, get in the car, just for a minute..." she was trying to sound casual, but she sounded desperate. *Who was this girl? She was definitely older than me...*

"Ahh," I sighed. My heart was torn... "I gotta go." I opened the door to the gymnastics studio and hurried in. I was alone in the waiting room. I sat there, scared. *What do I do?* I didn't want to scare my mom…I mean everything was okay…but I did not want to call the police…I had told the police about so many times Jack had followed me, and they hadn't done anything more than "write a report." I didn't want to miss a gymnastics class because I was busy writing a police report, and I didn't want to draw a scene to the studio…

I dialed my guidance counselor from school. She had given me her cell phone number in case I ever needed to talk, and I had been seeing her almost every day. I still spent my lunches in her office. She was one of my only friends.

I listened to it ring a few times, and I debated hanging up. Finally, she answered.

"Blair!" she answered cheerfully.

"Mrs. Clark…" I started. I wanted to just spit it out or I would never say it. "I just got to gymnastics class and on my way in someone told me to get in a car…that Jack was waiting for me…"

"Blair… where are you?" her voice was serious.

"I am in the gymnastics studio…I just went in and didn't listen," I told her.

"Blair, I need you to call 9-1-1 right now. This is something the police need to know about. There is a restraining order between you and Jack, and this is stalking and luring. Please call the police right away."

"But the police are scary, and I don't want to deal with them," I whined.

"Blair, please."

"Okay." I let a deep breath out.

"Are you going to do it right now?"

"Yes," I promised.

"Okay, call and then call your mother. Let me know how it goes. I am here for you."

I hung up with Mrs. Clark. Boy… I wished I had someone sitting next to me to support me through this. It was almost painful to dial the numbers 9-1-1. I listened to the phone ring, and I could hear my heart beating.

"9-1-1, what is your emergency?" a woman answered.

"Hi…um, my name is Blair, and this guy Jack who molested me just had someone try to get me in a car outside my gymnastics studio," I told the woman.

"Jack Campbell?" the women responded.

"Yes," I said.

"Police will be right out," she responded with urgency.

* * *

Before I knew it, there were three police cars at the studio. Both my parents had shown up, and the owners of the studio were there. I was so embarrassed to have caused such a scene. As if everyone did not already know I was the nameless girl in the papers who had an "affair" with Jack, as some town mothers called it. They all certainly knew now that I was that girl.

I sat and talked to the police and recounted what happened over and over again. They told me they were going to get him. This was a violation of the restraining order…blah, blah, blah…

The police had called Jack's wife to ask her where her husband was. She told police that she had no idea where he was during that time. *Perfect, he had no alibi,* I thought. *They really can get him this time.*

The next morning when I woke up, I would be disappointed yet again.

"Danielle retracted her statement," my mom told when I woke up. "She called the police back and said she had misspoken and that Jack had been at home the whole time…they did not arrest him."

I let out a sigh… *What in the world?* My mind could not get it straight. *I told the police the truth, and they still can't protect me? How wrong could any of this be if he still is stalking me? Did they really believe me? Did my safety really matter? Was this my fault? Was I being punished?*

My insides were boiling. I was angry and sad and embarrassed. I was ashamed. I was guilty.

MARCH 2019.

2 YEARS LATER.

I woke up that morning in my cozy bed, and in those first few moments when my alarm went off, I felt comfortable and secure in my warm pink plaid pajamas and wanted to snuggle back in. Those few seconds were fleeting. Almost instantly, my mind was flooded with thoughts. It was THE morning. The morning I had been dreading for the past two years. Since the day I told the police the truth about what had conspired between Jack and me, I had thought about this day. The day that I would arrive at the courthouse and raise my right hand to tell "nothing but the truth."

The past two years had tested me and my strength. I had lived my life with the constant presence of a lurking stalker. I had listened to Susie's mother call me a home wrecker, only for us to be sent to "mediation" with a lawyer and have a "no contact order" placed between our families. I had lost friends; I had made friends. But I was lucky. I had people who believed in me. Family, teachers, mentors, aunts and strangers who came out of the woodwork to support me. Their confidence in me pushed me through those years. Now it was time for me to take back my life.

I sat up in bed and rubbed my eyes. I had a huge exam at school this week. I could not interrupt my study schedule even for a day… especially since I was missing a day of school to testify. I hurried to the bathroom and then immediately sat down at my desk to do some quick practice. I had been studying forever, only for the trial to come up this week. Oh well, I would not let this man waste another moment of my life.

* * *

I remember sitting in the holding room with the prosecutor, a bunch of detectives and my mom. We waited for hours. Everyone in the room tried to distract me from what was about to happen. I cried a lot. I told them I changed my mind. I didn't want to testify anymore. I was fifteen years old now, but I felt like I was eleven and twevle years old again, reliving the experiences of the past in my head. I was dreading having to describe them out loud, in front of a courtroom of reporters, jurors, a judge, Jack's lawyer and Jack himself. I had begged my friends and family not to sit in the courtroom.

I did not want anyone to hear the words I was going to speak. I did not even want to hear them. When I pictured this day in my head, I imagined myself strong and confident. I thought I would be over the anger and the sadness and the guilt and the shame. The truth was, I did not feel strong. I did not feel supported. I felt alone and scared. I looked at my loving mother, hoping she could save me. She was brave, she was strong for me, she smiled and held my hand until finally, after hours of waiting, a courtroom police officer opened the door to the holding room and said they were ready for me.

I just wanted the jury to believe me. Maybe then, I would stop being so hard on myself. How could I make them believe me?

I shook my head from side to side. I did not want to go; I wasn't ready. I swallowed hard. People were saying all kinds of supportive statements that I was not listening to. I stood up and put one foot in front of the other until out of the holding room. I now stood behind the decorated doors of the court room. My chest felt like it was caving in, and I sucked in as much air as a I could through my nose. My chest filled with air. Two police officers opened the large double doors in front of me, and I looked into the court room. Tears poured from my eyes uncontrollably. I was directed to stand in the podium next to the judge. It took everything I had to regain control over myself, raise my right hand in the air and swear to tell nothing but the truth.

* * *

The first half was straightforward. The prosecutor asked me questions that I had excepted her to ask, and I answered them. I detailed every instance of sexual assault over the years and described the relationship between Jack and me. She brought out my old dairy, gifts Jack gave me and letters he wrote me, and asked to me to identify them. She asked me if I knew about the spyware on my iPad, and I said no. I told the truth. The latter half, when Jack's lawyer had a chance to ask me questions, was exasperating. I felt like I was a puppet being played with. I remember feeling like he was trying to trick me; I remember him embarrassing me and trying make me seem like a liar. When I was finally released, I was exhausted. I wanted it all to be over. I wanted to move on with my life. I had confidence that Jack would be found guilty, that by next week he would be locked up and I would not have to worry about him stalking me or assaulting anyone else. In the meantime, I poured myself into studying for my exam.

* * *

I was sitting in a club meeting after school when my phone buzzed. I opened a text from my neighbor Ann, the one for whom I had delivered magazines.

Ann: "Blair, this is not a reflection of you. You are so strong. I am so sorry this happened."

My body went into emotion overload. I looked up from my phone and around at the meeting going on. I smiled and put my phone away. I knew what must have happened. The verdict must have been read today. My family did not know when the jury would come to a decision. The trial had gone on for three weeks, and we had no way of knowing when the jury would come to a verdict. But this text told me it wasn't good.

I stayed silent for the remainder of the meeting, not wanting to draw any attention to myself. *Did anyone else know what happened?*

When my mom finally arrived to pick me up from school, I was given the news. Jack had been found not guilty. He was now a free man.

AUTHOR'S NOTE

Through listening to the stories of survivors of childhood sexual assault, I learned that there are many "endings" to their situations. Truth be told, most survivors I interviewed did not report their assault to the police. For the ones who did, the situation did not always end the way they would have hoped. Many survivors, including me, would turn to sources outside of themselves to find worth or comfort. Some used self-harm, alcohol and/or drugs. Others would dedicate themselves to school and accomplishment as a way to gain some sort of authority over their life. They gripped hold of anything they could to gain control and external validation. For some, eating "healthy," exercise and achievement became a basis for self-worth. Survivors may hang on to these things seen as "good" to validate their existence as good and worthy and rely on achievement for confidence, instead of using these outlets as a healthy way to cope. Their minds are groomed. They do not trust themselves. They believe they can work tirelessly for perfection in hopes of redeeming themselves. They work to hide their shame. Each accomplishment gives them a small boost of confidence, only to want to grasp at more and to feel worthy. Brandilyn Tebo's *The Achievement Trap* makes the connection between people's feeling of "not enoughness" and their unrealistic visions of perfection for themselves. These visions keep people who are stuck constantly striving for a sense that they are worthy because of what they do and not who they are. She tells readers, "You are enough. You always have been."[62]

Yet, survivors are warped in feelings of shame. As survivors, we look to the world to give us back our sense of worthiness and to validate our experiences.

This search for validation looks different for every survivor. Survivors are searching for ways to make it through the day. They are searching for a way to push down their feelings, to numb the shame and give them a reason to keep on pushing through with the guilt they carry. People who are sexually assaulted are more likely than the general public to use drugs. According to RAINN (Rape, Abuse,

62 Tebo, Brandilyn. *The Achievement Trap: The Over-Achiever, People-Pleaser & Perfectionist's Guide to Freedom & True Success.* B.C.Allen Publishing and Tonic Books, 2018.

Incest National Network), they are six times more likely to use cocaine and ten times more likely to use other major drugs than the general public.[63] The NSVRC (National Sexual Violence Resource Center) reports that 81 percent of women and 35 percent of men report significant short- or long-term impacts.[64]

What I know to be true today is that we are not defined by what happens to us. You are not defined by your sexual assault, your friend's assault or your child's assault. You are defined by your actions and reactions. You have the opportunity to practice gratitude and focus on what we have, to realize that *you* are enough. Together, we have the opportunity to be a light for someone struggling. We have the opportunity to open up to others about our struggles and learn about resilience, healing and joy. We have the opportunity to come together and heal—to realize that the struggle of one person is the struggle of the world. When we practice having empathy and love for one another, we can finally watch out, step up and speak out to change the culture around sexual violence. We can learn about our rights regarding sexual assault; we can educate others on our rights; we can have a healthy curiosity about people in our lives; we can stop

63 "Victims of Sexual Violence: Statistics." www.rainn.org. https://www.rainn.org/statistics/victims-sexual-violence. (May 2019).

64 "Get Statistics." www.nsvrc.org. https://www.nsvrc.org/es/node/4737. (May 2019).

blaming victims; we can start listening to survivors. Survivors need to find solace in the fact that what was done to them was not their fault.

Thank you for taking the time to read my book.

Genuinely,
Samantha Leonard

ACKNOWLEDGEMENTS

Crafting this book has been special journey for me and would not have been made possible without the support of my friends, family and the brave community of survivors and advocates that stand by my side. Thank you for teaching me to persevere and ask for help. Without you all, I could not have made this book a reality.

Thank you to each of the survivors I interviewed for this book who will remain anonymous.

I would like to acknowledge the experts, advocates and counselors supporting survivors that I interviewed:

Angela Seguin
Abigail Glasgow
Amy Estland
Nidhi Idnani

Matt Mahon
Megan Masterson
Olivia Blythe
Eric Garrison
Sage Carson
Zainab Shah
Annika Synnestvedt
Amy Hopkins

I'd like to also thank everyone who pre-ordered my book. Your financial support made this book and it's publication possible. I'd like to take a moment to individually thank everyone who pre-ordered my book:

Casey Moore
Julie Millisky
Emily Pizzimenti
Eric Koseter
Nicole Caulfield
Cara Cifelli
Madison Poff
Mary Grundy
Rachel Lawrence
Raymond Blanchard
Iris Tonti
Karen Plantarich
Lauren Healy
Rebecca Robbins
Mark Smith
Linda Richmond
Lisa Levine
Hayley Penrose
Ursula Montis
Kayla Herbert
Kim Herbert
Andrea Meindl
Jennifer Eady
Michele M. Symcak
Samantha Fortunato
Gillian Williams
Lori Tonti
Maura Meehan
Amanda Nashed
Renee Kontos
Natalie Pagenstecher
Anne Pierson
Dawn Sullivan Baliko
Faith Ausfresser

Jordan Gross
Celeste Osworth
George Wieber
Kristina Mannino
Robert Carroll
Juli Weitzen
Sandy Neumann
Molly V Dimas
Sarah Milbury-Steen
Rebecca Glinn
Lauren Miller
Zully Darby
Rachel Crow
Laura McClintick
Melissa Miller
Lynn Worden
Debra Siwczak
Tina Neely
Lisa Treshock
Cindy Holland
Tawrye Mason
Krissy Smith
Valerie Lane
Laura Eisenman
Marley Duchovnay
Holly Pyles
Katie Johnson
Molly Laterza
Stephanie Clampitt
Katherine Filliben
Jaime Renman
Laura Stemmler
Cheryl L.Stump
Claire Breyta
Amanda Giordano
Madison Mucha
Roderick Carey
Stephen C DiJulio
Kiera Schaindlin
Melanie Sipko
Emily Langsdorf
Lindsey McAleer
Debbie Nemirovsky
Molly Thames
Carolyn Byrne
Emily McKeon
Ginny King

I'd like to especially thank the people who invested more in my publishing and pre-ordered multiple copies of my book.

With special thanks to:

Denise and Ray Leonard
Emily Tonti
Kristen Kenna
Jennifer DeLucia
Karen Jobes
Wells Carter
Iris Tonti
Debbie Hill
Royce Dick
Joy Tozzi
Dave Fried
Allen and Mary Carter
Claire Carter
Cynthia Stratis
Kim Stout
Ozana Castellano
Zainab Shah

Thank you to everyone. Your financial support allowed me to transform countless pages of notes and interviews into the book you are about to read.

Last, but certainly not least, I would like to thank Jaclyn Digregorio for connecting me with Eric Koester who made it possible for me to actually publish this book. I also owe Brian Bies a huge thank you for being my cheerleader every step of the way. Each of you uniquely, inspired me everyday to keep writing!

RESOURCES

- Childhelp National Child Abuse Hotline
- 1-800-422- 4453
- https://www.childhelp.org/
- Victim Connect Resource Center
- 1-855-484-2846
- https://victimconnect.org
- National Suicide Prevention Hotline
- 1-800-273-8255
- https://suicidepreventionlifeline.org/
- Rape, Abuse, Incest National Network
- 1-800-656-4673
- https://www.rainn.org/

BIBLIOGRAPHY

INTRODUCTION

"Behaviors of Sexual Predators: Grooming" www.icmec.org. https://www.icmec.org/wp-content/uploads/2016/05/Behaviors-of-Sexual-Predators-Grooming.pdf. (May 2019).

"Children and Teen Statistics" www.rainn.org. https://www.rainn.org/statistics/children-and-teens (May 2019).

H, Hannah. "Internet Safety: A Mother's Story of How a Pedophile Groomed her 11-year-old Daughter Online." *Independent*. 6 February 2017. https://www.independent.co.uk/life-style/health-and-families/internet-safety-day-hannah-h-mother-paedophile-online-grooming-11-year-old-daughter-facebook-web-cam-a7560801.html (May 2019).

"Resources" d2l.org. https://www.d2l.org/resources/ (May 2019).

"Sexual Abuse Facts & Resources" Cachouston.org. https://www.cachouston.org/sexual-abuse/child-sexual-abuse-facts/. (May 2019).

Uttaro, Robert. *To the Survivors: One Man's Journey as a Rape Crisis Counselor with True Stories of Sexual Violence*. CreateSpace Independent Publishing Platform, 2013.

PART 1

Georgia M. Winters & Elizabeth L. Jeglic. "Stages of Sexual Grooming: Recognizing Potentially Predatory Behaviors of Child Molesters," Deviant Behavior, 38:6, 724-733, https://www.tandfonline.com/doi/full/10.1080/01639625.2016.1197656

Huffman, Charlotte. "Two Child Sex Offenders Explain How They Picked Their Targets." www.wfaa.com. https://www.wfaa.com/article/features/originals/two-child-sex-offenders-explain-how-they-picked-their-targets/287-434667495. (May 2019).

Jackson, Kate. "How Children Grieve—Persistent Myths May Stand in the Way of Appropriate Care and Support for Children" *Social Work Today. https://www.socialworktoday.com/archive/030415p20.shtml.* (May 2019).

Ehmke, Rachel. "Helping Children Deal with Grief." www.childmind.org. https://childmind.org/article/helping-children-deal-grief/. (May 2019).

"Step 3: Talk about it." www.d2l.org. https://www.d2l.org/education/5-steps/step-3/ (May 2019).

"Talk to Kids about Body Safety and Boundaries." www.d2l.org. https://www.d2l.org/wp-content/uploads/2018/10/Talk-to-Kids-Body-Safety_-JTM.pdf

"Tips for Hiring Caregivers" www.d2l.org. https://www.d2l.org/wp-content/uploads/2017/03/Tips-For-Hiring-Caregivers-2017.pdf. (May 2019).

"The Childhelp National Child Abuse Hotline" www.childhelp.org. https://www.childhelp.org/hotline/. (May 2019).

Webster, Emma. "What Is Sexual Grooming?" www.allure.com. https://www.allure.com/story/what-is-sexual-grooming-abuse. (May 2019).

Weber, Gregory. "Grooming Children for Sexual Molestation." www.vachss.com. http://www.vachss.com/guest_dispatches/grooming.html. (May 2019).

PART 2

"An Adult Who Gives Gifts without Permission." www.dioceseofbmt.org. http://www.dioceseofbmt.org/wp-content/uploads/2015/05/ParentTraining28.pdf. (May 2019).

"Children and Teens: Statistics" www.d2l.org. https://www.rainn.org/statistics/children-and-teens. (May 2019).

Georgia M. Winters & Elizabeth L. Jeglic. "Stages of Sexual Grooming: Recognizing Potentially Predatory Behaviors of Child Molesters," Deviant Behavior, 38:6, 724-733, https://www.tandfonline.com/doi/full/10.1080/01639625.2016.1197656

"Grooming: Protect Your Child from Sexual Predators." www.boystown.org. https://www.boystown.org/parenting/article/Pages/victim-grooming-protect-your-child-from-sexual-predators.aspx. (May 2019).

Huffman, Charlotte. "Two Child Sex Offenders Explain How They Picked Their Targets." www.wfaa.com. https://www.wfaa.com/article/features/originals/two-child-sex-offenders-explain-how-they-picked-their-targets/287-434667495. (May 2019).

"Stop it Now: Everyday Tips to Keep Kids Safe." www.stopitnow.org. https://stopitnow.org/ohc-content/tip-sheet-4. (May 2019).

Webster, Emma. "What Is Sexual Grooming?" www.allure.com. https://www.allure.com/story/what-is-sexual-grooming-abuse. (May 2019).

PART 3

Courtois, Christine A. *It's Not You, It's What Happened to You*. Telemachus Press, 2014.

Huffman, Charlotte. "Two Child Sex Offenders Explain How They Picked Their Targets." www.wfaa.com. https://www.wfaa.com/article/features/originals/two-child-sex-offenders-explain-how-they-picked-their-targets/287-434667495. (May 2019).

McCall, Catherine. "How and When to Talk to Your Child about Sexual Abuse" www.psychologytoday.com. https://www.psychologytoday.com/us/blog/overcoming-child-abuse/201006/how-and-when-talk-your-child-about-sexual-abuse. (May 2019).

"Trauma." www.apa.org. https://www.apa.org/topics/trauma/. (May 2019).

Trauma-Informed Care in Behavioral Health Services. Substance Abuse and Mental Health Services Administration (US); 2014. (Treatment Improvement Protocol (TIP) Series, No. 57.) Chapter 3, Understanding the Impact of Trauma. https://www.ncbi.nlm.nih.gov/books/NBK207191/

van der Kolk, Bessel A. *The Body Keeps the Score:* Brain, Mind and Body in the Healing of Trauma. Viking, 2014.

PART 4

"Grooming and Red Flag Behaviors." www.d2l.org. https://www.d2l.org/child-grooming-signs-behavior-awareness/. (May 2019).

Georgia M. Winters & Elizabeth L. Jeglic. "Stages of Sexual Grooming: Recognizing Potentially Predatory Behaviors of Child Molesters," Deviant Behavior, 38:6, 724-733, https://www.tandfonline.com/doi/full/10.1080/01639625.2016.1197656

"Trust Your Gut." www.d2l.com. https://www.d2l.org/trustyourgut/. (May 2019).

PART 5

"Benefits of Sexual Abuse Counseling." www.betterhelp.com. https://www.betterhelp.com/advice/abuse/benefits-of-sexual-abuse-counseling/. (May 2019).

"Effects." www.nctsn.org. https://www.nctsn.org/what-is-child-trauma/trauma-types/sexual-abuse/effects. (May 2019).

"Grooming: What it is, signs and how to protect children." www.nspcc.org.uk. https://www.nspcc.org.uk/preventing-abuse/child-abuse-and-neglect/grooming/. (May 2019).

Georgia M. Winters & Elizabeth L. Jeglic. "Stages of Sexual Grooming: Recognizing Potentially Predatory Behaviors of Child Molesters," Deviant Behavior, 38:6, 724-733, https://www.tandfonline.com/doi/full/10.1080/01639625.2016.1197656

Huffman, Charlotte. "Two Child Sex Offenders Explain How They Picked Their Targets." www.wfaa.com. https://www.wfaa.com/article/features/originals/tw

Sands, Nicole. "Months Before Interviewing Michael Jackson Accusers, Oprah Winfrey Opened Up about Her Own Abuse." people.com. https://people.com/tv/oprah-winfrey-details-own-abuse-months-before-interviewing-michael-jackson-accusers/. (May 2019).

"Share Aware." www.nspcc.org. https://www.nspcc.org.uk/preventing-abuse/keeping-children-safe/share-aware/. (May 2019).

"Why Rape and Trauma Survivors have Fragmented and Incomplete Memories." www.time.com. http://time.com/3625414/rape-trauma-brain-memory/. (May 2019).

PART 6

"Information for Professionals: Abusive Partners." www.opdv.ny.gov. https://www.opdv.ny.gov/professionals/abusers/coercivecontrol.html. (May 2019).

Robin O'Grady & Nicole Matthews-Creech. "Why Children Don't Tell" www.lacasacenter.org. https://lacasacenter.org/why-child-abuse-victims-dont-tell/. (May 2019).

CONCLUSION

Brown, Brené. *I Thought It Was Just Me (But It Isn't) Telling the Truth about Perfectionism, Inadequacy, and Power.* Gotham Books, 2008.

Brown, Brené. *Braving the Wilderness: The Quest for True Belonging and the Courage to Stand Alone.* Random House, 2017.

Daly, Kathleen & Brigitte Boubours. R. "Rape and Attrition in the Legal Process." *Crime and Justice.* Vol. 39, No. 1 (2010). Pp.-565-650.

"Get Statistics." www.nsvrc.org. https://www.nsvrc.org/es/node/4737. (May 2019).

Tebo, Brandilyn. *The Achievement Trap: The Over-Achiever, People-Pleaser & Perfectionist's Guide to Freedom & True Success.* B.C.Allen Publishing and Tonic Books, 2018.

"Trauma Informed Sexual Assault Investigation Training" www.theiacp.org. https://www.theiacp.org/events/training/trauma-informed-sexual-assault-investigation-training-hoover-al. (May 2019).

"Victims of Sexual Violence: Statistics." www.rainn.org. https://www.rainn.org/statistics/victims-sexual-violence. (May 2019).